'History appears to be repeating itself in this astute, powerful and pacy novel about race, secrets, and whether it's ever good to return to old haunts.'

CLAIRE FULLER, the Costa Novel Award-winning
author of *Unsettled Ground*

'Complications of race and class make for a deeply compelling novel.'

MARGOT LIVESEY, New York Times
best-selling author

'A romance, a detective story, and a coming-of-age novel all at once.'

GENE SEYMOUR, former Kirkus
Novel Prize judge

'There's a pacy intensity to this small-town America story of love and reverberating tragedy that would rival any modern box-set drama... an electric, emotionally charged novel: it seethes with its own energy. Pick it up, and you won't want to put it down.'

PHILIP HOARE, author of *Leviathan,*
and *Albert & the Whale*

'This is subtly compelling story telling, as alert as poetry to the power of the unsaid. Opening a crack in the personal past to shed light on the conflicts of the present, it picks apart the many guises of forgetting and the complex layers of complicity.'

PHILIP GROSS, Winner of the
T. S. Eliot Prize

'Gripping from the first page and satisfying to and beyond the last, *The Same Country* is an intimate, intricate history of violence, race, community and love. What a thrilling debut novel.'

TOBY LITT, novelist, short story writer,
Granta Best of Young British Novelist

'A searing and timely portrait of America today. Burns captures the lasting effects of gun violence on family, friendship and community, and balances grief and anger and hope.'

DONNA HEMANS, author of *Tea by the Sea*

'A novel which somehow manages to be both a page-turner and an issues-driven exposé of twenty-first century society, *The Same Country* is an important and astonishing book.'

CHARLIE CARROLL, author of *The Lip*

'*The Same Country* is utterly absorbing. It's a probing, disturbing and gripping look at race, class and privilege in the US ... The two murders at the centre of the story and the attempts to cover them up kept me turning the pages, but it is also such an honest, thought-provoking and nuanced novel – really unforgettable.'

REBECCA SMITH, author of *The Ash Museum*

THE SAME COUNTRY

Carole Burns

Legend Press Ltd, 51 Gower Street, London, WC1E 6HJ
info@legendtimesgroup.co.uk | www.legendpress.co.uk

The opening three chapters of this novel were first published by *The
Masters Review*.

Print ISBN 9781915643605
Ebook ISBN 9781915643612
Set in Times.
Cover design by Sarah Whittaker | www.whittakerbookdesign.com

Carole Burns, a freelance reviewer for the *Washington Post*, was the winner of Ploughshares' John C. Zacharis First Book Award in 2015 for her story collection, *The Missing Woman*. An American ex-pat now living in Wales, Carole worked as a journalist, including for washingtonpost.com and the *New York Times*, for some 15 years before moving to the UK, where she is now an Associate Professor in English teaching Creative Writing at the University of Southampton.

Her early years as a local journalist in Connecticut were influential in the writing of this novel, as was her perspective as an American living in the UK. Her short fiction has been longlisted in the BBC's National Short Story Award and published in *Mslexia*.

Follow Carole on Twitter
@Carole_Burns

and Instagram
WriterCaroleBurns

and visit
www.caroleburns.com

To Paul,
of course

OPHELIA
Sings
He is dead and gone, lady,
He is dead and gone;
At his head a grass-green turf,
At his heels a stone.

Hamlet, Act IV, Scene V

"It is the innocence which constitutes the crime."

— James Baldwin

I

2013/1992

There Is No Beginning

CHAPTER ONE

On my first morning back in Newfield, I drove to Aggie's old house again, drawn like a woman to her secret lover's grave, as if this were the sole purpose of returning to live in my hometown. It was Joe who compelled me to go – not Aggie – Joe who appeared to me that morning as just a flash, my waking dream, his face wavering near mine as I stirred, closer to me than he ever was in life. I heard him, next, as I made coffee alone, his voice rumbling into the still-empty rooms of my still-empty condo, disappearing into my gasp. Why had I thought Aggie might haunt me here? Aggie wasn't dead.

And now he was sitting next to me in my car and talking, talking as I drove down the leafy streets of Newfield, passing old haunts – the Palace movie theatre, the Friendly's where we used to linger for hours – before turning to head toward Aggie's. The houses became smaller, older, closer to the road as we approached the Bridgeton city line, yet I barely noticed with Joe beside me, animated, though I couldn't hear him this time, the same way I couldn't remember what we all talked about twenty years ago at late-night diners, at our lockers, on Aggie's back porch no matter the time or weather, night after night that I couldn't remember. And maybe that's why his words weren't coming through, just his lips moving, his head nodding and tilting, his quick smile between words, his swerving shoulders as he swivelled to glance at Aggie then back at me, though Aggie wasn't there either.

We were just a few blocks away from the house. So quick! This clutch of streets that led from our little town of Newfield to the more urban Bridgeton had seemed to me like an entrance to another world, back then. I passed her road in hope of first finding the feminist bookstore and café where we'd sometimes browse the shelves and sip lattes like we were college students, or, across the street, the tiny gallery that once held an exhibition of portraits made from old radio parts – art, we learned. I braced myself for this world – once so alluring, so sophisticated – to look small, dowdy. This was just Connecticut after all. I crossed the city line into Bridgeton.

The neighborhood had changed drastically. Lawns were untended, houses had not been painted in years, the blinds and curtains in windows were tattered and faded. Here was the Connecticut divide, sharper than I'd remembered. The shell of a car lay strewn in rusting pieces in someone's yard. At a light, I spotted the short block of shops where the Readers Feast used to be. It was now a pizza joint. The gallery? A "checks cashed" store. A couple of teenage boys swaggered by in high tops and baseball caps worn backwards and looked my way as if I didn't belong. Rich and poor, this divide. Also white and Black. I knew, of course, that Obama now being president wouldn't alter this new/old reality. So why was I surprised? The light changed and I avoided the boys' gaze as I pulled into the old gallery's parking lot to turn around and head back to Aggie's. "But I used to live here!" I said to no one, to Joe, though it wasn't even true.

And Joe had disappeared.

I took a left at the next corner and parked outside Aggie's old house. How many times as a teenager had I pulled in to pick her up, or drop her off, or stay for dinner with her magical parents in that once-magical world where, if there wasn't school the next day, I'd spend the night and practically the entire weekend? If I was expecting to find some clue about what happened that night more than twenty years ago, I would be disappointed. Nothing was the same. The stone steps that made a wiggly line from the street to the front door – Mr. Whitcombe's doing, not his more conservative wife's – were cracked and overrun with weeds. The wraparound porch was empty of the wicker patio chairs where we used to sit playing rummy 500 and listening to REM or some indie band Aggie had discovered. Just the chair swing remained, its vinyl cushions ripped, the foam yellowed and mildewed.

I stepped out of the car and stood at the edge of the yard, as if I was going to walk up the stone path and knock on the door as I had so often in high school that I couldn't possibly count the times, and then again, in vain, on at least a dozen days in the weeks after Joe died, determined to gain admittance once more, to see Aggie.

But I was shut out then, as I was shut out now. It looked like a place I'd never been – like I'd never opened its blue colonial door, never eaten at its table off the huge, ramshackle kitchen, never slept in its rooms with their wood floors and curtains thick as tapestries, never looked out its windows on to the street where I was now mutely standing, staring back at myself from twenty years ago. Of course that world was gone – I'd known that for years – but no one else had taken our place. No other girls, white or Black, were flinging their schoolbooks on the porch so they could flop into the chair swing on the first warm day of spring. To see it so abandoned almost implied that it had never existed at all, that the promise that we felt in our young lives, Aggie's and Joe's and Jess's and mine, had been an empty promise, that such a world never could exist. That was worse than our lives being destroyed.

As if Joe had died yet again.

But I was desperate to begin my new life. At least, that's what I told myself as I dressed for my first day of work at the statewide newspaper in Bridgeton – my ostensible reason for moving back – donning my new slim-cut black pants that looked exactly like the older pair in the closet, the slightly dressy T-shirt that was as close as I could manage to workwear. Long ago, I'd decided that the plainer my clothes, the less plain I looked. And wasn't my compact, slightly boxy frame lengthened, softened, under boxier attire? Only my hairstyle was new, cut on a whim on my last afternoon in Raleigh – asymmetrical, a longer strand on the right side curving under my chin. I'd been trying to convince myself that it rounded my angular face, made my mouse-blonde hair seem blonder, but yesterday afternoon, I almost slipped into a hairdresser to have the longer side chopped off.

Soon I was driving down busy Newfield Avenue toward downtown Bridgeton, passing the squat brick building that housed the local paper where I'd worked in the Classified section that awful summer that Joe died. At least I wasn't working there now. And then I was walking into yet another newspaper office in yet another decrepit area of yet another decrepit downtown, not unlike Raleigh's. I gave my name at reception and waited for the Human Resources person to arrive. I had insurance plans to choose and tax forms to fill out – sure signs this was a new job in a new life.

If this was my old life, I'd be going home to Maria.

A few hours later, Alex. Black straight hair over a pale boy's face, Oxford-blue Oxford shirt, sitting stiffly in a faux-leather café chair designed to look like comfort. My new colleague taking me out to lunch. Not my boss, just acting like it. In a few days I'd find out the newsroom called him Smart Aleck.

"Yeah, yeah, yeah," he said when I explained how the chance to edit the home page, as well as being a copy editor, was the main reason I'd changed jobs. "No one relies on the dead-tree edition anymore. That's so, you know, 1998." And he laughed a high-pitched, raucous laugh that rang out across the deli. A few customers looked over.

I left my girlfriend because I loved her too much. The truth sounded in my head, and I flinched. In secret, it'd come out blunter, balder, than I usually allowed.

"And this place is a good stepping stone," he went on. "I mean, who wants to stay in Bridgeton?"

Though I'd fled my hometown as soon as I could, I felt defensive. "Well, I grew up here."

He tried not to register his surprise. "Yeah." He was reassessing me. "You want to stay here."

"No…" I felt flummoxed. Did I? I'd thought only of fleeing Maria.

"Where you'd go to school?"

"Northwestern." I felt like I was being interviewed again. "You?" I asked.

Alex coughed. "Uh, New Haven."

It took me a moment to realize he meant Yale, like he was a character in *The Great Gatsby*. I laughed, but he didn't seem to notice.

"I was wondering why you left Raleigh," he said, "but it makes more sense now."

"Does it?" I said, not meaning to say it aloud.

The next night, another ghost. A slight, dark-haired woman was humming to herself as she shopped in the supermarket. Aggie? Her back was to me, but the way she moved, jumpy, animated even while merely sifting through red peppers, then garlic bulbs, was unmistakeable. I was stilled by her movement – the light stepping back as she thought, the brief rise of her shoulders and a little "Huh!" as she decided and popped the best pepper into her cart. Her quick steps to the mushrooms were like sparks of fast motion amid the slovenly mesh of other shoppers. Should I go up to her? What was she doing here? Then I was pushing my cart in her direction, the wheels as noisy and jangly as my breath.

"Aggie?" No response – but I was sure it was her. "Aggie? Aggie Whitcombe?" I said too loudly. Several shoppers glanced my way but it was only Aggie I could see, as she kept her back to me for another moment, stiff, before turning to me with her face pale and composed. I know she had composed it because it was expressionless in the way Aggie had never looked when I knew her – she'd always worn her heart on her face.

"Cassandra Jones," she said. Both carts were between us, which meant we couldn't embrace, or even shake hands. "Of all the supermarkets in all the cities in all the world… who'd expect we'd end up back where we started?"

"The scene of the crime," I said.

She blanched, and looked down, and I could see then how she had aged – her wan skin was subtly creased with wrinkles, her hair thinning like an old woman's. A spectre from the past she was, not the girl herself.

I had an instinct to put my hand over hers to soothe her. "I didn't mean—"

"You never did. Cassie."

That's when I found out she had moved back as well. We'd both arrived that week, we discovered as we chatted awkwardly, Aggie from Chicago, me from Raleigh. If it weren't for coming from different directions we might have passed each other on the highway coming in, or at the pizza place that night where I imagined we'd both gotten takeout, or at the hardware store the next day where she, too, must have gone to purchase picture hooks and a hammer. At least, that's what I told myself as I drove away from the supermarket, making up stories about how we might have bumped into each other on our first day back in Newfield.

"Jess is back, too," she said.

I hadn't known Joe's sister had returned as well, and we stood, silent, taking in the coincidence. "She came back last year. Working at the high school. I'm at the junior high, but I saw her at the staff day before school started."

I wouldn't have thought either of them would end up teaching, of all things. Weren't they more ambitious than that? For once I didn't blurt it out.

"Actually, you said your condo's in that old watch factory? I think that might be where she's living, too. I hear the architect did a pretty cool job."

"It's even affordable," I said. Something Jess would have to think about, too. I wondered where Aggie was living.

"Anyway," she went on, "my mother will be wondering where I am. She likes my cooking all of a sudden. Or pretends to. Dad was master of the kitchen."

Was. I wondered what had happened. I remembered Mr. Whitcombe in the midst of his final epicurean flourishes as we came down for dinner, his hair askew as he whisked together salad dressing, arranged the main course – pasta, maybe with sun-dried tomatoes – on warmed plates just out of the oven, his apron tied twice around and knotted in front, so it caused a fold on his stomach. I'd only heard "pasta" referred to as "spaghetti" in my house, and it was only ever served with meatballs.

"He has Alzheimer's."

"I'm sorry," I said. "I always loved your dad."

She nodded quickly, then gazed at me, tilting her head to one side. "I'm not sure I would have recognized you. Miss Stylish." And she smiled.

Stylish? Then I remembered my hair, and clutched at the longer strand. "I want to hack this off with scissors every time I look in the mirror."

Aggie laughed. "Don't. It looks good."

"Can I…" *Can I see you again*, I'd almost asked, like I was a long-lost flame rather than an old friend. "Why don't I call your cell phone? So you'll have my number."

How could she say no? I composed several texts to her that night – *Great to talk to you again. Wonderful to see a familiar face. Want to meet for coffee? I could cook on a Friday night* – but I didn't send any of them because I couldn't write what I wanted to write. *Are you OK?* Somehow, I knew she wasn't.

None of us would have come back if we were OK.

CHAPTER TWO

Occasionally, in these small cities and towns that stretch along Long Island Sound, just occasionally, you can tell you're near the sea. If you're far enough from the highway and the malls, the sky above the warm, dark asphalt of a Stop & Shop in Bridgeton will tint a clear, pale blue; the air in the fresh-cut grassiness of a baseball field in Newfield take on the slightest hint of a salty breeze. It was one of those days at my condo complex when a tall, elegant woman in a gorgeous yellow dress and large sunglasses was standing at the suite of mailboxes, tilting her face up to the sun before opening a box with the slightest flick of her wrist. Had she taken in the light, too, breathed in the scent of sea?

She didn't look like the usual hipster crowd that was beginning to populate this possibly up-and-coming but not yet expensive urban neighborhood of Bridgeton: the young women in wispy florals from vintage shops, the men in carefully distressed jeans and neat beards. Was this someone's sister visiting from New York City? Then I saw it was Jess.

Jess!

Of course it was. The one time I wasn't looking for her, she appeared.

I'd been wondering what to say to her if we ran into each other, worried she might not want to see me after all these years. But this fresh, clear day – wasn't that a good omen? I walked up and said hello.

If her emotions were mixed when she realized who I was, she was too polite to let them show. As we spoke, I remembered the last time I'd seen her: Joe's funeral.

Everything shy and awkward about her in high school had become quietly confident and graceful. Her once sweet, slightly pimply face looked wider somehow, her cheekbones bolder, her mouth fuller. Her skin, erased of its teenage imperfections, was smoother and darker. Her hair was not only longer but appeared thicker, too; she wore it pulled back with a '50s-style headband that made it seem she was only barely controlling its wildness. She was thin but curvy and soft, not skinny like Aggie. She looked beautiful.

But I could sense the old reserve in her. She talked about the high school in Bridgeton where she was working, instead of Newfield High where we'd gone – "Newfield's so pricey now," she said. "Those kids don't need any more help." I told her about my job at the Bridgeton newspaper ("Not the *Newfield Bugle*! Or *Bungle*, as we used to say," I quickly added). But while I cracked jokes about my paper not exactly being *The Washington Post* ("I'm editing *All the First Alderman's Men*," I said), she spoke vaguely about how much she loved working with the kids. She remained formal, and on script.

We fell silent, and I wondered, after all these years, how to go about mentioning Joe. "Is it strange living here again?"

She adjusted her purse – a narrow rectangle the same burnt yellow of her dress – and took out her house keys. She was ready to go. "I was back a lot anyway. For my parents."

"How are they?" I asked.

"Oh, you know, fine. Healthy."

Mr. and Mrs. Willis had seemed like the most old-fashioned parents in all of Newfield. The few times Aggie and I had picked up Joe and Jess before going out, we were told not to beep for them as we did with other friends; we always went into the house, and sat in the living room for a few minutes talking very politely with the whole family. Mr. Willis would be dressed like the minister he was, in a long-sleeved shirt and dress pants, a loosened tie his only concession to it being Friday night, and Mrs. Willis in a slightly shapeless wool dress, offering us cups of coffee which we always refused, wanting to get out.

"They were always so sweet when we picked you up," I said.

"More like embarrassing! Why my mother kept offering you coffee..."

"We should have just said yes. I regretted that so much after..." I hesitated. "After Joe died."

"After Joe was killed." Jess said it softly but firmly.

Murdered. The thought whispered in my head, or had I spoken aloud? But it wasn't true. Everyone had agreed it was an accident, Mr. and Mrs. Willis included. But Jess was right. Joe hadn't just died; he'd been killed. "Yes," I said quietly.

She jingled her keys in her hand for a moment, shifted them to the other hand, shifted them back. "Honestly? I don't think they've ever recovered."

Jess stood before me in her slim-fitting saffron-colored dress, her thick saffron-colored hairband with a silk black strip on either edge. Even her shoes – flats, but shiny patent leather – were saffron. She was everything her parents hadn't been, and trying very hard at it, too.

"And you?" I asked.

She turned her gaze to me, steady, clear, then looked away. I wondered if she would answer. Why should she?

"I keep thinking I see him," she finally said. "On the street. In Marshall's, yesterday. In the hallways at school."

Me, too, but I didn't say it aloud.

"The other day? A kid walked into the principal's office, carrying himself straight and tall. You know... how Joe used to cup his books in one hand by his hip, casual? Like he'd forgotten he was even carrying books?" She shook her head.

"So *cool*. This boy did that, too, then looked at me with that expression Joe'd had, not guarded, the way kids are with teachers, but curious. Open."

For a moment, I could see Joe again, too – his artless, easy manner. He hadn't been cool as in hip – I knew what Jess meant. He'd been cool the same way Aggie had been cool. He was just himself.

"Then" – Jess let the yellow purse dangling off her elbow fall to the ground as she made a *clap* with her hands – "crash! I dropped my coffee cup. Black liquid swimming across the floor, the secretary rushing over with paper towels, and this boy who wasn't Joe slowly picking up each piece of the broken mug, calm, methodical, and then holding all these pieces up to me. He says... he says, 'I didn't mean to startle you, ma'am,' in a voice so like Joe's, I..." She stopped, picked up her purse and hugged it to her torso. "Why are you back, Cassie?"

I felt accused. I needed to answer honestly, though I hadn't told anyone about Maria. Why I'd really left Raleigh. So I uttered Maria's name aloud to someone here, in Bridgeton, told Jess the bare bones of my breakup. "This was the first interview I had. The first job I was offered. And... I took it."

Carefully, she opened her purse and took out her keys and snapped it shut again. *Too much info*, I thought. From me. Maybe from her.

"I'm adopting," she said. "A young child."

"How wonderful!"

"Thanks." A smile lit up her face, and she looked sweeter, less polished. "I haven't told many people. But I thought, I don't want to be a single Black mother in America without my family nearby to help."

I was surprised, briefly, but of course it would be more difficult as a single woman – even for someone like Jess. I wondered if it would be a boy.

"You'll be a fabulous mother," I said. "Lucky kid. And how wonderful for your parents to have you back. And with a child!"

"That's exactly what they say. And then they add, 'If only we could have Joe, too.' "

She looked away for a moment, and I wondered if she was trying to compose herself, but when she turned back she was dry-eyed. "And I have to admit." She put her sunglasses on again. "I feel the same way."

How long and subtly loss lingers. I went back to my little condo with my lunch from the farmers' market in Newfield, imagining Mr. and Mrs. Willis sitting stiffly in their living room, Mrs. Willis holding a cup of coffee herself as if enticing us to stay, but older now, thinner, leaning back as Joe wavered into their vision again the way Maria appeared now to me. I unlocked my door, and she was waiting for me in all her vibrant softness, as if I'd let her in, too – coming out to greet me in a favorite red dress which hugged her plump frame, her hair black against her olive skin. She spoke my name but I couldn't hear her, could only see her lips shaping the sound. Then she disappeared.

But Maria was alive. I could call her, if I wanted to. I wanted to. But I didn't call.

Maybe one day, I could tell Jess all about her.

As I continued into the kitchen to find a plate for my lunch, it struck me that Jess and I had spoken to each other in those ten minutes in a more personal way than we ever had in all our hours together at Friendly's and at parties and at Aggie's house. Why hadn't the two of us been better friends? We were similar, Jess and I – quiet, smart, slightly nerdy. In the shadows. Aggie and Joe had held the best actress and actor roles, and I'm not sure we even were supporting roles – we were the backdrop, the *mise en scène*, of their story. Yet maybe we had a bond that I'd never recognized. Our own friendship.

And then I felt hopeful. Unlike Aggie and me, who would have to paper over the years and years of non-contact, the hurt I felt which she was likely completely unaware of – Aggie hadn't done anything wrong to me, had she? – Jess and I could start afresh. Our shared history was not about our friendship; it was merely shared. She wouldn't have to explain her brother, tell me that he was shot, where he was shot – in Aggie's bedroom. She wouldn't have to explain the horror of knowing the kid who'd shot him in the dark, too drunk or high to recognize it was Joe and not some intruder he hadn't meant to shoot anyway, just scare. All in the very house where we'd spent so much time.

We shared that, too.

I began washing the lettuce from the market (trying not to grimace as I removed a slug – *it's called organic!*), cutting the tomatoes, making a dressing from scratch the way Maria had taught me, slicing off a hunk of bread from the rich, dark loaf. I should have invited Jess over. She lived just two floors above me, we'd discovered as we walked back – as if, I thought now, Joe was throwing us together. So I decided I would invite her to lunch next time, if I ran into her at the mailboxes after the farmers' market next week, or I could even leave a note under her door. I put on Lucinda Williams's new CD and unpacked one of the boxes I'd left in the hallway for the past month, when I was wondering why I'd ever moved back. Maybe this was why. I knew people. It wasn't like we would go hanging out in Friendly's again on a Friday night. But maybe I could recover something of what we'd lost so many years ago.

CHAPTER THREE

A blue-grey light cast an eerie sheen across my hands, the keyboard, my face. Just the flickering shadows of three television screens, hovering over the news desk like a triumvirate of unreasonable gods demanding we pay them attention, heed their warnings. I didn't want to be a follower, yet tonight I could not ignore their signs. Five police cruisers on a residential city block, two ambulance drivers and, its irregular shape drawn with yellow police tape, the amoeba of a crime scene.

"Is it up yet?" Alex at my shoulder.

I hit send. "It's up."

The headline first – we were still waiting for a story, from the wire, or from our own cop reporter, who'd been sent out about twenty minutes before – so at first just the headline: *Male Shot in NE Bridgeton*.

"OK, so Stacy is at the scene," Alex told the night team a few minutes later, "and all the residents are saying the cops shot the kid."

There were six of us at the late news meeting, held around nine each night to see if any breaking news warranted our changing the front page. Ray was the night editor, in charge of making such decisions. He looked like a friendly bear, shambling around the newsroom with his rounded face and plump stomach that shook when he told jokes, but he was blunt, precise and exacting. I'm not sure I would have taken a job in Bridgeton if he hadn't been the one interviewing me.

"Shit," Ray finally said. "What do the cops say?"

"No comment yet."

Ray's face stayed calm, but his gaze darted left then right as if the factors he had to consider were being scrolled in front of him.

"He's Black?"

"Unconfirmed."

"His condition?"

"We don't even know his name yet."

Ray sighed. The news wasn't adhering to our deadlines. We didn't even have enough to justify a story, let alone a front-page story. Yet if we put nothing in, we risked looking completely out of touch if the news evolved in the wrong way.

These days such partial stories were underlaid with dread as well. It was a particularly American dread. A shooting by a husband. A shooting by a lone gunman at a movie theater. This time, possibly, another shooting of a man by a cop. What type of fatal shooting was this one? Was it a Black man, and a white cop? Ray drummed his fingers on his knee, looking across the newsroom. I imagined it would be especially important to Ray, as a Black journalist, to make the right call.

"OK." He stood, ending the meeting. "Just a headline on the front-page for now. Keep on it."

Alex's phone rang. We all watched, stilled from closing our notebooks, clicking our pens shut, getting out of our seats, as he answered. "Shit," he said into the phone. "I'll send someone else out." We waited after he hung up. "The kid's dead."

We went to work. I updated the headline, scanned the wire to see if the AP reporter had information we didn't, listened to the TVs, prepared a new layout to reflect the story's growing importance. "Don't mention yet that a cop might have shot him," Ray said. "Not till we know what we're deciding for the paper."

As I sorted through the swirl of information and rumors and rumors-turned-facts to write my headlines, the gods of the TV screens drew my gaze. The images looked like scenes from any troubled city in any troubled region in the troubled United States of America and, at the same time, this was Bridgeton. Behind the women thrust into the glare of the cameras to talk about their friend, brother, son who'd just died was the menacing darkness of urban night, the sometimes run-down, sometimes perfectly kept homes and shops of any American city. And then, from that murky darkness, a quick light revealed the corner store where Aggie and I had once bought wine as underage teenagers. As cameras panned a clutch of neighbors who had come out of their houses to see what had happened, the Puerto Rican bakery where Aggie's father would sometimes send us for empanadas came into view. The young woman talking to the news right now? Veronica, one of the baristas at my new coffee haunt, Cam's.

Bridgeton then, and now.

A few minutes later, large on the TV, the inevitable photograph of the victim flashed up: a snapshot of the man, now identified as Will Alan Haley, at a barbecue the summer before. He was indeed a Black man, with a tawny brown complexion and a face that was long, thin, and stubbled at the chin, older than we thought – twenty-three – yet young enough to have a few pimples. He had a sideways grin that looked like it would appear with little prompting.

Someone had taken that photograph – his father, a sister, a friend – and his death would now be contained in this photograph, taken when no one could have known how he would die.

"Do we have that damned photo?" someone yelled out.

Joe's photo, the one that had run in all the papers, was his senior portrait: Joseph Thomas Willis, the promising young scholar. Never felt like Joe to me when I saw it.

We obtained the "damned" photo. I added it to the home page. I hoped friends and family would think it captured the Will Haley they knew and loved. I checked the live page for errors but found instead the reflection of my own face superimposed over the face of this boy I'd never known.

I felt Ray's presence before I realized he was standing behind me. "It's fine," he said. I didn't know how long he'd been there. I was glad he hadn't said it was good.

We looked up to see Alex rushing over.

"Cops confirmed it," Alex said. "One of their officers shot him."

I woke early the next morning with the sense that I had been shocked awake – by a noise, by a dream, I wasn't sure. I felt exhausted and hyper-alert at once. The scenes from the TV the night before, the photos we'd put up, even the layout of the home page with my overlarge headlines, the letters black like beetles creeping across sand, kept flashing in my head. The room itself felt heavy, humid, as if the young man who'd died was taking up a physical presence in the space. Cam's. I'd get coffee at Cam's. I had to get out. I wondered if I wanted to see Veronica, to share what we had seen last night, as if I had been at her side rather than behind the news desk, watching on a screen.

As I reached the foyer to our building, Jess was trying to push open the door while carrying three boxes of what I imagined were school materials, and I realized, with the *kerplunk* of the obvious, why I felt so upset. It was Joe's absence I'd felt upon waking, like a physical, humming presence in the room – like a haunting. His death had little similarity to last night's shooting – he was nothing like the young man killed, and he hadn't been shot by a cop. Yet of course his image now wavered before me as if I'd just needed to focus on him to see again the softness of his features, the way his face seemed to form a question, as if he was open to any answers.

I rushed to get the door for Jess, and she allowed me to relieve her of one of the boxes – "Lazy man's load," she said apologetically – and carry it outside. We paused together at her car. I'd seen Jess a couple of times, once at the mailboxes, another time in the parking lot. Both times we had fallen into conversations more serious than the circumstances should have allowed, yet when I'd blurted out a lunch invitation, she'd demurred with quiet words about the weeks ahead being a little busy.

"You've heard the news?" I asked.

She nodded. The boxes were tilted awkwardly against her hip as she began to unlock the trunk, almost catching her chocolate-brown and black coat, a kind of wool that might snag, so I took them from her. Key turned, trunk opened, boxes inside. Though she was dressed as exquisitely as usual, she looked tired, as if she'd been hauling those boxes around for miles.

"You OK?"

She shrugged, a gesture I'd begun to recognize though I still wasn't sure how to interpret it. If she was trying to shake something off, it never seemed to work. "I should be used to it," she said. "I am used to it. But today, my students will be asking me what I think. And what they're really asking me is, what should *they* think? And I don't know how to answer that." She unlocked and opened her car door. "And then, there's my parents."

I remembered Jess saying that Mr. and Mrs. Willis always brought up, in passing, every Black man or woman or child shot or otherwise dispatched from this country in an untimely manner, at least those who made the news – "And every week there's another one," Jess had pointed out. They wouldn't start a separate conversation, but in the course of talking about an event at the church, a trip to the mall, a relative visiting, they'd mention the latest Black American wrongfully killed – Trayvon Martin, Anthony Lamar Smith – as if each one deserved his name, her name, to be voiced by them. I'd been embarrassed not to recognize every one.

"So tonight, I'll have to call them, too. Tell them what *not* to think."

I was glad I hadn't mentioned why I was awake so early. To tell her would feel like burdening her further. Like asking her what I should think.

How would Joe have turned out? I sometimes wondered. When I visited Florence a few years ago, I visited the Galleria dell'Accademia to see Michelangelo's *David*, but it was a series of half-finished sculptures nearby that captured my attention – half-formed men caught in transition, as if unable to become who they wanted to be. Made of unbending stone, their hands were not coming free, their thighs not running off into their future. An unfinished painting can seem mystical, can hold promise – it's teasing in an appealing way, the colors, the hints of shapes, a face barely sketched. It's like it's there, but you just can't see it. But these figures seemed stopped mid-stride as if struck by lightning, then frozen.

This is the state of us all – how many of us emerge from our blocks of stone to become our best selves without being trapped in some way, caught by the foot, the arm, and held back? But ours are psychological blocks. Joe was cut down. I wished I could see him fully formed, moving in the world, now more than ever.

CHAPTER FOUR

There's an evolution to news stories, how they take shape and grow, how they take sides then reverse sides. In the article that ran the first morning, Will Haley was simply a Bridgeton man in the headline, not named until the third paragraph. On the second day, a news story which tried to piece together what had happened at the scene didn't name him until the fourth paragraph, and even the profile of Will Haley didn't use his name until the second paragraph.

By the third day, as the story caught the attention of the national media, I used Haley's name in multiple headlines: *Community Groups to Protest Haley Shooting*; *Police Have Video of Haley Incident*; *College Student Gives Haley Statement to Police*. It took only three nights for him to evolve into a name worthy of a headline. I'd made the change instinctively, on deadline, and then, as I turned the home page over to my colleagues, what I'd done registered with me. Becoming a headline wasn't a good fate for most human beings.

When I arrived home shortly before midnight, Maria called again. We'd argued the last time, but tonight her voice, its lilt and timbre, were exactly what I needed to hear. And she knew just when to call, knew my routines even now. Maybe knew I'd be upset.

She'd seen the story online, she said, and wanted to "check in".

Hang up, I told myself.

But I couldn't send her away, not yet, so instead, I found myself recounting every detail of the Haley shooting. In a kind of out-of-order account that a newspaper didn't allow for, I veered from details about his mother, who'd spoken to the paper at length – "He went to church with her last month on her birthday. Why do I find that so sad? It was kind of him, wasn't it? And she was so hopeful, genuinely hopeful. And what if she had a right to be? What if Haley really was turning it around?" – to what little information we had about the rookie cop who'd shot him – "Ten weeks on the force. I'm glad I don't have to wield a gun. He's white, of course, but I guess you knew that?" – to how frustrated we were that we couldn't get an interview with Haley's friend, a college kid from Morehouse College in Atlanta, home for the weekend, who was with Haley the night he was shot – "So close," I told her, "that some of the neighbors said there was blood on his shirt, too." On and on I went, in the kind of excruciating detail that only Maria would listen to – she'd tell stories in the same way to me – until I was almost in tears when I told her that there wasn't a gun at the scene after all, that what the cops had thought was a gun was not a toy gun, as in other horrific police shootings, not a knife, not a cell phone even, but a tie. A necktie.

"Really, a tie?" she said.

It'd been all over the news – the tie had been the detail that finally caught the attention of the national media, along with the protest that was building for the coming weekend – so I was surprised she hadn't read about it.

"You must have been horrified," she said.

"Tonight," I said, "I put Will Haley's name into a headline for the first time. I mean, it's nothing compared to everything else. But, how cold it felt, how inhumane. It's his name, but it was like he became a number."

"But you wouldn't want him to be nameless?" Maria said, with that familiar rise at the end of her sentence. Soothing.

Her voice had always been so soothing. "Have you seen Aggie again?" she asked.

The question startled me. Maria knew all about Joe and his death, which was why I'd told her about seeing Aggie. I knew she would understand. But it felt almost as if she had called, tonight, only to ask that question. *Is she jealous*, I thought, hopeful despite myself.

"No," I said. "I guess this is a bigger city than I remembered."

"Well," she said as if something had been settled. "You were right, by the way."

For a moment I didn't know what she meant. Right about Aggie? Then I knew she meant us. How had she turned the conversation so quickly to talk about us?

"I should tell my parents about us."

About you, I thought.

"I should have told them. You know. Ages ago."

She said it as if this were new, though I'd heard it before. Many times. "Will you?" I asked, automatically, though I didn't want to hear the answer.

"I don't know how. Yet. Yet! But—"

"So nothing's changed."

"It feels different." She sounded excited, the way she did when she felt she'd had one of her "visions", as she called them, about her parents, about her religion, about her childhood, about whatever stupid part of her life she wanted to understand better, so then – then! – she could make the changes she needed in her life. "I—"

"Maria." I said it softly, letting the syllables of her name which I loved as much as I loved her linger on my tongue. "Maria. I've got a long day tomorrow. I have to go."

It wasn't as hard to do as it had been the last time. I had my role now, here in Bridgeton, however small that role was. Like the cleaner in a surgery ward, or a secretary in the White House, I'd do my part: edit for clarity, look for inconsistencies, write headlines in consultation with Ray. I'd be a cog in the wheels of the fourth estate, the tail of the *a* maybe, the cross on the second *t*.

And being from Bridgeton would actually help. I'd been dismayed to find I had a deeper knowledge of the city than my counterparts except for Ray, even those who had been covering Bridgeton for years. They misspelled street names, put shops in the wrong neighborhood, and I'd make the correction. I knew Will Haley could not have gone to Broadview Junior High if he'd lived in the Waterside area all his life, so we'd caught that error, too. Small mistakes, yet I knew how important they'd be to the family, a family living with the idea that their son was killed because he was carrying his friend's tie. I knew how angry I'd felt whenever something about Joe had been wrong. When no one cared enough to get it right.

The next afternoon, the fierce beauty of a brisk, sunny afternoon in Connecticut made me stop, and look, and breathe in as I walked into the office. I'd forgotten the crackling brightness of a clear autumn day in New England, the air fresh and smelling like the crisp bark of trees. These months in the South were soggy by comparison, without the snap to distinguish them from winter or spring. This felt familiar, and right, despite the Haley story. Despite the call from Maria. Despite the dirty, oil-spilled black of the parking lot, the weeds penetrating the misshapen city sidewalks, the dim light in the bays of the trucks that would, about three the next morning, commence the delivery of our newspaper across the region and state. Autumn as it was meant to be. What a tangle of emotions I'd been caught in with Maria, hot and murky, like someone else's bath. It felt good to be out of that, at least.

Ray had been taken away from other duties to lead coverage of the Haley story exclusively, and he looked harassed when I arrived, a red mark on his brow as if he'd been leaning on his forehead for hours. He was on the phone but immediately put up a finger for me to wait. "Cassie, I need to get out of here for a half-hour," he said as he hung up. "You guys can spare Cassie another few minutes, yeah?" he said to the news desk. People looked up blankly and nodded. "Let's escape the dungeon and get a coffee."

I was glad to be back outside, glad to be chosen by Ray as company on a break from work, even though we began talking about the Haley case right away. He had asked several reporters to run through the chain of command for police, both for the city cops and the state police, who not only had been brought in to investigate, but now were on guard to lead crowd control if a second, larger protest, scheduled for the next week, became violent. "It's a little early for this," Ray admitted to me as we sat in the small café in Bushman Park with lattes. The park stretched out from City Hall and other municipal buildings, and, during weekdays, food trucks serving lunches – pizza and souvlaki and Thai food – parked around its grassy expanse, a little oasis in the bleak Bridgeton downtown. "But we'll know who to contact, if shit happens. Though let's hope it doesn't." He laughed. "I know that's not very journalistic of me."

"Very noble," I said.

"The other thing I want is to get some audio. We're a website, too, but we still act like we're just a newspaper. And." He paused to take a sip of his coffee. "I'd like you to do it."

"Me?" I tried not to sound panicked. "But I've never done that. I've not even interviewed anyone since college."

"I know it's not part of your job description. Part of your print background," he added, teasing. "But you're a good listener. You ask good questions. That's all you need for this. I just want people's voices."

I never knew why I'd gone into copy editing instead of reporting. I'd wanted to write in high school, but once I'd arrived at the college newspaper I lost my nerve. All I knew was that I was good with words. Editing felt safe.

"But I really don't know how—"

"Listen." Ray leaned toward me, elbows on his knees, eyed the surrounding tables for someone he might know, stretched his head closer and spoke furtively. "Listen, this paper is full of people who barely fucking know Bridgeton. They're on the journalistic career ladder. Bridgeton is a stepping stone. But you've come back here."

I'd never told Ray the personal reasons why I'd left North Carolina. In my interview, I'd used my growing up nearby as a reason I'd applied for the job, even though in actuality it was the reason I almost didn't apply. But I knew what he meant. "Oh c'mon. Smart Alex wants to devote his life to Bridgeton. Don't you think?"

"Exactly."

I looked around the park. Even the curves of its paths, the big old oak trees, were familiar. When Aggie and I came shopping here in high school – or rather, when Aggie shopped and I watched – we always ate at one of the food trucks for lunch, no matter what the weather. The Thai truck was our favorite.

"But I've never been a reporter," I said.

Ray sat back in the stiff metal chair as if it were a La-Z-Boy, stretching his legs out to the side of our table, casual. "I've watched you, Cassie. As this story has unfolded. You're the only other person in that newsroom to whom this story feels personal."

I tried to remember what I had said or done that would make him think that. What had he seen? I laughed, and shook my head.

"And the story will disappear, you know."

I looked up at him. "Disappear?" The NAACP was expecting the national TV stations to show up for their protest next week.

"Give it a week, tops. This story will dis-a-ppear. One Black man. Shot by a white cop. Nothing new really. Is it? And, well. We can't let it."

I was going to say it wouldn't go away in a small, liberal

place like Connecticut. After Sandy Hook last year, we'd tightened our gun laws, even if Congress hadn't. But then I stopped myself. This was one person, not twenty elementary school children and six of their teachers. One Black man with a prison record. I thought of the high school students that Jess taught, students perhaps not so unlike we were at that age. How would they feel if the story was dropped?

"What if I talked to some kids at the high school?" I said.

"Yes. Yes. I know the principal at Whitman." He laughed. "Dated her while going to that very high school."

Jess's boss. Hadn't she mentioned her during one of our brief conversations in the lobby?

"Till she broke up with my sorry ass."

"So she owes you one."

He laughed again. "I will always owe her."

"Now *that* sounds like an interesting story."

"No asking her about that! Seriously, she'll be cool with us talking to students. Likes getting this kind of publicity. Pretty open for a school official."

"Felicity Ford," I said, remembering her name.

"See. You do know Bridgeton." Ray smiled broadly, and I suspected that this had been the purpose of our conversation all along.

Before reporters left for the night, all the people working on the Haley story gathered for a meeting, and the reporters went over what they'd heard that day, what they'd be working on the next day. Malik Washington, the friend who was with Haley, had traveled back to Atlanta and hadn't changed his mind about talking to the press. "So we still don't know his version of what happened," Stacy said.

"He's secured himself a smart lawyer," Ray said. "Nehemiah James. Malik Washington won't be talking to us until his lawyer knows it'll help him. OK, have we gone through the chain of command? I want to be prepared for that."

People threw out the names they'd tracked down while Alex took notes for a chart we'd put up in the newsroom: side-by-side columns of city and state police. Each had multiple departments: Internal Affairs, Major Incident Response Teams (called MIRTs, I learned that day), Community Relations, plus, for the city police, those in charge the night Haley was shot.

"Also from the state police, Hector Whitcombe," Stacy said. "He's a public safety guy."

Oh, god, I thought. Aggie's brother?

Alex laughed. "Aren't they all public safety guys?"

"Sorry. I meant MIRT."

"Hector Whitcombe?" I said. "Hector Whitcombe is involved with this?"

Ray was staring at me, his face getting sterner and quieter as he spoke. "You mean to say that our director of the Major Incident Response Team is Hector Whitcombe? *Hector* Whitcombe? The twenty-year-old racist bully whose drunken, racist friend shot a high school kid because they didn't want his sister sleeping with a Black boy?"

And that feeling I'd had for years after waking up the day after that summer party to find out that Joe had been shot – when my mother told me about the accident at Aggie's house the night before, "I'm sorry, your friend Joe is dead"; during all those weeks I didn't see Aggie because no one would let me near her; in the first months and years of college and sometimes even after – that feeling of guilt slithered through my body like venom from a snakebite, coursing through my veins, squeezing my heart, working its way up my throat until I felt nauseous – *It wasn't an accident*, I thought to myself, for the first time in years – nauseous with guilt as strong as if I'd killed him myself, because we were all responsible. Weren't we? All of us, every one of us, could have stopped it somehow.

"What are you guys talking about?" Stacy said.

"Jesus Christ," Ray said. "We'll have to keep an eye on him."

"Oh, you're not going to drag all that up again?" I thought

of Jess, the dread on her face the morning after the Haley shooting, and her parents, who still couldn't speak of their son's death. Would they now be forced to read after all these years another story outlining the ugly end to the life of their son and brother, Joseph Thomas Willis, some weird formal version of Joe who didn't seem like Joe at all? I thought of Aggie, home to take care of her ailing father – did she deserve being reminded again that her boyfriend was shot, naked, in her own bedroom? And I had to admit that I didn't want to relive those days either, those awful, confusing days when I lost not only my friend Joe but Aggie, too, and that entire world which, in the heady weeks after high school graduation, was still full of untarnished promise.

"Cassie, you're joking, right?" Ray said. "You really don't think Hector Whitcombe being in charge of any aspect of this investigation is a story?"

"I'm not thinking of him," I said.

Ray didn't hear me. "Jesus, I should have recognized him. That bastard should've been put in prison, too."

No, no, I don't want to hear this again, no. "I'm no fan of Hector Whitcombe, but it was that idiot friend of his who shot Joe—"

"That idiot friend got off pretty damn lightly."

"Oh, stop it!" I said. "Stop it! It was awful."

I thought of Hector's face at the party the night that Joe was shot as he asked me, casual, trying not to admit he was lowering himself by talking to me, offhand, yet excited, too: "Where's my sister?" His eyes glazed with drink and god knows what else. He knew exactly where Aggie was. Why did he have to ask me?

"Joe was my friend, they were all my friends. Joe, Aggie, Jessica his sister, we were all friends!"

Ray leaned forward, his elbows on his knees, then watched me without moving, quiet, like you might be with an upset child. Or maybe he was trying to assess my value to him. He was a journalist first.

39

"You went to high school with Joe Willis?"

I nodded, silent.

"Jesus Christ."

"Phone call, Ray," someone called over.

He looked over to acknowledge him, then stood up to go. "Meeting's over," he said, then turned to me. "At some point, you'll have to tell me what else you know."

CHAPTER FIVE

There is no beginning. All of the events from that year progress and elide so that there is no starting point: it had already begun. Which doesn't mean that Joe's death couldn't have been prevented – happenstance alone could have altered the outcome of that night – but the Whitcombes could have made the biggest difference. I think that now, though I also know that for Joe to be alive today, the Whitcombes would have needed to change something so inherent in who they were that I don't know whether to believe that would have been possible, or impossible. So I'll begin again with the Whitcombes, because so much for me – my teenage friendship with Aggie, my innocence, her innocence, if any of us are ever innocent – ended there. And Joe ends there.

"Cassandra?" Mr. Whitcombe's bushy eyebrows flitted above his black-rimmed glasses when he heard my name for the first time, and he clasped his hands to his chest. "How marvelous."

Aggie looked at me and smiled. Her father was a classics professor, and she'd predicted he'd be delighted that my name was Cassandra. If he'd had his way, her own formal name wouldn't be Agatha – as her mother had insisted when she turned out to be a girl – but Agamemnon. "He'll act as if your parents had invented the name 'Cassandra' and written the *Iliad* themselves instead of Homer. He'll be *that* excited."

I smiled back at her uncertainly but mainly stared at Mr. Whitcombe. He was unlike any parent I'd ever met, with glasses that looked like Kevin Costner's in *JFK*, before those glasses were cool, and a tweed jacket that resembled something out of *Brideshead Revisited*. This was a *parent*? I'm still not sure if Aggie's father had adopted this look – if it was a conscious demeanor that he strove to attain – or if he had simply never changed his glasses or attire since going to graduate school in the 1960s.

He took off his glasses and rested his chin on his hand, considering me for a moment, then held them in the air, waving them exuberantly. "Yes, it is fitting you are Aggie's friend," he said, then frowned, troubled suddenly. "Even if she ended up with Agamemnon as a war prize at the end of the Trojan War. Poor thing. It was not Agamemnon's finest hour. He should have protected her from Clytemnestra."

"Yeah, she knows, Dad," Aggie said impatiently. "She's taking Latin."

But I hadn't known.

"Latin!" He was made exuberant again by the mere word. "Latin! My dear, you must take Greek next, but yes, persist with Latin for a few years. Indeed you are fortunate to have found each other. Cassandra and Agamemnon."

Mrs. Whitcombe had been standing at the edge of the room, leaning against the door frame in flowing, silky pants and a tunic that at first I mistook for a long dress. The only time I'd ever seen my mother in a dress that long was in her own wedding pictures and her sister's.

"Her name is Agatha, my love," Mrs. Whitcombe said.

It would become our nickname for Aggie's mother. "Her Name's Agatha says I can't go out tonight – my aunt's visiting." "Her Name's Agatha says to come over at seven." "I suspect Her Name's Agatha might just disapprove of Joe, not that she'll ever admit it."

Mr. Whitcombe went on, oblivious to his wife's correction. "Cassandra is much maligned. She is, after all, a truth teller, and the world is never kind to truth tellers. So, Aggie, you must remember to listen to Cassie when she speaks. And, Cassie, you are fortunate, too, as the word Agamemnon in Greek is literally translated as *steadfast*. Let me be more precise: *very steadfast*. So Aggie will be a good friend."

"God, Dad, enough," Aggie said, before I could stop myself from saying:

"Wow."

They all laughed.

The next time I visited, Aggie's parents were arguing – discussing, they never argued – over which rendition of Chopin's waltzes to play on their CD player. They owned three. "I like one best," Aggie's father said, "Diana likes another one best, and this one received the best reviews." Aggie rolled her eyes but I was enchanted. All the floors in the house were wood, even the kitchen – unlike the wall-to-wall shag carpet and linoleum that covered every floor surface in my house – except for the bright blue and yellow tiles they had brought back from Mexico for the foyer. Did we even have a foyer? We barely had a hallway. Real paintings by painters that Aggie's mother had known in art school hung on the walls, including a few nudes – I'd only seen nudes on school trips to museums. They had two living rooms but called one the library, and Aggie's father had a "study" upstairs as well. Every one of those rooms had walls and walls of books.

I became their little project. "Has Cassie heard Billie Holiday yet? Shall we start with early or late Billie? Oh, just put on *Lady in Autumn*." "We must take Cassie to off-Broadway. I mean, I imagine you've seen *Annie*, dear, but what about *Dancing at Lughnasa*? The five sisters are both wildly exuberant and desperately sad. Every young woman should see it." (I hadn't even seen *Annie*.) "Let's put out the camembert for after dinner – I'm sure Cassie hasn't tasted camembert." I didn't even know he was talking about cheese until, after dinner, Mrs. Whitcombe carried into the dining room a wooden cutting board laden with a crusty white circle, round crackers I'd eventually learn were oatcakes, and tiny little knives. Since when did cheese come *after* dinner?

I revelled in it. I did not sense the condescension, the self-congratulatory air of their attention. They took it upon themselves to give me a cultural education, and their world was too fascinating, too alluring, for me to notice that their distant amusement – Mrs. Whitcombe's in particular – was at my expense. No one could please Mrs. Whitcombe anyway, except maybe Hector.

But it was Mr. Whitcombe I most liked pleasing. The glow of his passion for poetry, fiction, art, music, film, shone around him like the brightest lamp, its light falling on anyone within range, interested or not. And I was wildly interested. Here was a world I'd known only in books and movies, yet I couldn't imagine it in my world, the way one can't really imagine the smells and sounds and dirty reality of Chaucer's England or the Brontës' Yorkshire. This was not a place one could travel to. And then, suddenly, I walked into Aggie's house and I was enveloped by it – embraced even, coaxed along so that I might someday feel like a native. Like I belonged.

I still know I became the person I am because of the time I spent at the Whitcombes – the freedom I glimpsed, the culture I inculcated. Whenever I've set up a new home, and installed another IKEA bookcase or two, which is the closest I'll ever get to floor-to-ceiling shelving, Aggie's house has been present, her father's small pamphlet of poems, which he gave me on my sixteenth birthday, given a treasured spot at the center, its narrow spine nearly invisible to anyone but me. In that home, I experienced life the way I wanted it to be.

At least, I thought I did.

It wasn't until years later that I wondered: had Joe ever felt this way? And I could not decide which would be sadder: Joe feeling like he belonged, or Joe knowing that he would never belong.

CHAPTER SIX

Mainly, though, I liked Aggie by herself.

Here she is in her room at her old-fashioned mirrored vanity with matching stool, wearing a thick turquoise silk robe – one of the expensive items her mother had purchased that Aggie professed a ludicrous luxury while nonetheless using it constantly. I'm behind her, sprawled across her bed, watching her apply makeup.

Eyeshadow was a new concept for Aggie, and her mother had splurged on two expensive sets at a shop in New York City the weekend before. "I love these colors!" Aggie said. The case sat in front of her like a box of chocolates: dark chocolate, milk chocolate, caramel, cream. "Apparently, these will bring out the green in my eyes," she said, but her effort was rather haphazard as she chattered away to me. Once or twice, she forgot what she was doing altogether, like her father, and just sat at the dressing table and talked.

"Oh my god, it's hot!" She opened a window further to the early spring night, then took off her robe and sat in her bra and underpants, her body luminous in the falling light. She was completely unselfconscious but I felt fine-tuned to her nakedness – the gentle knobs of her spine, the fine hairs on her arms, and, in the mirror, the slight roundness of her breasts under her bra, a lacy pink thing entirely unlike Aggie. That, too, must have been for Joe.

"Look!" she said, sticking her chest in my direction. "My new pretend bra!"

"Pretty," I said.

"It might as well be a handkerchief," she said. "Unlike you, I don't actually have breasts." But I could tell she was pleased with it, and it suited her, the delicate fabric around her delicate breasts.

She frowned into the mirror at the result of the dark brown eyeshadow, then wiped it off. She sighed. "This one's awful on me. I'll have to try again. I'll bet you'll look good in the darker brown, though." She made room for me on the narrow seat.

I didn't really like makeup – still don't – but I sat next to her. She handed me the case and a brush, and our two faces stared back at us from the mirror, hers pale with a dishevelled halo of black hair, mine olive and framed sharply with straight, thick, paler hair. Our elbows and hips kept bumping against one another. I tried the darker brown as Aggie cleaned her lids to start again, and I kept watching her: her pale lips pursing sideways as she applied the two paler colors, her tongue licking her lips as she tried to blend the edges. She caught me looking and I made a goofy face.

She examined what I was doing. "You're crap at this," she said.

I stared at my eyes in the mirror, then at hers again, trying to see what she had done. "Honestly, I can see yours is better, but I have no idea how you did it."

"Let me," she said. "Move."

She directed me to the edge of her bed and leaned forward on her stool, one hand holding my chin, angling me left or right as she applied three shades of shadow – "Apparently, this is called sculpting," she said – then started putting a sheer foundation on my cheek – "No, I don't want that," I said. She wet a cotton ball with her tongue to take it off, then insisted on putting on gloss with the tip of her forefinger, her gaze intent on my eyes, my cheeks, my lips.

"You're just not patient enough. See, you need to apply eyeshadow slowly or it's like a sandstorm." Her words blew against my cheeks. "You're blushing. I can't see how it looks if you're blushing."

This made me blush more. "I can't help it!"

"You're hopeless – it's just me!"

"It's embarrassing – you're looking at every pore."

But she could have had her eyes shut, and I'd flush from the feel of her hands and fingers on my face, the heat of her breath on my cheek.

"You want to try anything on?" she asked.

Although Aggie was skinnier, we were almost the same size, so sometimes we wore each other's clothes. I shook my head. I just wanted to watch her.

She began trying out combinations of different jeans with different tops. She wasn't happy with any of them. I held up one of my own shirts, which I'd brought for tomorrow, knowing we were really late for Joe and Jess now, not bothering to point that out. But she shook her head, and put back on the first ensemble she'd tried, slim-fit faded jeans and a tight tulip-yellow T-shirt. "Do you think these are too tight?" she asked. I wiggled my hand in her waist to see how much room she had, feeling the softness of her skin against my fingers. "Tons of room," I said, reluctantly releasing my hand from her waist.

This was teenage bliss – or, at least, *my* teenage bliss. Innocent; casual; pre-sexual. Given what I know now about the joys of sex, I'm sure it isn't Aggie's idea of it, if these girlish memories remain with her at all. Her bliss was with Joe. When I remember them together, how their bodies always moved toward one another, their hands and arms touching and exploring and entwining – it was so natural. It wasn't pre-sexual, but so newly sexual that it, too, had an innocence, a lightness that's impossible to maintain as life gets more complicated. I want to tell her she would have lost that teenage bliss no matter what happened to Joe. That what she had wasn't sustainable. But Joe was killed, and so a normal loss became an abnormal, unreconcilable loss. It will never make sense. Even as I write this, trying to make sense of it, trying to tell our stories, I know it will never make sense.

We brought Joe and Jess back to Aggie's, and it was warm enough to hang out on their back porch if we all wore sweaters, except Joe, who always seemed impervious to the cold, in a dark blue cotton T-shirt. "Male metabolism," Mrs. Whitcombe said, eyeing him briefly as she asked if we needed anything else before she "retired". Aggie must have won the tug of war on what music to play because Tracy Chapman was coming quietly out of the outside speakers. Her new fave.

"Cassie," Joe said. "I think maybe Luke, you know, has the hots for you."

Luke was Joe's friend and, by now, our friend, too – it was unusual for him not to join us. Aggie and I had been in classes with him throughout high school, and now that we knew him, it seemed odd we hadn't been friends sooner. But Aggie and I had been somewhat exclusive, more so, strangely, than Joe and Aggie were.

Aggie, on the swing, rolled her eyes and took another sip of a glass of wine. The Whitcombes, being enlightened sophisticates, allowed us all to drink – "In moderation!" her mother would emphasize as she brought out one bottle and four wine glasses on a round metal platter from the '50s that they'd found in an antiques store.

"Luke? Like, no kidding," Aggie said.

I blushed. "I don't think so."

At the front of the house, a car squealed to a stop. Hector? He was supposed to be out for the night. I doubt we would have stayed at Aggie's if she'd thought he'd be around. Joe looked up, too, from his seat on the steps of the back porch, a foot now on each of the two steps, as if ready to take off. But then the car continued past the house.

Joe looked back at me then pulled another tall strand of grass that must have sprouted up since the lawn service's last visit before winter.

"OK, I'm a guy, yeah? And I can tell."

I'd forgotten for a moment they were talking about Luke.

"It's pretty obvious," Aggie agreed.

"Which is half the problem with Luke," I said. "Everything is obvious."

"Not really."

"He's obvious about everything. The music he likes, his clothes, his sense of humor."

But I didn't mean it. The truth was, I liked Luke. As the five of us had become friends, these two sets of friends shuffled into a different pair of subsets – Jess, Luke and me together making up the third wheels to Joe and Aggie. We found all five of us had the same sense of humor, a similar taste in movies and books and people. We disdained Daisy Dixon, the most popular girl in the class, who might have been smart if she wasn't so spoiled, and her set of acolytes, including Bill Henderson. We didn't understand why we were supposed to care about the characters in *The Great Gatsby*, and thought it appropriate, and hysterical, when Gatsby says about Daisy: "Her voice is full of money." Among all five of us, it became a running joke applied widely. Our English teacher's voice was full of semicolons; Mr. Simon, who was teaching us politics in the spring semester, had a voice full of chalk. Kathleen Turner's voice was full of butter. Dan Quayle's voice was full of mashed potatoes. Bill Clinton was running then, with his bimbo scandals exploding every other week – "I mean, is he *that* handsome?" Aggie asked – and his voice was full of flowers. "And not just Gennifer Flowers," Luke added.

But I didn't like Luke in *that* way.

"He's brilliant in physics," Aggie said. "Apparently. Right, Joe? No one in class understands what Mr. Miller is talking about except for Luke."

"Yeah, well."

"So?"

"So why are you guys trying to talk me into liking Luke? I don't think he's my type anyway."

"That's what Jess says all the time," Joe said.

Jess was sitting on one of the padded wicker chairs, her feet tucked up under her, the high rounded white wicker back making her look as small and self-contained as a contented cat. "Hmmmm. I think what I say is that the reason I don't 'like' someone is hard to explain, but the fact that I *don't* like them is very clear."

"Right," Joe said. "He's not your type. C'mon, Cass, isn't there anyone you've had a crush on?"

I shook my head.

"You know – you're right," Aggie said. "I can't think of a single guy you've had a crush on."

"I don't like any guys," I said.

They all stared at me. "What are you saying there, Cassandra Jones?" Joe said.

"No! I didn't mean *that*!" Did I? "I just… I don't know. I guess I haven't met the right one yet."

"I know who you had a crush on!" Aggie said. "That exchange student who was here last year. Francois!"

Jess giggled. "He was gay. Does that count?"

"Why not?" I asked.

Francois had been a hoot. He had this adorable French accent and jet-black hair that he would swoosh back with a flounce whenever anyone said something stupid. "*Mon père*, you are – *je ne se quoi* – *un dunce*." He wore wild floral shirts and horn-rimmed tortoiseshell glasses way before that look was in. I had been fascinated by him.

"He was pretty gay," Aggie admitted.

"No," Joe said. "I think he counts. He was cool."

"Not you, too," Aggie said.

"Seriously – he was different. I like your type, Cassie." He smiled at me as if he knew something – as if he understood. Had he guessed? Maybe he guessed I was gay even before I

50

did. I wonder if he even guessed I was in love with Aggie, and still made me his friend.

At Aggie's house that night, as we drifted off to sleep in her double bed, Aggie asked, her voice softer than usual, barely audible, "*Do* you like any guys?"

We'd opened the windows, and I could hear the crickets and the occasional car rush by. "I like a few people of the male persuasion."

"You know what I mean." She kicked me gently, her bare foot soft on my leg.

I couldn't say anything, as if my throat was filling with air, blocking me from speaking. I couldn't think either, a blank sponge expanding within my head as well as air filling my throat.

"It's OK," Aggie said.

I shrugged but still couldn't speak. "Sure," I finally said, but she might have been asleep by then.

By the next morning, though, I was secretly pleased. They were talking about me. I was a topic of discussion. I liked being a topic of their discussion – as if I were an object they considered, picked up and turned round and round in their hands. Contemplated. I liked the sensation of being under their gaze, Aggie seeing me differently as Joe turned me round and round for her, inviting her to see me in this light, then that, instead of in the usual light. Joe making me more interesting.

And then I began to notice Luke more, too, or at least notice his interest in me. How often he sat near me at lunch, at parties, in the car to the movies. How he was often the first one to laugh at my jokes. I found a photo from the year before at a party, before Joe was really part of our circle, and Luke, smiling widely, had his arms around me. I didn't remember him hugging me, had no recollection of the sensation of his arms around my body. I contemplated all this with a kind of detachment – a detached pleasure, a detached hyper-awareness, from which was absent any excitement. I just took stock of it. I was the focus of someone's attention, and even if it was from the wrong person, it made me feel more solid, somehow. Now that my best friend had a boyfriend, a defection every best friend hates, maybe I needed that.

II

2013/1992

A Wound Reopened

CHAPTER SEVEN

Half in sun, half in shadow, a slender hand cupped over half her forehead so she could read the book held flat with her other hand, one elegant black pump half off one foot, Jess basked in what was left of the sunlight at a table near the window at Cam's.

I'd not seen her since the morning after Haley's shooting, so I was pleased when she'd called and suggested we meet here after her workday ended and before mine began. But I also wondered why she'd asked. In the careful way she sat, her hand protecting her from more than the sun, I sensed in her the desire for reprieve. Not a reminder of all things bad in the world. I'd be such a reminder.

Ray hadn't heard back from the school principal yet about interviewing students, and I'd been thinking of asking Jess. I wondered now if I should hold off.

I chatted with Veronica as I ordered, and Jess heard my voice, smiled and put her book to the side.

"Cassie," she said as I walked over with my latte. She stood as if she might hug me, but then sat back down. "I didn't see you come in."

I took the seat across from her. Jess sat straight in her chair, occasionally playing with a ring on her finger. If I'd been expecting something casual I was going to be disappointed. She was her formal Jess.

"So, how are you? Must be busy at work," she said.

I wondered again why she'd called. "Crazy," I said.

She began twiddling her teacup, staring down quizzically as it rattled quietly in its saucer as if she didn't know what was causing the noise. "Listen, Cassie," she said without lifting her gaze. "I'm going to get right to the point. My principal has asked me to help out a reporter who wants to come talk to some students. And then I found out it was you."

"Yes, that's right," I repeated cautiously. "My venture into multimedia."

No response.

"So if you were involved, that'd be a fantastic surprise."

She stilled her hands and looked up. "You didn't know?"

"Well, no," I said. "I mean, my editor knows your principal from high school…"

She laughed, and I could see her shoulders relax, as if she'd put down a heavy bag. "I'm so relieved. Honest. When my principal came to me I thought you had mentioned me to the paper. Mentioned Joe."

I shook my head. No need to tell her Joe's name had come up without my help.

"And it felt like kind of a breach of… you know. I mean, it's silly because it's not like it's a secret." She put her hands to her face for a moment as if in tears, then I saw she was just embarrassed. "I'm sorry. I really got the wrong end of the stick."

"It's fine," I said, Ray's voice in my head. *At some point you'll have to tell me what else you know.*

"Let's start over," Jess said. "Cassandra Jones. How *are* you?"

Once we settled in, Jess and I talked like old friends. It was as if each of us tiptoed up to the other, wary, hesitant, then forgot about those hesitations once in each other's company. When I asked about her adoption, she ordered a glass of wine. "I'm at the end of my day," she said, "and right now, this topic requires alcohol."

Jess was feeling frustrated by the bureaucracy of adopting a child. The day I'd seen her at the mailboxes was the day after she'd gotten approved for a license to adopt – "Eleven months that took. And that was considered quick. I mean, no wonder more people don't do this…" – and she thought the matching phase, in which she'd be matched with a child, would begin immediately. Instead, she discovered, this prompted a further series of interviews about what kind of child might be suitable for her. Most of the children being adopted were coming from difficult situations, and so the state needed to determine what "needs level", based on a child's background, would be appropriate. Jess had one last consultation before the actual matching process could begin, and she still didn't have an appointment yet.

"It's awful," I said, "but this is good bureaucracy. Isn't it? The state taking care of their charges. And you."

When she asked about my breakup, I joked that I was proceeding through the de-adoption process with Maria. Jess was a quiet listener as I confided in her about Maria hiding her sexuality from her Catholic Puerto Rican family, but still seeing them almost every day – about the times I went for a hike, saw a movie, or sat at home alone when Maria went to family dinners, weddings, christenings. Her own birthday. "You must have loved her very much," Jess said. "And you must be very strong to have dealt with that for so long."

"Or stupid." But Jess's softness, her non-judgment, felt like a salve.

Yet I had to get to work. The second Haley protest was being held that night, and while I'd no longer be early to work, I certainly didn't want to be late. I moved to leave, and she reminded me we needed to make arrangements for me to come to the school. There was a new student group called One Whitman formed by two seniors who wanted to investigate and address the racial divisions within the school. Jess was serving as their advisor. "And that must be why Felicity came to me. They're wonderful. Articulate. Thoughtful. The problem is… I can't be in the paper."

I wasn't planning on quoting any teachers, but if Ray knew who Jess was, he might want me to. "OK by me. I want to focus on the kids anyway."

"Let's do it, then," she said.

We agreed she'd find out which afternoon next week the students would be available to talk; we'd meet at the school and use her classroom.

"Cassie," she said as I reached for my bag. "Can I ask you something else?"

I refused to look at my watch. "Sure."

"Is the paper going to write a new story about Joe?"

I thought about Ray's reaction to Hector's name. Would we? "Why do you ask?"

"My parents know Haley's mother – she's a member of Daddy's church. And then I began to worry when my parents told me that Hector works for the police now. Worry that it would all come back."

Mrs. Haley was a member of her father's church? Had I really not caught that detail?

"You know my mother? She's kept Joe's room exactly as it was when he was killed. Every embarrassing rock poster, his high school diploma, which she'd framed and made him hang up, still on the wall. His acceptance letter to Penn is taped over his desk, yellowing. I can't bear it. So a story right now?" She shook her head. "I want them to concentrate on the future."

I wondered which posters were in Joe's room. Which objects had been kept by him, then his mother. How painful it must have been for Jess to walk past. And yet I understood Mrs. Willis's desire, too, for a space where Joe was preserved.

"I'm sorry," I said.

"So you'll help?"

I didn't know what she meant. "Of course I'll help."

She held my hand in both of hers. "Oh, thanks. So much. I'll tell Daddy you'll do what you can to keep a new story out of the paper. He's worried, too."

It was then I realized what I'd promised.

At work, we watched the Haley protest on the TV screens above the news desk, Ray next to me. It was an orderly, quiet demonstration, and their case that the police officer had acted wrongly was becoming stronger. He was a rookie cop named Sean McCarthy, we'd learned a few days before, who at twenty-five was not much older than Will Haley. While they were refusing to release the video, the principal witness was extremely reliable. Not only was Malik Washington on a full academic scholarship at Morehouse, he'd been named Volunteer of the Year at his high school after helping inmates in Connecticut prisons learn to read. A family friend had said he'd been inspired to do this when Will Haley ended up in prison – Haley had been a friend of Malik's late brother four years earlier. "Will used to check on Malik after his brother died," the friend said. "Recently, Malik had been checking on Will."

But to everyone else, the story had lost its shine. Only about forty people were gathering outside City Hall with *Black Lives Matter* and *Haley's Life Matters* signs, and the media coverage was entirely local. A Black man killed for carrying a necktie was already old news. A mere week and a half after his death, the world was moving on. In truth, the world had barely even paused.

I began playing with the headline. *Protest Over 'Tie' Shooting Garners Zero Attention*, I typed, then erased it. Helpless. I felt helpless again, as I had after Joe died, when I felt the reasons given for his death didn't add up and I couldn't do anything about it. Hector and his friend Ed had known Joe was at Aggie's. How could Ed think he was an intruder?

And this time, I wasn't just an eighteen-year-old high school graduate. I was a journalist.

Ray sat down beside me to consult on the home page, I assumed, and I motioned to the TV screens. "No one outside Connecticut is even covering this," I said. "You were right."

He sat so still I wondered if he'd heard me. Or maybe he was just thinking about an actual headline I could write, rather than wallowing the way I was.

"You do know I don't actually *want* to be right?" he asked.

Now I felt even more foolish. "I'm sorr—"

"Don't Cassie. No need. But for my sons?"

Ray never talked about his sons. He was divorced, another journalist who'd screwed up his personal life, but that was all I knew.

"For my sons, I wish I wasn't right."

He stood. Conversation over, but I persisted.

"Will you tell them that?"

Ray grimaced. "They're with their mother," he said. "Oh, and I've just emailed you the contact at the high school. It's a Jessica Willis." He waited for a reaction. "Is that who I think it is? Joe Willis's sister?"

Now I knew the real reason for Ray's little chat. I thought about pretending not to know Jess was my contact at the high school, thought about what I'd promised her, but I nodded. On the screens, protesters began chanting, "Justice for Haley."

"I'd ask if this was a conflict for you, but we can't quote her anyway, or mention her name. It took me a second to figure out why."

I was glad the principal had made that rule. "I'm not really friends with Jess now," I said.

"Good," he said. "Because she'd make a good story."

This was true and I didn't try to argue the point. "Except she won't want a story," I said.

Ray shifted his gaze from the TV to look at me. "I thought you didn't know her anymore."

"I know her well enough to know that. She's..." I almost

told Ray she was adopting, but that was too personal. I already knew more than I could tell Ray.

"She's what?"

"Concentrating on other things. I guess. It's been a long time."

"Well," he said as he rose to leave. "Keep it in mind. You know those boys' tall tale about looking for coyotes to shoot that night was a bunch of bullshit. I'll bet Jess knows it, too. I mean" – Ray sat down again, leaned his elbow on his knee but didn't look at me, just spoke, quiet, familial, intimate – "maybe you got unfinished business here in Bridgeton, Cassie. I mean, I sort of wondered why you came back."

CHAPTER EIGHT

It was strange, a few days later, being in a high school again. Students were streaming into the Atrium for the lunch break as I arrived, some getting in line for food, but most just standing around, forming clumps of five or six. Lunch wasn't the point. One tall blonde boy approached a group with a kind of backward-leaning walk, smiling with a cool diffidence, as if he were being pulled along pleasantly without quite making any effort. He fist-bumped a Black kid wearing different-colored socks under his sandals: one dark blue, one brilliant blue. The Black girl next to him was wearing red and black checked jeans; another girl, white, crossed the Atrium in a pink and orange flowery dress, her long, '70s-style hair flowing behind her. She was among several white girls who had dyed her hair a light, beautiful grey, sometimes tinged with pale purple, that I'd seen a few times in town. Grey was the new blonde.

I'd been expecting school to feel different, but as dozens more students streamed in for lunch – a girl in drastically short cutoffs and mustard-colored tights, a boy in white sneakers with black laces – I thought: they're just teenagers. Had I expected them to hail from Pluto? They dressed more outlandishly than we had, and we were before the era of earbuds: it seemed like the white boys wore black earbuds, and the Black boys wore white ones. Everything was a fashion statement. Yet they could have been my friends. I could almost put on jeans and step right in, except that the poses of adolescence, its insecurities, were shining out at me. Every step seemed self-conscious, for the boys especially. I hadn't been aware of these emotions when I was in high school; I didn't know how strongly they drove us. But I could see them now.

How comfortable Joe had usually seemed. His array of T-shirts that were always a bit too large for him, the relaxed slump of his shoulders, their frown reversed by his ready smile. I tried not to look for him in the crowd.

An issue the students I was interviewing wanted to address, Jess had told me, was self-segregation: they were trying to encourage students to integrate outside the classroom, even if too often they ended up segregated in the classroom, as well as in the world. ("And it's not really *self*-segregation," one would remind me. "We make friends where we live.") It made me realize how few kids of color I'd had in my own classes, twenty years earlier. But the group of white kids I was watching now included two Black students; the one to their left included an Asian guy, a Latino girl and a Black girl. I was pleased. Then I noticed, deeper into the room, swaths of students who were all Black. Jess's students were right, of course. It had happened when I was a student, too. The Black tables. The Black seating area at the basketball game where I never would have chosen to sit. How I'd progress instinctively to a seat in the section I didn't think of as the white section, though it was. How uncomfortable I'd feel walking through a particular entrance into my own high school cafeteria where Black kids, mostly boys, tended to congregate.

I looked back toward the other part of the Atrium, and saw that the groups there were pretty much white. One or two kids of color in a group of mostly white students does not integration make. Though it passes for integration in the white world.

Then Jess was walking up to me, and as I watched the fashionable adult version of my old friend approach – orange was today's color, though with more practical shoes than I'd seen her in around town – I could not help but remember her when she was just another of these teenagers. Whenever I'd see her in the hallways in high school, she was almost always alone, her head down, not nervously, as if she were trying to avoid people's gaze, just quietly. I remember once standing in front of her path, smiling, waiting for her to notice me. She'd looked up just a foot from me and jumped a little, then giggled and put her hand before her face in embarrassment. "I was so somewhere else," she'd said, and in the middle of my next class, I wondered where else Jess had been.

As Jess had two free periods on Wednesdays, I waited in her room until Makayla and Stuart arrived for me to talk to. It was hardly my idea of a free period. As Jess sat at her desk working on her computer at the back, students congregated in her room. "I talk a lot more when I'm actually teaching," she told me later – yet her quietness gave her a presence, a sureness that the students seemed to check in with, occasionally glancing toward her, meandering to the back of the room as if to be closer to her for a moment.

A male student came in to say he'd finished *The Bluest Eye* by Toni Morrison. "I found it confusing," he admitted. "But I really liked it. I forgot to bring it with me."

"I'm sure I have another copy," she said. "Don't worry about returning it."

He left, and another sauntered by. "I did my homework today, Miss Willis," he told her. His manner suggested both compliance and aggression – begging for a compliment, daring her to suggest that merely doing one's homework wasn't worthy of a compliment.

"It always makes me happy when a student does his homework," she said simply. I thought again about what a great parent Jess would make.

Four girls were preparing for a discussion they were leading in another student group that Jess advised, the Black Students League. Next week, they were focusing on gentrification. One started reading out a paper she said she'd written when at another school. "Should I read it aloud?" No one answered. She began reading anyway. Then she stopped. "Actually, I don't have it all. Where is it? I wonder where it is?"

"Miss Willis," another said, "can we use your computer to show the PowerPoint?"

"On the day," Jess said. "I need it today. Can you read it out from your phone?"

"O.K. O.K.," she said to the others. "How to recognize when your neighborhood is becoming gentrified."

"You get gelato shops. Instead of just generalized stores."

"Yeah. Gluten-free bakeries."

"It's not just race," one student said. "It's income. Tied to race."

"That's what Miss Whitcombe says."

Aggie, I thought. But she didn't teach at the high school. I looked over at Jess and she nodded. "Advising at the junior high," she said quietly.

"No more liquor stores," the student continued. "Just 'Wine and Spirit' shops."

Two more students walked in, a tall white boy, lanky in jeans and a T-shirt, and a Black girl in black jeans and white top, a red band across her thick hair à la Michelle Obama. I had a feeling they were Stuart and Makayla even before Jess introduced me. They were the least unusually dressed of the students I'd seen, and I wondered if they were quieter, like Jess had been, or established their identity in other ways. By doing things such as founding One Whitman.

Makayla and Stuart recounted how the group came to be. It was Stuart who was in the diverse class, not Makayla, and the difference, they found, was stark. "I remember we were talking about 'Letter from Birmingham Jail', " Makayla said, "and people would be saying, 'Oh, that was so awful,' and 'Oh, that was terrible.' It was almost like a pity party. I was trying to dissect what Martin Luther King was saying about why people were acting in this way, and they kept saying, 'That was awful,' like it was in the past. It isn't in the past."

"And that was partly because her class was made up of a bunch of white kids from the same neighborhood," Stuart said.

"I'm glad you said that," she said.

"Well, you coulda said it."

"I would've."

They began addressing me again. "So, like, for them," Stuart said, "racism is in the past."

"Because they've never experienced it," Makayla said. "And they don't know people who have experienced it, who are experiencing it. Or they don't know them well enough. They think they know them. But they don't."

"So we wanted to address these issues at Whitman. To counteract the segregation in the world. Which of course is reflected here. At Whitman."

"And then we had a cop shooting a Black man. Right in Bridgeton." Makayla said it matter-of-factly, her tone even and calm. "And it's like, it's here now. It always was here but it's really here. Now. And we can't ignore it."

We talked for an hour until the protest was about to begin. It was much more than I needed, but I liked listening to them. I'd be struck, when I was editing the audio the next day, how they finished each other's sentences, amplified each other's ideas. Helped each other out. One Black, one white; one male, one female; one's parents both attorneys, the other's mother a nurse; they had forged a synchronicity out of different lives— shared a view of the world that encompassed each other's experiences. Wasn't this what we wanted? This?

And then, only about twenty students showed up for One Whitman's protest in the Atrium – and ten of them even I recognized from my hour in Jess's classroom. A few teachers had turned up, too, and I moved closer to them, hoping I might spot Aggie. But not even Aggie made an appearance. Maybe she had something to do that afternoon. I felt bad for Makayla and Stuart. Afterward, I saw them talking to Jess, and went over to thank them.

"We're a little disappointed," Makayla admitted, then registered Jess staring at her with her eyebrows raised. Makayla laughed. "Yeah, I know. Everything's a learning experience."

I decided to write up a few paragraphs to insert into the roundup for the next morning's paper. Makayla and Stuart deserved some sort of success from the day. A story about Jess, the sister of a slain Black college-bound high school graduate coaching her students on how to protest Haley's death, would make a better story – a front-page story – but I pushed the idea out of my head.

With an hour before work, it didn't make sense to go home, so I stopped at the Latin American café I'd spied on my way to the school, the Bolivian Expresso. I didn't know if the "x" was purposeful, but it sounded like you could get a nonstop flight to another country just by walking in the door. You almost did. The fittings were American – Formica counters, those chrome napkin holders from the '50s – but the orange walls, the scent of burnt sugar, and the song of Spanish words trilling from many tables was Latin American in flavor. Maria would love this place!

I'd taken my place in line when I heard my name, and I turned to see Aggie. She was standing between her chair and table as if trapped there, motioning me toward her, animated, smiling. "Cassie! I wondered when I'd see you again!" She gestured around the café. "It's a great coffee shop, isn't it? I do love the Latin American thing."

How easily I'd been ready to find an excuse for Aggie's absence. *I think she had something to do.* Get coffee, apparently, at the Bolivian Expresso. I walked over to her, doubtful, this time, that I really wanted to see her.

"I don't usually put sugar in my coffee, but their Cubano!" she went on. "Do you know they put the sugar in with the grounds? When they brew it? I never knew that."

As I mentioned the student protest, she went on about the sweetness of the Latin American palate as if she were her father, and it came to me: she hadn't had anything else to do. She could have listened to the students and still come for coffee after. And she was trying to mask her absence with chatter. What was that about? Aggie had been, as a teenager, strong, forthright, direct. Now, she hid in a coffee shop two blocks away from a rally by students she knew and avoided the topic of her absence entirely.

I brought it up again, telling her about the piece I was doing about the One Whitman students. "Aren't they great?" she said. "But if you tell them that, they get irritated these days. They're sick of adults congratulating them all the time."

I smiled to mask my anger, which welled up in me, sudden and fierce. "Is that why you didn't go?" I asked.

"No, I... I just..." She stood, silent, her face a blank again.

"Listen, I have to get to work—"

"But you haven't had a coffee!" she said. "My treat." She pushed back her chair and it toppled over with a clattering clang. She raised her hands, "Oh, for goodness' sake, I'm sorry," looking at the chair, as if apologizing to it. She righted it and then was off to the counter. "Here, hold our table. I might have another coffee, too. And one of those rolls before they run out. I'll get two."

She was ordering before I could resist.

She was just as chatty when she returned, talking animatedly about the students now as if I hadn't just interviewed them, as if she hadn't seen another person in days. "What I like about them is, I feel they're honest, in a way we adults seldom are. They're really looking at their world." As she mentioned specific details of the Haley story, I could tell she'd been following it closely. It didn't make any sense. "And Makayla and Stuart see all this so clearly. I mean. We didn't do that. Did we?"

Her gaze was direct now, level. She waited for an answer. She was right, of course. "Then why weren't you there?"

"Couldn't," she said. "Wanted to. Drove over. Then I came here."

She closed her eyes, put her hand over her forehead, then swept her hair from her face and looked at me again as if that moment hadn't occurred.

"Listen," she said, "there's something I've been thinking about asking you, so I couldn't believe it when you walked in, because I swear I was just sitting here thinking that I have to ask Cassie to do this. I have to ask her. So, I was wondering. Would you come and visit my father? I mean, you know how fond he was of you."

Her father? My head was so full of the students and the Haley shooting that it took me a moment to understand: she was inviting me to the Whitcombe home. After all these years. The rest of the world fell away for me, too. *Yes!* I wanted to say, eagerly, as if I'd be going back to their beautiful old house in Newfield on the outskirts of Bridgeton. And then, I didn't want to go at all. I remembered standing at their door after Joe died, knocking and knocking, absolutely certain as I walked away again that they were all present in the house. I'd felt not that the Whitcombes didn't hear me, not that they didn't see me, but that I no longer existed.

Aggie told me more about her father's illness. He barely left his room, except for dinner in the evenings, which Aggie's mother, in the Whitcombe manner, tried to make a special occasion each day. They'd hired a nursing student to watch him about ten hours a day in exchange for free rent and a small salary – "The poor woman is going to the community college for her associate's degree, but I don't know how she has a single minute to study," Aggie said – and her mother watched him the rest of the time, with Aggie stepping in one or two nights a week, and Hector on Sundays.

"My father says crazy things – they make no sense whatsoever. And then sometimes he says half of something but can't find the word to finish the sentence. *My father*. Can't find a word. Sometimes I think it's easier for my mother when he makes no sense whatsoever than when he's almost there. Because she'll completely misread what he means."

Aggie recounted a dinner they'd had the week before. Wine had been banned from the Whitcombe dinner table when Mr. Whitcombe was present – alcohol would apparently interact badly with his medication – yet Mrs. Whitcombe still put out wine glasses for water. And Mr. Whitcombe held up his wine glass with this wide smile, and said, "Hey, don't we have any…" It was obvious that he wanted wine, or, at least, was fondly remembering having wine.

"Do you want more water, darling?" her mother asked.

He shook his head, then smiled again. "Hey, shall we have some… what do you think about having a glass of…"

"There's water in your glass already, my love," she said ever so sweetly.

"No, there…" And then he screamed it: "No!"

"So I said, 'Mom, he wants wine. You want some wine, Dad?' And he looked up at me with the saddest, most grateful, warmest look I'd seen since I came back to Newfield. It's just so…" Aggie sighed. "I mean, I understand it would make him ill. But why can't she tell him that, instead of pretending to not even know what wine is?"

It was hard to connect the people she described with the people I'd grown up knowing – the urbanely outlandish Mr. Whitcombe, over the top before the phrase turned into an acronym, and his charming, doting wife, the role Mrs. Whitcombe usually adopted around her husband.

"Why do you want me to come?" I asked.

Aggie fiddled with her bun, which she hadn't even tasted, then pushed it away. "Maybe he'll remember you," she said.

Remember me? But they'd all forgotten about me, the Whitcombes. Even Aggie.

"I came by your house," I said. I tried to sound casual – as if this were a by-the-by for me, as if not seeing Aggie for days and weeks and months then never hadn't been a devastating blow. "After Joe died. I never knew if your mother even told you. But I stopped by every day."

Aggie nodded, quick. "I think I knew that," she said. "But I don't really *remember* it, if that makes any sense. It's like those months are a blank for me. Like I was in a coma."

"And after?" I asked. "You went away for a while. Didn't you?"

She nodded. "Dad sent me to Europe. Like I was a character in a Henry James novel! I was just glad he helped me escape. I think my mother would have kept me in bubble wrap forever."

I didn't know what to say. Had I not been even a thought in her head? Did she not think once, *Gee, I wonder how Cassie is?*

"So," she said, toying again with her roll. "Are you up for it?"

I thought about saying no, but as Aggie glanced up at me to hear my answer, she looked almost afraid. Afraid of what? Aggie had never been afraid of anything. "OK," I said. "I'll come." Maybe I wanted to be remembered again.

CHAPTER NINE

"As from your graves rise up, and walk like sprites, to countenance this horror! Ring the bell."

"Macduff," I said, responding to Aggie's overdramatic reading. "After the king has died. Act two, scene... three?"

"Oh my god, you're so good at this!" Aggie said, and I couldn't help being pleased, even if it was just a quotation exam on *Macbeth* that we'd been studying for four days straight because our English teaching kept calling in sick.

"It's an abject lesson in how to study," I said. "It's frightening how much more I remember now than I did four days ago."

Aggie was smiling at me the way her father might. "Object lesson," she said softly.

Then her brother Hector was sauntering down the stairs. He paused, for once, to look at us, but as if we were two oddities in a museum. I hoped he hadn't heard. I thought about asking if he'd had to take this test, but I didn't dare. I stared at my book, determined not to meet his gaze and give him an excuse to make some comment.

"Isn't it sweet?" he said. "Two studious students studiously studying their studies."

Since getting thrown out of Colby College that autumn after failing several classes, Hector was now a constant presence at the Whitcombes', even when he wasn't in the house. I hated it. He was as removed from us, as superior, as he'd been when we were mere sophomores and he was the star quarterback in his last year on the football team, swaggering through the halls surrounded by a coterie of bulky boys, pecs jutting out from tight T-shirts, and one shining girl, usually a blonde, grasping his hand as if she were afraid she might disappear if she let go. Once, for a few days, it'd been Daisy Dixon by his side. Now, he had a quiet, angry sullenness that seemed laden in his gaze, his brief sentences, in the way he held his body, leaner, more muscled, than he'd been in high school. And yet, he was catered to, cajoled; no one in the family except Aggie dared to disagree with him.

That afternoon, he lingered, staring at us, one hand in his pocket, jingling something metal like he was Captain Bligh in *Mutiny on the Bounty*.

"You're going to get some kind of weird reputation if you keep playing with the keys in your pocket," Aggie said without looking up.

"They're not keys."

"Yeah, that's what I was afraid of."

What was it about his demeanor that was so off-putting? All he was doing was standing at the window, a hand in his pocket, tousling his hair with the other, yet I felt judged. His default mode was derision. I was grateful when he left for the kitchen; the fridge door opened with a sigh and then shut again. Then he was back in the living room, holding a sandwich. He sat on the couch and ate it as if we weren't there. He stood up, looked in our direction, sat down again, then began inspecting the plate his sandwich was on. He held it above him and looked beneath it, as if he cared which brand of dishes his mother had bought.

Aggie put her pen down. "What?"

He stood. "Want to see something?"

"No," she said, and picked her pen up again.

"I'll bet you do," he said.

"I'll bet I don't."

72

"What, are we in third grade?" I asked.

They ignored me. "I'll bet you do," Hector said.

"OK," Aggie said, "I'll look as long as it's clear I'm looking so you'll leave us alone. What?"

Hector brought his hand out of his pocket as he stepped closer and held out his palm to us. In between the dimes and quarters were two small cylindrical metal objects, which took me a few moments to identify. Bullets. Were they really bullets?

"You've got to be kidding me," Aggie said. "What, this turns you on?"

"Are they real?" I asked.

"Live ammo," Hector said, then brought them closer to his face to look at them more closely.

"*Live ammo*," Aggie mimicked. "Wow, you're really getting the lingo down."

I kept staring at the objects in Hector's hand. Such small items – not even half the length of Hector's thumb, and barely the width of a pinkie. They were mostly a brassy gold color, with shiny silver tips slightly narrower than the base. They glimmered even in the dark library.

"Can I hold them?" I asked.

If Hector was surprised by my interest, he didn't show it. "Sure," he said amiably, picking them out from the change and putting them in my hand. They were warm from his pocket, hot even, but at the same time their smooth, shining surface felt cool on my skin.

"So people call these bullets, but these are actually cartridges." He picked one up to show me. "This brass part is the casing, the silver – well, silver in color, but it's lead covered in tin – is the actual bullet. Also inside the casing is the gunpowder." Hector spoke of the bullets – the cartridges – as lovingly as his father spoke of Homer, as if they contained the world's secrets. His voice was softer, almost affectionate, and as he spoke it was like he'd been taken to another world. And this was just a bullet. What would he be like with a gun?

73

He handed it back to me, and I smoothed my fingers around it. The tip, the bump where it fit into the casing.

"They look like lipsticks," I said.

Hector laughed, but not caustically. Did he actually think something I said was funny?

I pushed at the bullet. It looked like it wanted to come out, as if, if I gave it a strong enough push, it would go shooting across the room.

And then I didn't want to hold them anymore. I gave them back to him quickly. Hector noticed my discomfort.

"I think they look like dicks, actually." He fondled one of them in his palm before putting them back in his pocket.

"Great," Aggie said. "No wonder you like them. Fabulous. Where'd you get them? Ed Marshall?"

His friendship with Eddie Marshall was a strange twist to Hector's strange year back at home. Ed was in our class now after being held back two years in a row, but if we saw him at school at all, it was in the courtyard where the druggies hung out, or, in cold weather, lurking near the blue metal doors near my math class, lighting a cigarette before going to class, if he even bothered going to class. It amused us all enormously that the biggest pothead in the school was a cop's son.

This was Hector's new best friend.

Hector hadn't responded to Aggie's question. "You didn't steal them from Mr. Marshall, I hope," she asked.

"No telling."

"Mom'll go apeshit."

"They're just bullets. They're harmless without a gun."

"Yeah, well. Enjoy carrying harmless metal objects that look like tiny little dicks around in your pants."

But Hector was already gone.

His enraptured gaze, the fond way he tucked them into his fist, protective, like a man holding a young girl's hand. I'd think about this a lot in the first years after Joe died, how much like love it was, the attention he gave those bullets. And they were like a drug, too, giving him a self he didn't have at the time. "Where's my sister?" he'd ask me at the house party the night Joe died, as if he wanted me to tell him so he'd hear the words themselves in another person's voice, hear another person's voice remind him that Aggie and Joe were at Aggie's house, his house, where else would they go when her parents had, finally, gone away for a weekend? Where else would a teenage couple go? Hector's gaze unfocused, with drink and drugs probably, leering at me. Sexual, somehow.

CHAPTER TEN

In school – in public schools, at least – we are thrown against people of all types. Even if our classes are divided in a way similar to society – and how stupid I feel now for not seeing that, like Makayla, Joe and Jess were pretty much the only Black students in our honors classes – we nonetheless crowd the same hallways; we eat in the same cafeteria, even if we usually sit at separate tables; our lockers are not segregated based on grades, socioeconomic status, or race.

But as adults, we move in separate worlds – different neighborhoods, different shops, different restaurants. There is an entire universe of people in our town whom we may never share a space with, or not much notice. So it was a surprise to begin seeing Ed Marshall the day after I'd run into Aggie at the Bolivian Expresso. The first time I was leaving the paper at midnight, and he was loping out of the dive bar next to the dive bar where, once upon a time, not so often anymore, the reporters used to hang out after filing their stories. He was not walking a straight line. The next week, he was two people in front of me in the checkout line at Deep's, the local supermarket I'd rediscovered, a can of baked beans, a rotisserie chicken, and a six-pack of Bud sliding past him to the cashier. A bag of fresh spinach tagged along late. For a moment I thought it was the next customer's, but the cashier balanced it on top of the Bud.

Maybe he was health-conscious in a bodybuilder kind of way; maybe he was a Popeye fan.

The day after the protest over Haley's death, I saw him come into the CVS drug store as I was about to go to the front counter to pay. I paused and watched him from two aisles away as he limped past and headed toward the pharmacy, hunched over in his jean jacket, a packet of cigarettes in his hand as if reminding himself he could have a smoke as soon as he was outside again. I skulked down my own aisle and pretended to look at diapers and baby rash medication. I don't know if it was some journalistic instinct nagging at me, compelling me toward him despite at the same time feeling repelled by him. Even the way he carried himself repulsed me: his chin tucked in, his eyes staring up, his gaze left and right as if he were hunting, or being hunted. Yet I drew in close: in case he said something, in case I decided to try to talk to him sometime about Joe. The day before, the separate Freedom of Information requests filed by the Haley family and our newspaper to release the video had been turned down, but the story hadn't appeared on the front-page – Ray could not convince our executive editor of its importance. "Releasing the video is front-page news," she'd said. "Not releasing it a second time isn't." Those of us working on the Haley story were angry, but Ray remained calm. "This is the stage we're at now with this story," he'd told us. "The news now is incremental. To get on the front-page, we'll need to turn to investigative pieces. Play the long game." Maybe this was the long game. That was how I justified it to myself anyway, as I eavesdropped on Ed Marshall.

"Repeat?" said the pharmacist, a young woman with straight dark hair and glasses. Ed nodded, then stood to the right in his small sunglasses, staring blankly in my direction.

"Sir?" the pharmacist said, taking off her glasses to speak to him. "I'm sorry. I can't refill this for another" – she put her glasses back on to peer at the prescription – "ten days."

He turned to her but didn't lift his sunglasses. "I'm out," he said. "They're just painkillers."

"Pretty strong painkillers, too. You'll need to speak to your doctor, sir."

Ed didn't move. From between the boxes of diapers, I watched as he flipped the cigarette packet to his other hand, then back again, clenching his empty fist. I waited for him to mix it up and crush the cigarettes as they arrived.

"Did you speak to your doctor last month?" the pharmacist asked, her voice light, like a bell, trying, I imagined, not to sound intrusive. "Am I right in thinking you came in early then, too?"

A slight muttering came from Ed, and he put up his hand and turned around. I ducked to look at the baby oil on the lower shelf.

"You may need your prescription tweaked," the woman said, a helpful ring in her voice. But Ed was walking up the aisle and out of the store, pulling out a cigarette as he went. He was lighting it as he pushed open the glass door.

He must have been out of prison for fifteen years by now, yet he reeked of it still the way he used to reek of pot, of failure.

In high school, Ed Marshall had curly, pale hair that was cropped close to his head and a small, heart-shaped face sprayed with pale freckles that would have been described as a baby face if not for the lopsided grin that resembled a sneer as much as it did a smile. He had a limp that I'd always thought was part of his demeanor. It made him lope like a prizefighter worn out from a match. Later, I found out from Aggie that his father had run him over when he was four, when backing the family car out of the driveway. Eddie was supposed to be inside with his mother, and no one noticed he'd followed his father out the door. His father only braked because he'd heard his son screaming. His right ankle had been crushed.

His father was hoping he'd make the police force, eventually, otherwise Ed would have probably been in the vocational high school in town, or even dropped out. His father wanted him to go to college so he'd have better promotional opportunities, especially if he ever wanted to be a state cop, at least according to Hector. But it was hard to imagine Eddie Marshall as anything but a fuck-up. He was always the one carrying the keg into the house party, always the one you'd see smoking pot outside the garage. He was oddly respectful of parental rules, however. I never spotted him smoking inside anyone's house, and I once saw him diligently soaking up a spreading splotch of red wine that a girl had spilled on a white carpet, using first dry paper towels, then salt, then a wet cloth. It was pretty pale by the time I passed by a second time. Aggie and I figured this was simply fear of parental authority rather than general thoughtfulness.

That year, held back again, he was in our homeroom, though "in" would be an exaggeration, as he was barely ever there, and when he was, he still seemed absent – eyes bloodshot, head hanging, reeking of pot. By chance of alphabetical seating, Aggie's desk was at his right. "I'm gonna get high just sitting next to him," she said.

One night, Aggie and I were waiting for Hector so we could all drive home from a party after Joe, Jess and Luke had already left. Joe and Jess had an earlier curfew than the Whitcombes did – the same curfew I'd have if I were spending the night at home instead of at Aggie's – and Luke had taken them back. Finally, Hector showed up.

"We need to give Eddie a lift home," he said.

"He lives ages from here," Aggie said.

"Yeah, well. Still. If he walks home, he'll be even later."

"That was his master plan, was it? Walk home?" Aggie said. But Mr. Marshall was notoriously strict with Ed – the rumor was he had to call his father "sir" – and Aggie was always more likely to help someone than not.

Hector sensed her softening. "I'll drive if you want."

She harrumphed. "No way. You've had too much to drink, bro. Let alone smoke."

I was relieved when Hector climbed into the back seat to sit with Ed. I didn't mind giving him a ride, but I didn't particularly like the idea of sitting in the back seat with Eddie Marshall.

Ed lived out in the country, or what we thought of as country in Connecticut, farther from the Sound, at the outskirts of town. We drove out of the tightly packed development where the party had been, out of what I'd thought of since junior-year English class as *ticky-tacky houses* thanks to a folk song our teacher played one day, cut through the older, more modest part of town, crossed my own street, then headed further out to where the homes became remote mansions behind hundred-year-old oaks and tall wooden fences. And then the houses began getting smaller again, scrappier, single-story ranches with carports instead of garages. After the expansive, richly lawned homes of town, or even the smaller lawns like my own with do-it-yourself landscaping – just some grass and a few un-exotic flowers like zinnias, irises, and plantain lilies – these looked like empty lots with a building on them. Most of them were unlit, and uninviting.

Aggie and Hector had begun joking around. It always made me uncomfortable when they got along. Hector was haranguing Aggie from the back seat about her driving – "Little Miss Slowpoke. How's your horse today?" – and Aggie just laughed. She knew she was an awful driver, but didn't really care that much, and so she was going along with his teasing. It would have really pissed me off. And pissed off Hector, too, if he'd been the butt of it.

"I think I'd be better on a horse," Aggie said. "Don't you? I mean, don't horses learn their way home anyway? I wouldn't have to navigate, so I could just concentrate on staying on."

Ed spoke up. "Man, I could use a horse."

Hector looked at him. "A horse?"

Ed looked back at Hector then stared ahead as if he'd said all he meant to say on the matter. I could almost see Ed working in a rodeo, a lasso roped around his shoulder, a hat making him look not less squat but more so, in a way that would suggest he'd keep his balance on a rearing horse, a Texas twang sneaking into his few words. A word popped into my head from my SAT practice tests: *laconic*.

Then we reached the woods. Ed lived out here. It was darker, with few streetlights, and I could feel Aggie tense up. The trees were sparse and looked lonely in the night, with their thin trunks and only half their leaves. And then they began to come closer and closer to the road, as if man had lost the battle against nature and the trees were encroaching on civilization. Maybe this was where the coyotes being spotted more and more in backyards, town parks, the beach, normally lived. Maybe we'd hear them yowling if we opened our windows, the way we'd heard them at that party the other week in that house at the edge of the woods as we sipped beer on the deck, quiet for a moment, not wanting to miss their howling and the fear that shivered up our spines.

"All right, rodeo star," Hector said to Aggie. "You should probably pick it up to a gallop at some point."

If anything, Aggie should slow down, I thought.

"Ed's going to miss his curfew," Hector added.

"Ed's got a curfew?" I said.

"My old man's a fucker about it, too," Eddie said. "Don't worry about it." That these were contradictory statements didn't seem to occur to him. I guessed he was used to getting into trouble.

And that's when Aggie began to speed up. I doubt she would have if Ed had been complaining. I became aware of how close the trees were to the road, as Aggie's wobbly steering took us too far to the left, then too close to the curb. Luckily, there was no oncoming traffic.

She turned a corner a bit close, and then we felt a big thud. The car juddered. Aggie swerved to the left and almost hit the embankment on the opposite side of the road – I saw a tree approaching fast – then she straightened out, and began driving faster.

"You've hit something!" Ed cried out.

"What was that?" Aggie said.

"Was it a tree?" I asked.

"You gotta go back!" Ed insisted. "You hit something."

"It's probably just a squirrel," Hector said. "She's the worst driver I know," as if to an audience.

"That wasn't a squirrel." Ed leaned forward and began tapping the back of Aggie's seat. "C'mon. It could've been somebody's cat. You gotta stop."

"It's past midnight," I said.

"Someone's dog," he said.

Aggie stopped. The darkness closed in around us. There were no houses in sight, just the trees hanging over the road. The only streetlight shone dully a good quarter-mile ahead of us, a pale yellow light that merely made the woods around us seem even darker and more menacing. Shadows loomed misshapen across the road, and it took me a moment to see they were the shadows from the trees cast by the barely illuminated night.

What if it's a coyote, I wondered.

"Should I reverse?" Aggie asked.

But Ed was already out of the car and running back toward the curve where we'd heard the bump. Aggie pulled the car haphazardly to the side of the road and we followed Ed.

We heard the whimpering before our eyes adjusted to the dark and we saw Ed on one knee, then what lay in front of him: a small white and brown dog in the middle of the street, on its side, its eyes open, panting with its tongue out. "You're just a pup. Aren't you, girl?" Ed spoke reassuringly to the dog. Its eyes darted in Ed's direction – it couldn't seem to turn its head.

"Oh, no!" Aggie said.

"We gotta get you out of here, pooch, don't we? I don't

really want to move you but you'll get killed for sure by the next car if you stay here in the middle of the road."

So will we, I thought.

"She might just be in shock" – it took us a minute to realize he'd transitioned to talking to us – "but we have to play it safe and move her carefully in case she's hurt her back. Cassie, can you help me?" Ed was looking straight at me with a big smile that was oddly reassuring. "Do you think if I put my jacket on the ground, and get the pooch on it, you could help me keep the jacket stiff for her all the way to the car? Just hold it as tight as we can?"

"Let me move the car closer," Aggie said.

"Hector, maybe you could back the car up a little. Do you think? Aggie's probably a little shaken up."

And so we began following Ed's directions. He spoke to the dog the whole time – it must have been the most I ever heard him speak – sometimes cooing, sometimes chatting, sometimes giving us directions – "Aggie, if you could open the hatch now, thank god for a hatchback" – and Ed and I loaded the dog in the back. I was proud to be able to keep the jacket taut. It didn't look like the dog was jiggled at all.

We all stared down at the pooch. She was quiet, but I could see her panting, quick and deep.

"I'm so sorry," Aggie said quietly.

"Not your fault, really," Ed said. "Owners shouldn't let her out on her own at night. No collar either."

"I would never have stopped," Aggie said.

"Sure you would've," Ed said. "We can just take her to my house. My dad's friend is a vet."

"And she would've died."

"That was really nice of you," I said to Ed.

Hector laughed. "Nah. He was just finding an excuse for being late again."

Ed refused to let us wait when we dropped him off five minutes later at his house. Aggie and I watched from the car as Hector carried the dog in Ed's jacket to the front porch. Ed bent down and rubbed the dog's ears as Hector walked away. As we began to back the car out, the front door opened and we had a glimpse before we drove away of Detective Marshall in his pajamas, his crew cut silvery in the porch light as he dropped into a squat to examine the dog.

"Maybe Ed would make a good cop?" I said a few minutes later.

Hector, driving now instead of Aggie, laughed. "He'd stay busy arresting himself."

Ed wasn't in homeroom on Monday, but when I saw him near my math class that day, skulking at the doors, I stopped to ask him about the dog.

"How is she?" I asked.

He said he didn't know, but didn't offer any explanation. His eyes were bloodshot, and I thought about the rumor that he had begun taking mescaline.

"That was really nice of you," I said again, but he just stared at me blankly, then blew out a puff of smoke and shrugged.

CHAPTER ELEVEN

"Listen, Ray," Alex was saying as he waved his card at the bartender at Kenney's, "I can't let you buy every round."

"I just thought you might get carded," Ray said, to hoots from the rest of us, gathered at the local dive at his insistence. "You've been working hard," he'd told us that night at the news meeting that marked, we all knew, exactly three weeks since Will Haley was killed. "A couple of drinks won't hurt."

And it did feel good to pile together into this dimly lit bar, a classic local newspaper dive – every paper had one – and nestle around its rundown dark wood tables over a dark wood floor near the long dark wooden bar that took up an entire wall. Once, newspaper reporters and editors had gathered in these places nightly. As the team settled into a soft chatter, I wished I hadn't missed that era so completely.

I suspected all of us were secretly revelling in the series of stories we'd been working on for nearly three weeks and had finally run that Sunday. We'd investigated the procedures being used by police departments across the country aimed at combatting excessive force, including body cameras and dashboard cameras and de-escalation training for officers, and the articles were gaining national attention. The Associated Press picked them up first, and the New York Times ran its first story about Haley on Tuesday. Today, the local NAACP and ACLU had announced they were holding a press conference the following afternoon to call on police departments state-wide to adopt the same procedures we'd reported on. We were having an impact.

And then, I noticed the falseness of Ray's smile as he clapped Alex on the back, sat at the edge of our group and pulled out his phone. Was he bothered by the suddenly festive atmosphere? I could understand why – too often, a journalist's success depends on another's misery. But of any of us, Ray was the one who most deserved to feel good about our Haley coverage.

I maneuvered to his table to sit across from him. He looked up from his phone, then back down again, his frown deepening. "Hey," I said. "This was your idea."

He took one more glance at his phone then slipped it into his pocket. He glanced behind him at the Obama press conference on the TV, then back at me. "I'm not good at parties."

"I noticed. But, it's not really a party. A bunch of journalists does not a party make."

Ray smiled, and shook his head. On the screen behind him, Obama, slender and sleek in a dark blue suit, shook his head in the same manner in much the same way, slow and serious, and as if he wasn't saying everything he wanted to say.

"Then what?" I asked. "What would cheer you up?" I motioned toward Obama. "He still makes me happy."

"Thanks, Obama."

"I mean, I know he isn't perfect."

Ray smiled ruefully. "Yeah, of course. Sure. But. The war isn't over. You know that. Right?"

Did I? I raised my eyebrows. "War?"

"OK, do you mind me saying this? White people don't get it. Obama being president – just a blip. The right wing is digging in. This is war, and it's never gonna be over. Not really." He sipped his beer.

"Yeah, OK, but. He was re-elected last year. We won that battle."

"The Republicans – they're relentless."

"But it didn't work this time."

"We have a long way to go. And we might go backwards first."

I didn't know what to say. He was probably right. But was it so bad? "You want another beer? My favorite pessimist?" I teased.

"Realist," he said, and clinked my glass.

And then, the publisher took the story about the NAACP's press conference off the front page.

Ray explained the decision at the next day's news meeting, not a hint of the pessimism of our conversation the night before coming through, although he would have found us a pretty receptive audience – we were all pissed off. The story was a result of our own coverage, the very type of article that papers usually like to promote. It didn't make any sense.

"The powers that be felt the story wasn't strong enough," Ray said. "The groups are merely making a request."

"Yeah," Alex said, flicking his finger at the color photo of two bearded hipsters holding mugs of amber ale, "and the German-style market that Connecticut's craft beer association is holding Thanksgiving weekend is so much more newsworthy."

"We are all aware of our publisher's affinity for local businesses—"

"And local cops," Alex said.

"—and the need for a mix of news and photo-rich features on page one," Ray said. "Especially as we head into Christmas. OK, listen, we need to remember what this means: people are getting tired of the Haley story. If we can't convince our editors the story is important, how are we going to convince our readers? We need to make sure we follow through so this shooting doesn't go away."

"So we just need happy photos?" Alex said, grumpily.

"Good stories," Ray said.

And then I realized he wasn't hiding any pessimism. It'd been realism after all.

Ray went round our group to check on different angles: yes, Stacy had tried again to get Malik Washington to talk – "He's already preparing for finals," she reported his lawyer, Nehemiah James, as saying; James, also the Haley family lawyer, still had no comment on a potential civil suit, although he'd said off the record they might not file that until the cop was or wasn't indicted; yes, Alex had checked with the state's attorney's office about progress on indictment, and a decision still wasn't expected for months, so no luck there either. "Cassie, we may need you to interview our high school friends again," he said, and I saw Stacy roll her eyes. My audio report had gotten a good number of hits, in part because the kids put it on Snapchat, annoying my colleagues doing hard news.

I couldn't blame them. I felt my own frustration growing. Sean McCarthy, the rookie cop who had shot Haley, was on leave—paid leave, as required by the union contract. And a beer festival was on the front-page. Before the meeting, I'd been editing a photo package on the city's independently owned shops in time for the first days of Christmas shopping. Everything was going back to normal, as if a young man hadn't died for no reason. As if Mrs. Haley wouldn't be celebrating Thanksgiving and Christmas without her son.

"So what do we have for tomorrow?" Ray asked.

There was an uncomfortable silence. I remembered that Jess had said Haley's mother had gone to her father's church. Mrs. Haley hadn't spoken to us since the funeral on advice of her lawyer, but maybe, if Jess asked her father... I started to speak, then stopped. Mr. and Mrs. Willis didn't need anything else that might remind them of Joe's death. As the prospect of an adopted child had progressed, Jess's parents – her mother, really – had begun voicing ideas about how the new child could be integrated into the family. She wanted the child, for instance, to stay in Joe's room when spending the night at their place. "I've told her the child can stay in Joe's room only if they redecorate it," Jess said. "A taboo subject. You can imagine. OK, fine, but my child is not sleeping in that room."

"Cassie?" Ray said.

I shook my head. I was supposed to be keeping the Willis family out of the paper, not putting them into it.

"What about that Hector Whitcombe angle?" Stacy said.

Everyone but Ray looked at me, and I felt myself stiffen. As much as I wanted Haley to stay on the front-page, a story on Hector meant a story about Joe. And I'd made a promise. "Daddy remembers you, he'll be so grateful," Jess had murmured that evening as we left the café, catching my hand and giving it a squeeze as we walked outside.

"The powers that be feel he's not relevant here," Ray said. "Whitcombe isn't really involved with the Haley case. Not yet, at least. But we haven't forgotten that angle. Have we, Cassie?" Ray glanced over at me as he stood to end the meeting. "Anything else?"

Silence.

"Stacy, is your analysis on the frequency of cop shootings in Connecticut versus nationally gonna be ready for the weekend?"

"Getting there," she said.

"OK. I want to see copy today. Meantime, we all need to be thinking more about longer-term pieces. Christmas is a great time to run these kinds of stories – nothing fucking else going on – but after New Year's, too. Let's reconvene tomorrow to see what you all can have ready for the Christmas period, and discuss stories for January as well. The news is bound to dry up, and there may be days, like tomorrow, where there are no stories at all. But we have to keep the story live."

I went back to the news desk and, after adding a link to our food guide to the beer-festival package, I began typing up some investigative ideas. How police were trained seemed to me a possible focus. Given Haley had spent time in prison, the incarceration rate by race in Connecticut versus elsewhere came to mind. Yet I found these generalized stories frustrating, too. I wanted to know about Will Haley. Wasn't he what mattered here?

I'd asked Veronica at Cam's Coffee about him, but she didn't have much to say beyond what she'd said the night of the shooting. How well did Mr. Willis know him? Did Jess? I'd never asked Jess. He certainly wasn't Joe – a quick look at his Facebook page, full of trash talk about girls and drugs and, in one post, guns, had left me shaken. I was so far from his life, so separate. I could bridge the gap to a working-class, trash-talking white man – at least, I thought I could. Why did race make such a difference?

It was then I received a text from Aggie. She wondered if I could come to her mother's for dinner and see her father on Sunday night. *Just Mom, Dad and I*, she texted, as if suspecting I wouldn't want to see Hector.

As we returned to our desks, I texted back. *What can I bring?* I thought of the strange look Ray had given me when he'd mentioned the Hector story. I wondered what he'd think of my dinner invitation. But I wasn't going to have dinner with the Whitcombes. I was going to help Aggie.

Though I was late when I arrived at the Whitcombes' house, I hesitated before knocking. The iron knocker on its door was the same shape they'd had on their old house, though smaller. *Fleur-de-lys*, I remembered her father calling it – I hadn't thought of the phrase in ages. I wondered if he'd remember the term now.

Their new home was modest in scale compared to the rambling old house they'd owned on the edge of Bridgeton when we were in high school – newer, neater, and probably twice as expensive given its location in Newfield's most exclusive neighborhood. As a teenager, I'd been told to "just come in" if my knock wasn't answered right away, and the time I waited before walking into the house had grown shorter and shorter the longer I'd known Aggie. Of course I wouldn't do that now, but it felt like the house itself wouldn't allow it. Though cuter, with a triangular roof and rounded arts-and-craft door – red, as if decorated for Christmas – this house was more forbidding, like I was paying a visit to a very mean grandmother. I'd already been nervous about having dinner at the Whitcombes: about how ill Mr. Whitcombe would be, about how receptive Mrs. Whitcombe might or might not be twenty years after she'd turned me away; I'd feel like a spy if Aggie's brother suddenly appeared. By the time I knocked on the door, I felt like a child again, unsure what to do, who I was.

Mrs. Whitcombe opened the door immediately, as if she'd been lingering in the short hallway, waiting for my arrival. "Cassandra, it's good to see you," she said unconvincingly and, after hanging my coat in the hallway, she led me immediately into the kitchen, where Aggie was chopping something at the counter. The two of us stood watching Aggie as she lowered the flame under her pan, Mrs. Whitcombe with her arms crossed in that loose, graceful way she had even when just standing. She wore a sleeveless charcoal-colored dress, long and straight, under a darker grey knitted jacket that matched the trim on the dress. *She hasn't aged a day*, I thought at first, then quickly saw I was wrong: she looked unsteady somehow, and her face, smoothed over with what I could now see was a very pale foundation, shook slightly as she stared blankly in Aggie's direction.

The oil sizzled as Aggie threw garlic into the pan. It was still a strange sight for me, Aggie as an adult, doing adult things. "Aggie, I don't believe I've ever seen you cook," I said. "Not once. Except when you'd burn chocolate chip cookies in high school."

She laughed. "Oh my god, I was hopeless. Still am half the time, unless Mom's around. She keeps me focused. Really, Mom, I'm not going to forget I'm cooking with Cassie here."

"Now, Agatha, dear, you're a marvelous cook. I'm certain you are, too, Cassandra." Her mother smiled briefly, as if not sure she really meant to smile. "Call me when it's ready, dear. I must read that email from Dr. Means," and left. She was gracious as always, a cool that was just on the border of cold. I could see it more clearly than I had been able to as a child – the purposeful aloofness. I wondered again how she and the colorful Mr. Whitcombe had ever married.

Aggie watched her leave, then turned the burner off. "I think you should see Dad now, in his room," she said. "While Mom's in her office. He's not always at his best at dinner."

"OK," I said, not understanding all the dynamics. Some things never changed for me in the Whitcombe household.

"I don't know whether to tell him who you are right away," she said. "Let's just see how it goes."

I followed her upstairs and she knocked on the door. A petite Asian woman in blue scrubs sat reading in a chair by the window – *Anatomy and Physiology for Nurses* – in a vast, beautiful room that was every bit a Whitcombe room. A still life of lemons and a blue pitcher hung on one wall; a couch covered in a brilliant blue fabric against another wall. Wood floors gleamed along the borders of a lemon-yellow carpet. The nurse stood up when she saw me, her arm held out as if stopping traffic.

"Mrs. Whitcombe doesn't like anyone else in here," she said in a strong accent.

"Shh, Milani," Aggie said. "Dad knows Cassie from ages ago."

It was then I saw Mr. Whitcombe. He was lying on the opposite side of the room in a double bed overflowing with sheets and quilts the same blues and whites and yellows that were in the painting and the rug and the curtains. At first all I saw was his head, as if it had been placed carefully on one of the nearly dozen pillows scattered along the back, positioned to seem as natural as possible. His hair had kept its warm chestnutty brown color, piles of it still in his dishevelled debonair poet look. I wouldn't have recognized him otherwise: his face was gaunt; his skin pale. I made out then the rest of his body, clad in white and blue pinstripe silk pajamas. *Is this what he wears all day*, I wondered.

He didn't look in our direction but continued staring toward the window, as he had been since I'd walked in.

"Dad." Aggie went over to him. "Dad, how are you doing?"

He turned toward her, then smiled widely.

"He's having a good day," the nurse said.

"I'm glad. I'm glad you're having a good day, Dad."

"Mrs. Whitcombe wouldn't want him upset," the nurse warned again, quietly.

"Of course." Aggie motioned to me. "Dad, you remember my friend Cassie."

As I approached the bed, I was appalled not so much by his thinness, by his gaunt, haggard face, but by the blankness of his gaze. His blue eyes looked up at me and might as well have been looking at the sun, the air, random stars, the rug.

"Cassandra," Aggie then said.

He smiled vaguely and resumed staring out the window, then shifted his gaze higher.

There were books everywhere, lining the top several feet of the room on every wall, well above where Mr. Whitcombe might actually be able to reach, pull one down and read it. The shelves were painted the same creamy white of the walls and so it looked as if the books were hovering in the air above Mr. Whitcombe. There were dozens of them, and yet I knew Mr. Whitcombe had owned many more books than this, and I wondered where they were, and if anyone had chosen which books to put near him and which to put into storage, or give away.

Aggie saw where I was looking and came closer to me, talking quietly, so that Mr. Whitcombe wouldn't hear. "He stares at them half the day, as if they're people outside on the street. At first, Mom had put the shelves lower, but the first week he was here, he began pulling the books down, helter-skelter, standing on his bed at one point and falling onto the floor. He was lucky not to break something. Anyway, she was going to get rid of them all but I convinced her to do this. He stares at them more than he looks out the window, more than he ever looks at that painting by the artist Mom knew, even if it is now worth a fortune. I like to think he's reading them – looking at the title and watching them unfold, like a film. He certainly knew some of these books well enough to do that."

"Do you ever read to him?"

"I've stopped trying. Too often he'd end up getting really upset. I'd start reading and he'd become so agitated."

"Cassandra!" he said suddenly. "What a sweet girl she was. Whatever happened to your friend Cassandra?"

"This is Cassie, Dad. She's right here."

He stared blankly at me, said nothing, then stared up again at the books.

This is a good day? I thought.

Aggie sighed as if she'd heard me. "OK, I should finish cooking. See you at dinner, Dad. Dad?"

No response.

94

CHAPTER TWELVE

The bringing down of Mr. Whitcombe for dinner was an amazingly complex, almost ceremonial activity. First, Mrs. Whitcombe prepared his place at the table. She cleared an entire side of the rectangular table – the two other placemat/napkin combos apparently there just for show during the day (for showing whom? I wondered) – and even replaced his cloth placemat with a plastic one like parents might use for their children, along with a plastic water goblet and a specially made dull knife and fork. The three chairs on that side were taken away, and she wheeled in a special chair, with hard white plastic and rounded edges. She then stood over the chair, surveying the table, putting one wine glass, the vase of flowers, farther out of his reach.

"I'll prepare Dad's plate," Mrs. Whitcombe said. "Can you tell Milani to bring him down?"

Aggie went upstairs and returned quickly, but it was ten minutes before Mr. Whitcombe had been ushered down the stairs. No wonder it took so long. Milani supported his back with one hand, gripping his arm with the other as they walked, side by side, one step at a time, down the stairs. Mrs. Whitcombe walked over and waited at the bottom, then took over from there – Milani stepping back to allow Mrs. Whitcombe to slide her arm behind her husband and take over. Why didn't they find him a room on this floor? Did he have to do this anytime he left his room? They shuffled over, Mr. Whitcombe leaning heavily on his wife, as she then wheeled out the chair, placed him in it, then pushed him closer and locked the wheels. His meal, no longer steaming, was waiting for him.

Everyone sat down except for Milani, who pulled a chair near Mr. Whitcombe and then sat, sentinel. Apparently, she would eat later.

Aggie and Mrs. Whitcombe helped themselves to hot food, so I did the same, though I felt ill. Mr. Whitcombe sat there, his arms hanging on either side of the chair, staring down not at the food, it seemed, but at the table. Milani finally put a morsel on to a fork and held it up to him. He accepted the fork then put it down.

Mrs. Whitcombe sighed. "This is why he's so thin," she said, as if she suspected I was wondering.

"Mom," Aggie said gently. She'd complained to me about how her mother always spoke about Mr. Whitcombe in the third person, as if he wasn't there. "Shall I try?" Aggie stood up.

"You'll get thin yourself, dear, if you don't eat either."

Aggie leaned over the table on her elbows and put her face right in front of her father's. "Daddy. Daddy, Daddy. Don't you want to eat?"

"I saw your friend Cassandra today," he said.

Mrs. Whitcombe looked up quickly.

"Yes, Dad, she's right here."

"Don't say that, my love," her mother said. "He'll just get confused."

"She knew your friend Joe. Didn't she?"

Aggie stared at her father in astonishment, then reached across the table, trying to tap his hand, but it was out of reach. "Yes, she—"

"Don't be silly, Agatha," Mrs. Whitcombe said. "You can't upset him. He'll be ill for days if you upset him."

"He's already ill for days," she said in a fierce whisper,

then in a normal voice again, soft, cajoling: "Daddy, you remember my friend Joe."

"We should have had him for dinner more often, I always thought. But your mother said, 'He's just a boyfriend. We can't act like they're engaged. It's not like Cassandra, dear, she'd say, boyfriends come and go.'"

Aggie sat back in her chair, turning to her mother, then her father again. "What?"

"Did you say Cassandra was here?" He looked around frantically. "Gosh, I'd just love to see her."

"Yes, Dad, she's older now, she—"

"Aggie, no. Milani, please take Mr. Whitcombe upstairs. We cannot upset him by confusing him."

"Mom, he's understanding—"

"I've been around him much longer than you, Agatha. I've seen the ramifications – oh, why am I bothering to—"

"Diana." Mr. Whitcombe spoke to his wife in a gentle voice – his old voice. He stared at her directly, unlike the vague gazes I'd seen so far. Mrs. Whitcombe stared back, silenced.

"Shall we invite Joe for dinner, too, this time? Diana?" He stared down, then looked back at her sideways, smiling his old smile for a moment, his beguiling, charming, poet-scholar-lover look. "Diana?" Then his face crumpled. In a second, he was crying. "How did Cassandra get so old? I don't understand! So old." He looked at his wife. "You're as old as I am now. How?"

Mrs. Whitcombe swiftly stood. "*Milani!*"

Milani jumped up, unlocked his chair and began wheeling Mr. Whitcombe away.

"No, bring him to the patio, Milani, not upstairs. The outdoors might help tonight." She spoke as if Milani had misheard her the first time. Milani didn't object, and Mr. Whitcombe was whisked out of the room. How long it would have taken to get him upstairs. How much time it would have given him to ask about me or Joe again. Mrs. Whitcombe knew how to handle a crisis.

"Why did he say Cassandra's name?" Mrs. Whitcombe demanded. "Agatha? You said you wouldn't mention her name."

This was news to me.

"He must have recognized her."

"He didn't even look at her. I'll find out the truth from Milani later." She stood up, her plate still full. "You cannot toy with him, Agatha. He's an ill man. Do you understand?"

Aggie moved her head in a way that was neither a yes nor a no, but it was enough for Mrs. Whitcombe, who picked up her husband's plate and followed him outside.

I felt like a storm had passed and I was sitting in the wake of it, although the table, and our food, were in complete order. Hadn't the flowers been knocked over? Even Mrs. Whitcombe's napkin was folded perfectly next to her plate. I didn't remember her doing that. Aggie looked as stunned as her father, staring into nothing next to me.

"How long has it been like this?" I asked.

She kept staring, then stood up and took my plate and hers. "It?" she asked. "You mean my father?"

"No, I mean this. Your mother. You. Him talking about Joe."

"He's never mentioned Joe before."

Aggie brought her plate to the sink and started wiping the kitchen counters furiously, as if they held decades of grime instead of a few crumbs and a layer of last night's antibacterial spray. I should have started bringing over the rest of the dishes, but I sat there.

"And you might guess," Aggie added, "that it's the first time I'd ever heard about any family discussion about having Joe to dinner. Since you would've been the first to hear of it. Back then."

"That's awful," I said, like we were still in high school.

"I feel outraged. It's stupid. I mean, Joe's dead. But, at the same time. Joe's dead."

I began to help her clean up. No one had eaten much of their meal at all, and it felt wasteful to throw it all away, but

Aggie insisted no one would eat leftovers. Occasionally, I'd hear a scraping, or a step, and I'd think Mrs. Whitcombe was coming back, and I would look up nervously. I didn't want her to return while I was there.

I told Aggie I needed to get home, and she walked me to the door. She came outside and stood on the step with me. It had strangely turned warm again that afternoon, and a fog was thickening over the lawn. I felt overdressed in my wool coat, a little sweaty. I wished Aggie and I were leaving, going out to a party, meeting Joe, but not coming back here. Not to this house.

"Why didn't you tell me your mother didn't want your father to hear my name?" I asked.

"Do you remember when Joe and Luke had gone bike riding and Luke fell off his bike and was knocked out?" she asked as if she hadn't heard me. "He could remember just before falling off, and waking up in the ambulance, but not what made him fall."

"Yeah?" I took off my coat and folded it over my arm. We'd all been fascinated by it, Luke especially – Mr. Brain, not being able to figure out how the brain worked.

"I don't know what happened that night. To me. It's like I fell off my bike and hit my head and can't remember what happened between going to the bathroom and waking up in an ambulance with Joe dead."

"So it's like shock?"

"That's what my therapist says. But it doesn't make sense to me. No one says I fainted. I thought…" Hugging her arms to her body underneath a long sweater that for a moment I thought was the one her mother had been wearing, she stared out into the night. "Everyone tells me what happened – my mother, Hector. 'Thank god you don't remember,' my father used to say. 'Be grateful you don't remember.' But I don't. Feel grateful."

"I saw Ed Marshall the other day," I said. "I hid in the

aisles of the CVS so I could listen in on his conversation with the pharmacist."

"I don't know what I'd do."

"Do you think he meant to kill Joe? Went to your house with a gun with that purpose?"

"Do you know," she said, "I thought if I moved back to Bridgeton, I'd remember what happened. Thought just being here, day in, day out, might do it. And, you know. Nothing."

I thought about whether I was remembering more about Joe after being back – but the truth was, I hadn't ever forgotten.

"If Dad was himself, I think he'd help me. I wish I'd asked him. I wish I'd asked him while he still could help."

"Why didn't you?"

"I wasn't well enough," she said. "I mean, I was on some pretty serious drugs for a while. I would have been ashamed, really, if you'd seen me. If anyone had. By the time I'd weaned myself off them – by the time I realized I wanted to know more – my father was the one on drugs."

It was the first time Aggie had alluded to the years after Joe died, to the years she was never in touch. I felt strangely unaffected. I'd wanted this kind of explanation ferociously, for so many years. Now that it had come, it no longer mattered.

"And then sometimes I think, maybe Dad still can help. Help me remember." She looked at me, waiting for me to remind her of the version of her father we'd just both seen. "Even if he can't remember." She stared out again into the night, hugging herself tighter, as if the thought comforted her.

I spotted Ed Marshall again at Deep's the next day, at the checkout line adjacent to mine. The boy swishing my groceries across the reader kept blocking my view of Ed, but I had clear sight of his cooked chicken, bag of spinach, and six-pack of Bud. How bad could someone be who eats spinach? Maybe I could gain his trust. Maybe he'd tell me what happened that night. He had a strange mark on his chin, beneath his right jaw. A bruise? A growth? I wondered if he was ill. He'd have no reason not to tell me what had gone on; he'd served his two years, couldn't be tried again. Right? As my checkout person moved to help me bag, Ed turned his head just enough for me to see what the mark was: a tattoo in the shape of a swastika. I looked away, back into the store, afraid now he would have seen me looking, recognized me, challenged me. Shivers crept up my back.

"Ma'am?"

The teenage assistant was looking at me. He was Black, and I'd been ignoring him. Joe and Jess used to tell us about customers like me. "That's thirty-eight dollars and twenty-four cents."

I looked down and fumbled for my wallet. I shook my head. "Sorry," I mumbled and handed him my card. I was afraid to look up in case Ed was there, staring at me. A cart rattled by but Ed would just be carrying those few items, wouldn't he? I penned my signature on to the electronic keypad and accepted the receipt before daring to look up. An elderly woman with white hair and a sky-blue dress was checking out, and I felt myself breathe out.

"Have a nice day," the boy said.

I hadn't meant to ignore him. "Oh, I'm sorry! Thank you!" I glanced at his name tag. "Thanks, Daniel." Trying to make up for my rudeness. *It wasn't you*, I wanted to say. *I wasn't pretending not to see you.*

"You're welcome, ma'am," he said affably enough. I wondered if I'd become a story he'd tell his friends that night, the way Joe and Jess would occasionally admit to rude treatment by a customer when they'd worked here, laughing it off, Joe standing up, sometimes, to exaggerate the customer's blank stare, his own overeager politeness. At least the kid hadn't had to serve Ed Marshall, I thought, with his swastika tattoo. I wondered what Joe would have made of that.

CHAPTER THIRTEEN

I look back now and the dreadful moments from that year shine out like warning beacons on a rocky coast, blinking, blinking, in the foggy night. How could we possibly not have changed course? How could we have not understood that we were navigating tricky terrain and we had to be very, very careful? Or turn around.

But the beacons were not blinking so brightly then, so incessantly. They were sporadic warnings that were cloaked by the everyday experiences of being a teenager in a moderately wealthy suburb of Connecticut in 1992. My mother would drive an extra five miles to Target to save five dollars on my father's favorite brand of socks, or to get double coupons at the supermarket in the same shopping mall – and she sometimes ran into Mrs. Willis doing the same. I never felt any need was unmet. It was true we didn't do the things the Whitcombes did – weekends in New York to see a play, spring vacation in France – but it seemed to me the Whitcombes did these things because they were cultured enough to want to, not because they had the money to do so. We enjoyed our New England thrift.

And so as the school year progressed, my mother and I made a trip to Marshalls to buy new towels, and then to T.J. Maxx for a new pair of jeans for me, but not a pair of boots although they were half-price – still too expensive for my mother. Aggie and I hung out after school listening to new CDs that she had an endless supply of cash to purchase, until I went home for dinner and homework. One week, we were pulled into a bit part in a skit in the school variety show, in which three friends were playing Bill and Hillary Clinton out for dinner with a buxom blonde named Gennifer as their waitress; Joe, Aggie, Jess and I were guests at another table, and we enjoyed a week of late nights at the high school and a cast party on Saturday night. Most weekend nights, we simply picked up Jess and Joe for a party or a movie or just hanging out at Luke's house, where the basement afforded us the most privacy. So nights like the one I'm going to describe now, nights like this at the Whitcombes, were so seldom they seemed like the aberration, the accident on the side of the road that we'd drive past and leave behind.

It was unusual by late spring for Hector to be around for dinner. He was spending more and more time with Ed Marshall, and, since the Marshall family ate at six o'clock, Mrs. Whitcombe had begun making Hector a sandwich early so he could be out the door before Mr. Whitcombe was even in the kitchen cooking, before Mr. Whitcombe was around to ask any questions. Hector was left to do whatever he did with Ed Marshall each evening – smoke, drink, drive around while smoking and drinking.

But for whatever reason – maybe Ed Marshall had been grounded again – Hector was present that evening. That night, as dark clouds spread across the sky outside, a forecast storm taking shape, his mood was palpable. He sat motionless at the table, his arms draped on the table in a way that took the most room possible, and he pointedly ignored the activities around him: Aggie setting the table, Mr. Whitcombe scurrying around the kitchen, calling out for a potholder, then, as I eagerly rose to help him, saying, "Never mind! Never mind!" and waving the one he'd found before going back to the stove. Mrs. Whitcombe switched on a light against the dark then pulled shut the floor-length drapes, their thick fabric swooshing against the wood floor. "Light some candles, dear heart!" Mr. Whitcombe called out from the kitchen. "It's a Gothic kind of evening."

Mrs. Whitcombe obliged. "Aggie, get some candles out of the sideboard," she said, and Aggie went obligingly to the chest of drawers along the far wall. *Sideboard* was now a word I knew, thanks to the Whitcombes, and I liked hearing it, liked that it had become familiar.

If only Hector wasn't here, I thought. Because I sensed the promise of an expansive evening, the kind I loved, with Aggie's father including me in the adult discussion on literature or art or music as if I were an equal, though I almost always knew nothing about what he was expounding upon. I'd race to look it all up the next day, sometimes guessing at the spellings of names, so the next time, if I was brave enough, I might contribute to the conversation. Maybe tonight, Pat Metheny or William Burroughs or Marguerite Duras might come up again and, if Hector wasn't there, I might at least be able to say I'd read *The Lover*, even if I wouldn't venture an opinion. But everyone else seemed to be ignoring Hector. I guessed I could, too.

Dinner was served and the conversation was already continuing, picking up from before I arrived, political this time. The Democratic debates were going on, and it looked more and more like Bill Clinton would be the candidate. He'd just won Georgia, and the exit polls suggested that it was the Black vote that had helped get him over the top. At first, Hector sat silently, eating his dinner, not engaging. I wondered if he was high, then I forgot about him, as Mr. Whitcombe began to dissect Clinton's rhetoric: his plain language was in the Senecan style, and Clinton's use of specific examples was called *enumeratio*. "He's a master of epanalepsis," Mr. Whitcombe said. "He ends a very long paragraph with the same phrases he began it with, and yet he changes his stump speech every time he does one. He does it on the hoof, so to speak. It's possible he studied rhetoric at Oxford, and certainly at Yale Law School, but I think his learning is more instinctual. It's from the church. He was raised on it."

"Well, Joe said all the people in his church loved it," Aggie said. "Not that they weren't voting for Clinton already anyway."

Hector put his fork down with a sudden clatter. "*Joe said, Joe said*," he said in a high voice, a poor mimicking of Aggie. "You're pathetic, sis. And I thought you were a feminist."

"Now, you know he's teasing, Agatha," Mrs. Whitcombe warned.

Aggie didn't hear, or chose not to hear. "In this particular instance, it was Joe's experience I was talking about. I wouldn't want to co-opt his interpretation of something he was part of, not me."

Mr. Whitcombe sat back, stroking his chin, pursing his lips. "Of course, the African American community is indeed very loyal to Clinton."

I was glad to ignore Hector, too. "Why do you think they are?" I asked.

"It's an interesting phenomenon," Mr. Whitcombe said. "He's a single-parent boy from a poor background who's made good. I don't entirely understand it, though he certainly isn't Bush. He wasn't born with a silver foot in his mouth, as Ann Richards put it."

"Joe's father says he's a real advocate of civil rights," Aggie said. "But Joe thinks it's a working-class thing. People relate to him."

"So Joe's now the resident expert on Black America?" Hector said. "Mr. Middle America?"

"What, so Joe isn't Black *enough* for you now?" Aggie said.

"Now, children," Mrs. Whitcombe said. *Children?* I thought. *Plural? How about just Hector?* I could see Aggie fuming.

Mr. Whitcombe turned toward Hector – was he about to reprimand him? At last? – then spoke mildly. "I was going to say that I think Joe has a point."

The sound of rain against the window echoed through the thick drapes as the downpour started. The curtains were yellow, with an odd animal print: a lion, a bear and a donkey painted in a peaceful cluster under a bright green tree. Years later, when visiting a museum, I would learn it was a version of *The Peaceable Kingdom*. It was the painting which, in a survey taken of museum-goers, children had voted "the most beautiful".

Quietly, not wanting to interrupt her husband, Mrs. Whitcombe leaned over to Aggie. "Hector has never criticized Joe for being Black."

"Just for everything *but* being Black," Aggie said loudly.

Mr. Whitcombe coughed. "Joe is right to identify Clinton's affable quality. Now I'd like to think I don't vote for someone because he'd be great to have a drink with, but… thus is our electorate."

Hector stood to leave. "Dishes, Hector," Mrs. Whitcombe said. He picked up his dirty plate slowly, then put it back down to place his knife and fork neatly on top of it and picked it up again. *For Christ's sake*, I thought. Why didn't she just let him leave? The way Hector obeyed his mother always surprised me. If she asked him something directly, he did it.

He returned from the kitchen after delivering his dishes and was about to depart when he turned around. He stood there for a moment, as if deliberating. "I think I'm allowed not to like the guy," he said. *Clinton?* I thought for a moment, then figured out he was back on Joe.

"I don't care," Aggie said.

"Not everyone thinks he's the Great Black Hope."

A shocked silence. Hector stood still as well, as if surprised by his own words. No one spoke for a moment. The wind shook the window.

"Hector." Mr. Whitcombe spoke firmly, though his voice shook. "That's entirely inappropriate. I'm shocked at you."

Finally! Aggie and I waited to see what else he would say. Mrs. Whitcombe smoothed her hand over Mr. Whitcombe's arm, her head down.

Hector stood, half-victorious, smiling over us all, half waiting for a reprimand.

"Please exit this room," his father said. "Please. I don't know what to make of you. Just get out."

Mrs. Whitcombe squeezed her husband's hand, and he looked at her rather than his son, a pained expression in his eyes. Hector left.

Mr. Whitcombe slipped his hand away from his wife's and put his glasses back on. He smiled, gazing around the table, as if there were twenty guests instead of just me, Aggie and her mother. "Now, who would like some dessert?" he said, and went into the kitchen.

Mrs. Whitcombe poured herself more water, asked us if we wanted any – we were teenage girls, we'd really want water? – then said very quietly: "Now, Agatha."

"What? *I'm* getting a talking to?"

"I just want to remind you that your brother is going through a difficult time."

She humphed. "That's what you always say."

"Because it's true."

"It's lame."

"Now, don't cause trouble with him over this Joe stuff. It just upsets your father."

"I'm not the one—"

Mr. Whitcombe re-emerged holding a tart – the Whitcombes didn't make cakes, they always made tarts – and the discussion ended.

Aggie was quiet when we were getting ready in her room that night. I wanted to be soothed by Mr. Whitcombe's definitive statement, his trembling, outraged voice, but Hector's sarcastic, searing words kept repeating in my head. *The Great Black Hope.*

"Hector sort of got off easy. Don't you think?" I finally said.

"He's a bastard."

She was looking listlessly through her closet, fingering a tie-dyed gypsy shirt, a plain white blouse, a sleeveless black turtleneck. The Clash T-shirt she was wearing when I met her made a brief appearance before disappearing again into the closet.

"I thought you'd be more upset," I said.

She brought out a pair of jeans, as if they were armor she could use to protect herself, and the sleeveless turtleneck. "I can't let him affect my life. I won't let him. I love Joe." She pulled the black sweater over her head and the turtleneck outlined her face for a moment before she emerged again, tears in her eyes. "I can't believe I've just said that. But I do. I'm not letting Hector ruin that."

I nodded. Love. It wasn't something I could understand. It was as surprising as Hector's hatred. Both a little frightening. Both silencing. The two emotions mixing in one enclosed room, overwhelming anyone enclosed with them. Love. I was speechless again.

CHAPTER FOURTEEN

For years after, even the methodic rhythms of high school took on a hazy, gorgeous wonder for me, as if my life could never be happier than it had been in those final months of school before Joe was shot. Even now the mundane routines – the clamorous banging of lockers in between class, the crowding of friends around a small table in the cafeteria, the trips after school to McDonald's or the beach – can take on in my memory the hallowedness of ritual. Senior year glowed especially warmly because we'd established our group of friends and it was like the rest of the student body didn't exist; we all owned the school, separately, without knowing or even much caring if the people we didn't like owned it, too. The time was ours and in that calm enclave within a larger enclave we were able to grow. To stretch. To test out who we were.

Even as I write that I realize it's nonsense. I was a confused adolescent for whom, as the weather finally turned warmer and our weeks in high school became numbered, my walk with Luke from English at one side of the school to Politics & Society at the other had become awash with dynamics that made me feel awkward and self-conscious, but about which I was completely unperceptive. What had been just a walk with a friend – Luke could be funny, and it was always good to have company through the halls thronging with teenagers attempting teenage cool – had turned into a slightly self-conscious assessing of what Luke meant and what I felt. Did I like him? Did he like me? They were false questions – some part of me knew that, too – and yet I enjoyed the drama, though I kept it to myself. To Joe and Aggie, I was mainly mocking about Luke.

But they were beginning to wonder, and I liked making them wonder. Luke and I walked more and more slowly between those classes, any urgency dwindling as senioritis began to kick in, until teachers began shutting doors and we were the only ones left by the time we reached Mr. Simon's class. Aggie and Joe watched us come in late each day, and I'd see them smile at each other when we walked in.

This day, Mr. Simon was even later than we were, and as we took our seats in the front row – the only seats left, of course – I heard Daisy Dixon say: "Bill had better SAT scores."

"By like twenty points," Aggie said. "It's not significant."

"Twenty points in English alone," Daisy said. "It is."

College by college, we'd all been finding out who had been accepted where, but it wasn't really cool to discuss it with anyone but your closest friends. Who were they talking about? "Bill Henderson?" Luke whispered to me as we sat down.

"Listen," Joe said, turning to Bill, "you should've gotten in, man. I wish you had." His voice sounded affable, open, but he kept moving his chair, stretching his legs out in front of him, pulling them in, pushing his feet to the side, like he was caught in a trap.

Was Joe having to defend his getting into Penn? I couldn't believe it. He'd only just confirmed his place there the week before, right before the May 1 deadline, trying to give his parents time to get used to the idea. His father had wanted him to go to Morehouse.

I was surprised Bill Henderson had even applied to Penn. He must have known it'd be a reach school for him.

"Man, Joe deserved to get in," Luke said as we took our seats and Mr. Simon shut our door.

"Well, you got into RPI," Bill said.

"But I didn't get into MIT. That's not Joe's fault."

"Luke's brilliant," Joe said.

"And what if you got into RPI but Luke didn't?" Daisy asked Joe.

"Joe didn't take Bill's place, Daisy," Luke said. "It's not like there was a seat there with Bill's name on it and they gave it to Joe."

Mr. Simon looked quickly in our direction. He put his books on the teacher's desk, glanced over again, opened the notebook he used to lecture, then shut it again and stared out the window.

"But they had the same grades, same test scores, except Bill's are a little better, come from the same school..." Daisy said as Mr. Simon started writing on the blackboard.

"Joe's essay was great!" Aggie said.

"Aggie, it's OK," Joe said.

"Children and adults," Mr. Simon's voice carried above us, "for those of you who have reached the watershed age of eighteen."

"Yeah, he probably wrote about Martin Luther King," I heard Daisy mutter to Bill. I looked at Joe, whose hands were rubbing the corners of his desk as he turned to face our teacher. I couldn't tell if he had heard.

In huge letters taking up the entire blackboard Mr. Simon had written: *A Fair Society*.

"We're veering off course today for a real-life social studies lesson," he said, "which will feature the topics of ethics, of fairness, of institutional policies, of institutional bias, and of racism in the United States of America. As by now you've all gotten into your colleges of choice, be that first, second, third or eighth choice, I feel it's acceptable to delay our further discussion of the flaws in the balance-of-powers theory of the American political system until Friday so that we can discuss the related and very important issue of how to create a fair society.

"So." Mr. Simon paused and stood, for a moment, before

the blackboard, arms straight at his side. He'd always wait, silent, until all students were turned toward him and silent, too; we all knew by now he wouldn't start until we were. Even Daisy turned around. "Does everyone believe that creating a fair society should be one of the goals of a society – its government, its schools, its institutions, its citizens?"

We should have been used to Mr. Simon's seemingly simple questions turning into very complicated questions – but we all nodded our heads. A few people, including Aggie, very loudly, said, "Yes."

"OK. That was easy. Do we have a fair society now?"

Silence. I looked down at my book, on which was written, in thick, boxy letters I'd colored in with orange and red diagonal stripes, *POLITICS & SOCIETY*, which, seven months later, were beginning to look childish to me.

"Sort of," someone said.

"Sort of," Mr. Simon repeated. "OK, so I applaud you for speaking when no one else would speak, and for saying what you think, but 'sort of' is not an answer, although in some way it's an accurate answer. Do we have a fair society now, yes or no?"

More silence.

"OK, Bill Clinton was raised by a single mother in the small town of Hope – as you will all know from the propaganda film his campaign has put out – did well enough in high school to get into Georgetown, before going to Oxford on a Rhodes scholarship then Yale Law School and is now serving as the governor of Arkansas while running to become the Democratic nominee for president. Do we have a fair society?"

"Sometimes," Luke said. "But then that isn't fair."

"Correct," Mr. Simon said. "Have any of you driven down Newfield Avenue and left our fair downtown to venture into the Italian section of our metropolis? Taken a left away from the Sound on your way to First and Last Pizza?"

A few people nodded.

"Your cheap eats at First and Last Pizza in Bridgeton? And

on your way, did you notice the run-down houses between our shining downtown and the southern section of the city? Before you reach the next suburb? And did you notice the man who loves to sit on his lawn chair during the day, if you've gone some warm Saturday afternoon, his chair clamped to a chain? Did you notice when you went shopping at Filene's the man with this red-spotted sack of belongings with his tambourine singing in hope you might drop a few coins into his rather empty hat? Have you read about, in our neighboring city of Bridgeton, the slumlord in the northeastern section of Main Street who'd been charging six hundred dollars per month for apartments that have now been condemned because they were infested with roaches, had no smoke alarms, had floors that could break through to the apartment below, had indeed one hundred and ninety-one violations of city code, while his tenants were bringing home just six hundred and seventy-five dollars and seventy-eight cents a month in benefits for a family with three children?

"I think you know where I'm headed: we do not live in a fair society. But every single one of you agreed that we should live in a fair society. How does a society create a fair society?"

A clutch of keys jingled beneath his voice, the sound of class ending. Already? But the clock showed another twenty-five minutes remained. I looked back. Daisy had shut her notebook and was sitting on the edge of her seat, as if the bell was about the ring. She'd put her purse on her shoulder and was clutching her keys in her hand. I wondered for a moment if she would walk out, but she remained there, looking out the window, then at the clock, poised. I knew she was too chicken to leave. But other students began looking at her, too, including Joe.

If Mr. Simon noticed, he didn't let on. He went on, giving a broad sweep of the history of "fairness" or lack thereof since the mid-20th century, starting with the Great Society, running through the G.I. Bill after World War II ("Do you have any idea how many of our best poets went to college on the G.I.

Bill? Frank O'Hara? James Wright?") the civil rights era, then the sort of reversal under Reagan. "The right blamed the unions, but companies began using workers overseas – China, etcetera. – because labor was cheaper *than would be legally allowed in this country.* It wasn't because unions were asking for too much money, though sometimes maybe they did. The law wouldn't have allowed such low pay. What's plastered onto the wall of Clinton's campaign war room? *It's the economy, stupid.* A reminder of what to emphasize to voters and the press. That's fairness, too."

We'd all forgotten about Joe and Bill's argument when Mr. Simon finally returned to education.

"OK, so you're a university, with the task of educating the populace – one of the primary ways that a society can ensure fairness, by providing an education for every citizen – which we do in theory if not in practice – which is another forty-five-minute lecture but maybe another day – and as a university you want the best student body you can get. Yes, the smartest, but also the most dynamic, in part because that helps create a good learning environment and in part because universities are also to some extent businesses who rely on income from their students/customers and they want their graduates to become as successful as possible after graduation so they can point to that success to bring in even more successful students ten years down the line, at even higher tuition rates. They want a diverse student body because it's educationally sound to have a range of cultural experiences and points of view; they want an economically diverse student body – to a point, because they can't afford to waive too many tuition fees – they want a good balance of women and men. Etcetera.

"And so, you have two students who look almost identical in terms of grades, SATs, community involvement. Let's say they wrote the same exact essay. One is African American, and you're under pressure to admit talented African American applicants – because last year, for example, Black students made up only seven percent of the Yale freshman class,

114

although it's located in a city that is about thirty-five percent Black. Who do you let in?"

No one said anything.

"It's a difficult answer. Let's say they let in the African American student. That's not always what happens, but let's say they do. Is that fair to the African American applicant?"

"Yes," Luke said.

"Is it fair to the white applicant?"

"No," Luke said.

"And is the rest of the process fair?"

We all hesitated.

"No?" Luke said.

"An example. Did you know that about a dozen kids from Greenwich High School get into Yale each and every year?"

"Every year?" someone said.

"And the last time someone from this high school got into Yale was three years ago."

"But if they had better grades and better SATs, maybe they should get in," Bill said.

"Maybe they should. But does that seem fair?"

"Why do they get in?" I asked.

"Why do you think they'd get in? By the way, I can say with confidence that all twelve of them did not have perfect SAT scores and were not the class valedictorian. Even in Greenwich they don't have twelve valedictorians, though they probably would if they could, except that someone would complain about his child being denied the honor of being the only valedictorian like his grandfather had been. But I'm veering off point. Why do you think they'd get in?"

"Because Greenwich High School is considered better than Newfield High School?"

"Yes. Pretty much. There's a track record of Greenwich High School students succeeding at Yale." He paused to let it sink in. "Though, of course, Newfield students haven't had that chance. It's in effect a bias toward class, often mixed in with race, toward wealth and access to education that goes back generations. Here in Connecticut it turns into a bias toward Gold Coast communities, communities wealthier than ours. Did you know there are twenty-three languages spoken in this high school? Twenty-three languages in which our school needs to provide ESL classes. This is enriching to us culturally, but it's costly in terms of budget. Anyone who goes to sports events can see Greenwich has a better track, a better football field, better stands, and better uniforms than we do. Is it wrong to surmise they may also have better classrooms, smaller class sizes, better test-preparation classes, etcetera., all because their parents can afford the wildly high house prices and high property taxes – though their tax rate is much lower than Bridgeton's and even Newfield's – that residents find in Greenwich? I don't know about you. I don't think that's fair."

No one said anything. I wasn't sure what I felt, but next to me, Daisy rolled her eyes at her friend.

"I know. It's hard to take in. You're not used to being on the wrong side of fairness. So let's say you're Yale and you eliminate two of the twelve Greenwich kids because you decide it isn't fair and let in two kids from Newfield High School with pretty much the same profiles. Is that fair?

"Well, it's *more* fair," Luke said.

"Exactly. It's not fair, but at least it seems *more* fair. It mitigates this bias. And the profiles of the usual twelve Greenwich kids who normally would all get in – their grades and SATs and extracurricular activities – aren't much different from each other, so maybe Yale chooses to eliminate two men because they don't have a lot of women applicants this year, or let's say they 'fairly' eliminate one male and one female. Let's say one of the ten is a track star admitted on an athletic scholarship with slightly worse grades than someone whom they reject. It's a minefield. It can't be fair. And it's never fair if you're the one left out."

We were silent. Somebody played with a pen, the *chi-ching*, *chi-ching* as he closed and opened it clicking around the room, then stopped. I think we were shocked, uncomfortable with what Mr. Simon had said, because we could see he was right but couldn't accept it. It felt like choices should be clearer – if it were next year and it was Jess who'd been accepted to Penn, no one would have complained. They couldn't. I thought Joe was a lot smarter than Bill Henderson, but I was his friend. I wasn't sure his grades would show it.

"So I know some of you are disappointed because you didn't get into your top choices of colleges. I don't know how to say this, because of course you want to go to the best college you can, but it doesn't matter *that* much. You can thrive anywhere. I know a lot of people who went to their fifth choices and loved them. And it's still possible some of you could get in off the waiting list. With more students applying to more colleges every year, those waiting lists become more and more important. And what you all have to remember is: you are fortunate. Every single person sitting in this classroom is fortunate.

"I don't say this to make you feel guilty. To make you apologetic. But to make you aware. There are others more fortunate than you, but many, many more, countless more, so much less fortunate than you, and that's just in this microcosm of the United States of America. It will help you in life if you understand that. Nothing is fair, and most of the time life is fairer for you than it is for others. And I also hope that when you leave the beloved halls of this secondary school, the hallowed halls of Newfield High School, that you will also remember that at the age of seventeen and eighteen you thought that society *should* be fair, and not give up on making it as fair as possible for the rest of your lives. The End."

The bell rang, and the clatter of shutting books and the galumphing of chairs sliding back to release our teenage bodies from the confines of a school desk filled the room. Daisy was out like a shot, but then she paused to wait in the hallway for Bill Henderson and said to him loudly: "I don't know why we have to listen to his communist crap."

Aggie laughed out loud. "It's not communist, Daisy. It's not even socialist."

"Well." She pouted in that way that boys evidently found sexy. "He's trying to make us think his way."

"No, he's just trying to make us think," Aggie said.

"Like, right," she said. "Well, I'm not going to!" And she flounced away with Bill Henderson following like a pet dog.

All of us laughed except Aggie. "She's an idiot. Who thinks she isn't. The worst kind."

Luke scrunched up his face and waved his fists in the air. "I just refuse to think!" he said in a high voice.

"Man, you shouldn't make fun of her," Joe said.

"Why not?" I asked.

"You're too nice, Joe," Luke said.

"She's just sticking up for her friend. I mean, I don't like Bill, but I feel bad for him."

"You're a lot better than fucking Bill Henderson!" Luke said.

Joe looked down at the ground, then back up at Luke, serious for a minute. "You think?" he said, his voice quivering. Then he laughed. He shoved Luke in the arm. "Yeah man, no shit."

I didn't tell him Daisy's comment about Martin Luther King.

CHAPTER FIFTEEN

I received a text from Aggie the next day. *Tx for seeing Dad.* Then, a few seconds later: *For better or worse.* Then, as I was typing a response, another one: *A poet without words.*

It was the first of a series of texts that I would begin receiving from Aggie, a bit random in their frequency, but similar in pattern. She tended to send several in rapid succession, and so I always knew it was her when I'd hear my text tone sound three or four times in half a minute, as surely as if I'd assigned Aggie her own jingle. Though no one was texting when we were in high school, something about these quick missives reminded me of Aggie then – their offhandedness, their wry tone, their surety. Sometimes she commented on her family like we were still teenagers. *Mom just complained about my messiness in kitchen. Hello? I'm cooking.* Then, *I suppose it's *her* kitchen.* I was still texting *Thank god for that* – I couldn't imagine spending so much time in that house, so thank god Aggie had her own house with her own kitchen, but she beat me with: *do you salt water for pasta????* I sent the first, then a *No!* The intersplicing interested me. I liked this mix and match of meanings, the out-of-order receive and respond.

Her Name's Agatha thinks Dad needs more drugs, read one text that arrived when I was on deadline. *Like *more*??* arrived a few seconds later.

Is that humanly possible? I texted back in between headlines, then wondered when Aggie had last used that nickname for her mother. Twenty years?

HNA should get 2nd opinion, I texted after deadline.

Only one opinion matters to HNA, Aggie texted back. *Wanna guess whose?* Before I had a chance to text back, another one arrived: *Got it in one.*

While I enjoyed her texts, they worried me, too. Arriving so late at night, so randomly, their humor felt a little lonely. How was she not falling asleep while teaching? I doubted I was her only friend, but I might be the only person she was talking to about her parents. And texting was hardly talking. But it was as if Aggie lived in some parallel universe, another Bridgeton entirely, that looked and smelled like the Bridgeton the rest of us lived in, but wasn't.

I didn't know any of this the night after I'd seen Mr. Whitcombe. I was simply pleased to hear from her again, and relieved, too, that she seemed OK. I deleted my *no problem* response and thought about what to text back. *You need to get out of there* came to mind. *I hope your Dad is feeling better*, I finally wrote.

When I ran into Jess in the lobby of our condo complex the next night, working an earlier shift on my last day before flying to Arizona to see my parents for Christmas, she stopped me and touched my arm, smiling, as I crossed the threshold. "I've *news*, Cassie," she said.

"A match?"

"A *possible* match."

"Oh, fabulous!" I said. "That's wonderful!"

"I mean, I probably shouldn't be saying anything yet. Getting my hopes up. But. I can't tell my parents – nothing's final. I can't risk disappointing them. I know people who've been at this stage ten times before one worked out. But..."

But she had to tell someone. I felt pleased it was me.

She was beaming once she was out with it, rattling on like a child on her birthday. "I really shouldn't be getting my hopes up. But gosh. This one feels right."

"Listen," I said, aware of the extra food I still always found myself coming home with, not thinking of Maria, but forgetting she wasn't around. "Come up for dinner. I always buy enough for – three. I'm pretty sure I have some wine upstairs, too."

"Well, it's a school night, but – yes, that would be great, Cassie. I'm going to talk your ear off, you know that, right?"

I thought of the evening I would have had instead – putting on a CD when I first arrived home, getting out my ingredients, wondering, halfway through a complicated meal, why I was bothering; reading a novel as I ate, the circle of air around me feeling larger and larger, the world farther and farther away. The closer we came to Christmas, the worse it had become – I had more than one reason to take on extra shifts for the Haley story. This was often when Maria visited, always when I was at my loneliest, when the sight of her at the stove in her peacock-blue apron, across from me with a goblet of wine, her many rings flashing as if in candlelight, made me wonder what I'd done to myself moving back here.

"Do you have any idea what a nice change that would be?" I asked Jess.

Over dinner, I learned the boy's name was Antonne, and he was just twenty months old. Jess couldn't discuss his family background – "It's not allowed, not now, not later," she said – but told me that his upbringing, while difficult, was slightly less problematic than that of other children they had discussed with her. "You remember when I said they'd be talking about matching me to the right type of background a child has? Assessing how difficult a set of circumstances I was willing, or able, to deal with? I would have thought I was ready for anything. Turns out I wasn't. I'm not. So Amy feels this child is the best match we've found yet, because of that."

I would have thought Jess would be the ideal parent for

an especially troubled child. Calm. Direct. Loving. Stable. "I guess raising a child at all is hard enough," I said. On your own. I wondered if that had been a factor.

"I feel guilty sometimes," she said. "Shouldn't I be strong enough for a more troubled child? Be able to help more. But." Again that gesture, her fingers flicking away whatever she was about to say as if batting away a speck of dust. "They're looking over my complete file now. So maybe… maybe for once Joe's death leads to something good. To this boy."

Joe's death? I thought. *What does she mean?*

The logic didn't make sense to me, but I didn't probe Jess further. Nothing about Joe's death was logical. I thought of Aggie outside her door, her face dreamy in the blackness of the evening, seeking comfort where there was no comfort. Then her father's face appeared before me, his blank stare wrinkling into tears. *Shall we invite Joe for dinner, too, this time?* It wouldn't have surprised me if Mrs. Whitcombe had discouraged welcoming Joe into their house – she'd only tolerated me because she thought, knew, I was harmless. Yet what light could Mr. Whitcombe shed on all this now?

And then, Aggie's blank in place of memory. In the year after Joe's death, after being turned away again and again from the Whitcombes', after learning Aggie hadn't even showed up at Smith, I'd pored over the many newspaper stories for about a year, until Ed Marshall went to prison, looking for some clue, any word at all of Aggie. She was barely mentioned. All I could learn was that she had been in the bathroom when the shooting occurred. By the time she'd run out, Joe was dead. I'd always thought it strange. But I never imagined that she couldn't remember what she saw. What she heard. That was stranger still.

Behind Jess, I saw the flickering of car lights on my window, then a siren. The outside world. How the five of us always forgot about it.

"I saw Aggie the other night," I said.

I'd been wanting to talk to Jess about Aggie, and holding

off, not wanting to upset her. I certainly hadn't thought tonight's celebration would be the time. But tonight no longer felt like a celebration. If normally these days Jess looked invincible in her perfect outfits, her sculpted expressions, tonight, over dinner, she had softened, like a flower just peeking out of its bud. By now, crumpled deep into her chair, she looked deflated.

"It's always weird seeing Aggie," she said.

"Do you know she has no recollection whatsoever about what happened that night?"

Jess nodded dully. "Like she blacked out. My therapist then said it might be shock. You know. Our memory stops a few minutes before a car crash, comes back when we're at the hospital. Protects us from the trauma we experienced."

"That's exactly what Aggie says," I said, excited despite myself. "How do you know this?"

"I read the police report. Went through FOI to get it. Years ago."

And here I thought I'd tried every option.

"The only other witnesses in the report are Mr. and Mrs. Whitcombe. How they'd come home a night early because Mr. Whitcombe wasn't feeling well. Heard a loud bang as they were walking into the house. Raced upstairs. The first thing they saw was Ed Marshall holding the gun. Mrs. Whitcombe told him to put the gun down. It was when he put the gun down that she saw Joe. I, uh... I'd never read that in the paper."

Neither had I. One small piece put into place. One more dreadful detail. I tried not to picture it, and then I couldn't even when I tried. I couldn't see Joe. Yet a tingling – fear? Horror? Simply knowledge? – crept up my back.

"The prosecutor used it in his opening statement, though Mrs. Whitcombe never testified."

"She would have made a powerful witness," I said.

Jess nodded. "Maybe that's why Ed Marshall pleaded guilty. It all ended then. Thank god. I think now."

I'd read the trial coverage, too – had looked it up again the other day during a slow half-hour on the news desk – and she was right. Ed's guilty plea, filed the afternoon of the first day of the trial, dominated the stories. The prosecutor's opening statement was barely mentioned. I wanted to read it. Obtaining the police report would take a few days. But I might be able to get the court transcript by just walking into the courthouse. I might be able to obtain the transcript the next morning.

"Did learning all that help?" I asked Jess.

She looked at me briefly then sighed, staring back out the window. "My parents convinced themselves, right away, that the shooting was entirely accidental. It hadn't been racism that killed my brother. God forbid. Guns are deadly toys. Hector and Ed Marshall shouldn't have snuck off with Mr. Marshall's guns, but it hadn't been racism that made them want to shoot coyotes at the beach that night. Two boys made a horrible mistake. So I just accepted that. Except…"

"Except what?" Though I wasn't sure I wanted to hear.

"I'd be at my locker at school, right? And I'd want to smash the slatted metal door against my face. When I took the SATs I had to tie my shoelaces together because I wanted to just fly out of that room. Out of the school. Off the earth. I was so *angry*!"

Why hadn't I called Jess? Why hadn't I called her in those days and months after Joe's death?

"Thank god I enrolled at Howard. Very first day, my story began oozing out of me like a wound unbandaged, and my roommate says: 'No Black boy gonna get less than the death sentence for shit like that.' And I say, 'Shit, that's right.' And then the next week, an upperclassman at a party trying to pick me up. 'What, those white boys think they *own* that beach?' I bled over him, too. And then, my African American Studies II professor. I asked what she thought. Very precisely, she told me: 'You are aware, Miss Willis, how unlikely it is that a Black man could shoot and kill the white boyfriend of his Black friend's sister and not be charged with murder?'" Jess emitted a small, bitter laugh. "I became aware."

How far I felt from the Whitcombes now.

"There were times I felt Aggie was part of it, too," Jess went on as if she'd heard my thoughts. "Never for long. I'd spend a day being absolutely sure of it. Walking angrily around the Howard campus convinced she'd maneuvered the entire relationship, was part of some weird Whitcombe cultish plot."

"You're joking."

"So at least I don't think that anymore."

Other details about that night – how long Hector and Ed were in the house, when Aggie left the room, when their parents appeared – could be in that police report. Did it mention Hector knowing Joe would be there that night?

"What else did the report say?"

She looked at me. "The *what*?"

I felt embarrassed. "Never mind."

"You still think the *police* report is going to answer any questions?"

I did. Part of me did. In the face of evidence to the contrary. Something undetected, or maybe the court transcript – I had to get that, at least.

"And like a cop's son was ever going to get convicted of killing my brother? I still wonder why the hell he ever pleaded guilty." Jess covered her face with her hands and leaned over, as if hiding or protecting herself. From this old/new pain. Maybe from me, this time. *He shot Joe on purpose*, I thought. I didn't say it aloud. I had no basis for thinking it. But I felt it, as clearly and as viscerally as I'd felt it when I was eighteen.

Jess sat up again and spoke without heat, her eyes closed. I watched her face, the renewed calm of her expression, her emotions not tamed – they raged, I knew – but they were hers. She wasn't theirs. "It took me years to really understand the fiction surrounding Joe's death. The pure fiction of it being a fucking accident. If you're angry at a fiction, it vanishes into air and you're left being angry at yourself."

Suddenly she was staring at me, and I stared back. What did my face say to her?

"I thought I got over that. And then" – Jess looked away and smiled, at me, or at herself, I wasn't sure – "and then, I go to adopt a kid, and find out I'm *still* angry. I'm..." She shook her head. "In the end, Amy decided my needs level for an adoptive child should be pretty low. She suspected it was because of what happened to Joe. Too much of my own trauma."

The cost of Joe's death was always rising. "I'm sorry."

"It's been a real stumbling block. But this child? She feels I can handle this child's needs level."

As she took a sip of her wine, I raised my glass. Fuck the police report, the court transcript. Fuck Ed Marshall with his Nazi tattoo as if he'd been the fucking victim. I felt hopeful again. "Listen, you're fabulous. This boy, or whichever child you end up adopting, will be lucky to have you as his mother. So to Joe. And to you. Too."

With the black night outlining her face she turned toward me again, sighed, but softly, affectionately. Jess lifted herself to the edge of the chair to reach my glass, then leaned further forward and kissed me chastely on the cheek. I felt myself flush with pleasure. "Thank you," she said, "but you're wrong. I'll be the lucky one." We clinked our glasses.

III

2013/1992

Waking Dreams

CHAPTER SIXTEEN

"Your friend. Joe… Sweetheart. Your friend. I'm sorry. Cassie, your friend, Joe… your friend Joe is…"

My body jerked and I was wide awake. Dark still. Not a glimmer of dawn through my blinds. Another morning – no, night, not close to morning yet – another night woken by bad dreams, though this time it was my mother's voice, soothing but not able to soothe, my mother's voice waking me again on that morning twenty years ago.

For weeks now, this had been happening: ever since I'd finally read the transcript of Ed Marshall's trial, I'd been waking to voices I sometimes knew and sometimes didn't, though I always recognized Aggie's mother's voice and understood what she was saying. Hers were the words the prosecutor had used in his opening statement, repeating and repeating now until I could barely get them out of my head, the prosecutor who said Mrs. Diana Whitcombe had acted with a soldier's calm that night, arguing that she might have prevented more deaths when she'd told Ed Marshall simply to "put the gun down, Edmond". She'd never needed to testify, yet I could hear her speaking those words to Ed, precise, formal, firm. "Put the gun down, Edmond. Edmond. Put the gun down." Intermixing with her voice was another, also from the past, though I'd heard it just a few months before. "Shall we have Joe to dinner, too, next time, Diana?"

I dreamt of Joe's voice, once. Though I didn't wake soon enough to remember what he'd said or if it really was his.

I understood, then, why I'd not obtained the transcript until after New Year's, then avoided reading it for weeks while we were working so many hours on the long-term Haley pieces. Nothing to do with Haley. Everything to do with the dry, legalistic language of court transformed into images that floated in front of me as if they were my own forgotten memories. Joe's blood swimming across the floor, no one seeing it until the police turned on a light. Both arms above his head as he lay there, as if he'd held his hands up in surprise, or self-defense. Sometimes I wished I'd never read the court record at all.

Because there was nothing new in it. The smoking gun was out in the open, in Ed Marshall's hands, and then, thanks to Mrs. Whitcombe, on the floor of Aggie's bedroom. What had I thought I would find out? So what if Aggie's parents hadn't been as accepting of Joe as I'd thought – if her mother had made me complicit, somehow, using my friendship with Aggie as a pretext for not fully embracing her relationship with Joe. Would Joe be alive still if he'd spent more time with the Whitcombes? Of course not.

Put the gun down. Edmond.

I put the transcript down again, not aware of having picked it up. I made myself a cup of tea. I looked online for news on Haley, though there'd been no news on Haley for weeks now. Until the state's attorney investigation decided whether to press charges against Officer Sean McCarthy – which might take a full year, Stacy reported the other week – there wasn't anything new to report.

I learned only that it was the first day of spring.

So I promised myself that on this first day of spring, that I would not detour past the Whitcombes' new house again in hope of finding some clue. I'd seen Ed Marshall the week before in an old sky-blue pickup truck exiting their road – *Why?* – and spent a day devising conspiracy theories until I looked up online where he lived and saw their street would be a perfect shortcut from his house to Deep's, avoiding the traffic on Newfield Avenue. Foolish. I would not be foolish again. I would not drive past on the first day of spring.

Though I had Ed's address now. He was oddly missing from his own court transcript, and his own witness statement was either too garbled, or too legalistic, to sound like him at all; I never heard Ed's voice. Maybe because I knew he'd never talk to me now. Unless I thought of a question he might be willing to answer. A kind of secret question, with implications he wouldn't understand.

Maybe I could trick him into revealing what he and Hector were up to that night. But the record was clear. Why did I still think he would tell me that he'd known it was Joe that night, and shot him anyway? And maybe that wasn't even true.

"There's news on Haley," Ray said as I sat down at my desk.

I shouldn't have felt happy. But I did. Actual news would be a relief. "Shit," I said, trying to think what it might be. "The family is suing?"

Ray chuckled. "No. But right ballpark."

"What is it?"

"Our shy witness is finally giving an interview. We're out there now."

"Is it exclusive?"

Ray nodded toward the TV screens over our desks. On a local TV channel, a slick-haired woman was standing outside a house with red lettering on the screen beneath her: *Witness in Haley Case to Give Statement*.

We watched as an older man in a suit – Nehemiah James – and a younger man in a crisp shirt came out to the microphones. James read a lawyerly statement: on or about 8:30 on October 9, 2013, William Haley Jr. was shot and killed by police, allegedly after they attempted to stop him for questioning. His friend Malik Washington, age twenty, also of Bridgeton, was with him. "Mr. Washington made a statement to police at the time, and now publicly, about the half-hour he spent with the late Mr. Haley before he was shot that evening. Mr. Washington could tell Mr. Haley was becoming agitated. He was worried about him provoking the police. And so he was talking to him and holding him in an effort to keep him calm. This is when Mr. Haley was shot."

"Mr. James, does this mean that the police account that Will Haley was 'moving toward them in a threatening way' is not accurate?"

"Yes, it does."

"What, have the police just been *lying*?" I asked.

Ray looked at me. "Don't tell me you're shocked."

The lawyer continued. "We've been hoping that the police would be required to release the video recording of the incident, and hoping that video recording would make Mr. Washington talking directly to the press unnecessary. But as you know, it doesn't look like that's going to happen anytime soon. If ever. And so here we are today. Both Will Haley's family, and Malik himself, felt it was time to speak out. Now, I know Malik would like to say a few words."

Haley's friend began talking, so quietly at first I could barely hear him. Reporters began peppering him with questions, and though he looked up at Nehemiah James a few times, he spoke calmly and steadily throughout. Dryly, even. He was almost too calm. I remembered a politician analyzing the performance of a new candidate for his own party as being too much lawyer, not enough heart. It came to mind as I watched the witness speak. The news cameras would lose interest without any drama.

Ray humphed. "Give the kid a sound bite, Nemy."

"Why did you wait so long to come forward?" someone asked.

Nehemiah James interrupted. "We would have preferred not to be speaking at all. Mr. Washington is a sophomore at Morehouse College in Atlanta. He gave his testimony to police. The Haley family, and the Washington family, felt he should concentrate on his studies. But the decision not to release the video made us change our mind."

"That was a month ago!" someone shouted.

"Both families wanted to wait until Mr. Washington was not in class. This week is spring break at Morehouse."

"Why should we believe you after all this time?" another voice shouted out.

"His testimony has not changed since he gave it to police the day of the shooting," the lawyer said.

"Let him tell us!"

The young man paused, looked out at the reporter, breathed. Anger flashed in his eyes. He looked away, then looked back. "Listen," he finally said, still careful, still measured. "Will was a hothead. Everyone knows that. I knew that. That's why I had him. I had him tight. He wasn't going anywhere. And then they shot him."

"There's our quote," Ray said.

"He was my brother's best friend. And then he was my best friend. After my brother died."

The reporters at the press conference had grown silent, the whirring of cameras now as loud as the clicking of crickets on a summer night.

"So I visited him whenever I could, after he got in trouble. He was teasing me about my looking white when I took off my tie. Gave it to him. Told him maybe he should try wearing one sometime." He laughed, or maybe coughed. A thought crossed his face that he didn't share. He glanced at his lawyer, who nodded. "And then there's blood. Blood on my shirt. Will's blood."

I tried not to picture Joe's blood, pooling beneath him, around him, on Aggie's floor.

"He dropped out of my hands. Just dropped. My ears were ringing and I didn't understand why there'd been a loud bang, the shot. I know they say there were four shots fired but I just heard the one, and then Will, you know…"

He looked at the lawyer again, as if waiting for him to say something else, but the older man just nodded for him to go on.

"And I looked up and they was like five guns pointing our way. Where they all come from? And the cops were screaming, '*Stay where you are!*' And my hands felt so empty. I just stood there looking at them and my friend, my brother's friend, on the ground, the cops screaming, '*Don't move!*' All of them pointing guns at me and Will. Five guns. There were just two of them and then like they was five."

"Or maybe that's the quote," Ray said.

Put the gun down. Edmond.

A dozen people had gathered in front of the TV screens, watching silently, the only sound the press conference and Alex's typing as he updated the home page. "OK, it's out," he called out. "Just a headline. Do we have a story yet?"

Nehemiah James was raising his hand, signalling the end of the press conference. "Mr. Washington's testimony is very clear. Very precise. The truth is, there could have been two Black men killed that evening. That's how close this young man was. Thank you."

And they filed inside.

"The cops are sticking to their story, according to the wire," Alex said. "They say the college kid's account corroborates theirs entirely. Except they say Haley broke free first."

"Let them release the fucking video, then," Ray said.

I took over the home page as Ray coordinated coverage throughout the city: the new general assignment reporter going to Haley's neighborhood, the cop reporter talking to the police, Stacy given the task of getting an interview with Malik Washington (she wouldn't succeed). The cop reporter called in from police headquarters to say people were gathering outside and a crowd was building – "He needs help," Ray said, and he found another reporter and a photographer to send out, then placed another on call. We developed three separate stories for the next day's paper – the breaking news, an analysis, and a profile of Malik Washington, despite not getting an interview, a graduate of Walt Whitman High School whose mother was the principal at a local elementary school. I texted Jess to find out if she'd known him, but he'd graduated the year before she started.

I've always been proud to work for a newspaper rather than TV. Our sources are better, our judgment stronger, our reporting less sensational. But at times like this, newspapers become inadequate – people want to see it, not read about it – and so TV simplifies and sensationalizes, and social media now amplifies and distorts. Black bodies dominated our screens: young kids with skinny arms and legs, heavy-set older women, the teenage boys with hardened muscles and hardened faces and a way of talking that I was embarrassed sometimes not to understand. My own countrymen, and I couldn't understand their words.

A CVS miles from where Haley had lived was broken into that night, its wall-length glass shattered. There was no obvious connection to Haley, but TV showed this incessantly in the ensuing days. Its windows were smashed again and again, the slightly balding, pudgy Black pharmacist jumping over his counter the same way each time, tripping over the falling Tylenol boxes as he ran once more onto the street.

As Ray came over to discuss headlines for our stories, we watched two sixteen-year-old boys turned media antiheroes showing off their guns, talking crap about how they were going to go out and "kill the next white cop they see". A depression came over me like a force pushing my body into the ground. "This is going to do wonders for race relations," I said.

Ray said nothing.

"Is it racist to be scared of these two? I mean, I'm no fan of the cops but I don't want vigilantes running around killing anyone wearing a uniform."

"You're missing the point."

"My point is that every white person watching this is going to miss the point."

"We've created them."

"Yes and no. You're not like this."

"It's harder now."

"You were born when the Voting Rights Act was passed. When Black men were still being lynched in the South. It's harder now?"

"There weren't the gangs. There weren't the guns. There wasn't television showing off every single fucking material object you couldn't own."

"I don't believe you would have been like this. Ever."

He turned to look at me. "You have no idea how close that future is for a Black man. For a Black boy. No idea."

"I don't think they should report it. Do you?"

"I don't know. We're stuck with it now, though. Doesn't matter if we fucking report it or not. Doesn't make a..." He walked away. His bulky form swerved around tables, reporters, past the greying bob of our executive editor as she opened the door of her glassed-in office, around the corner and, I imagined, out the door.

A while after he returned, we went through the headlines and photos for the home page, trying to balance conveying the importance of the story against sensationalizing the story. We decided against *near-riot* – "We might as well say 'riot'," Ray said – discussed *unrest*, and went for *Witness Statement on Haley Shooting Prompts New Anger and Unrest*.

He pulled over a chair to wait until the page was live, then drummed his fingers on the desk as he stared at the screen. I wondered what change he was considering. He didn't linger without a reason.

"You know," he said, not taking his gaze from the home page, "my two sons will be looking at this. Twelve and fourteen years old. Trying to figure out what they think of this world."

"What do you want them to think?"

He laughed, then shook his head. "So the younger one is angry. Already thinks the world sucks. No. Knows it. And the other one – he's more like his mother. He's pissed off, but patient. Hopeful." He stood up to leave, then added: "Is it too much to want them to be both? Both of them? For both of them to be angry *and* analytical?"

"Maybe they'll rub off on each other."

"Oh, and careful. Because the younger one's right. The world sucks." He paused another moment. "And speaking of hopeful? Stay close to your high school friends. I like that angle. I like their take on things. Talk to them."

Jess and Aggie? I felt a moment of panic until I registered that he'd meant the students. I nodded. I'd thought of Makayla and Stuart too a few times that night, of the world they were trying to build, of the world we lived in instead.

Once the new home page was out, I went downstairs and stepped outside. I needed some fresh air, some quiet time away from the drone of TV news, but I also wanted to feel the city's pulse. The night was chill but opaque, as if the dust was still settling from a dirt road filled with horses and carriages rather than pavement and cars. The low clouds reflected light back on to the street and revealed air thick with dust, exhaust. I imagined, if the anger took a turn for the worse, the mist might be tear gas. It was always quiet when I walked to my car at 11:30 to drive home, but this was oppressive. The clouds were hanging low in the sky, making the light yellow, muting the sounds of night.

I ventured further from the building and looked up and down the street. Nothing. Not a car, not a person. A rat ran across the road – could they survive nuclear war, just like cockroaches could?

I shivered in the cold – I'd forgotten to wear a coat. Though it was now officially spring, winter was lingering, and, for a moment, I missed the South. For all its slowness, spring arrived on time, and summer was the season that lingered.

A cop car turned into the street, but I stood, not moving, as if in a trance. He pulled past then paused. I saw him and his partner look at me, then at the paper's logo behind.

His window began flowing down. "Do you need help, ma'am?" he asked, and waited. It didn't feel like an offer of help. It felt like a threat.

I didn't want to answer. I stood for a moment, staring back at him. His partner coughed. I wondered what they'd have said if I was one of those Black kids on the TV tonight. And then I wanted to run at them, screaming, *This is my city!* Couldn't I stand on the street, take in the air, of my own city, in peace? Was I a criminal for just standing on the street?

Yes, I couldn't just stand here. No, I was a criminal.

I turned and walked into the building, feeling defeated.

"That's how my boys feel," Ray told me when I was upstairs, "every day."

The next night, as I was drifting off to sleep, a single text: *Will you come with to talk to Ed Marshall?*

Engulfed in the Haley story, it took me half a second to take in what Aggie wanted. Hadn't she been watching the news? I remembered finding her in the café after the students' protest. Did these outside events agitate her? Or was she this self-involved?

And then I remembered that I had wanted to talk to Ed Marshall myself just the day before.

Why? I finally asked, wondering what she wanted to accomplish.

Can't do it alone

Had she purposefully answered the wrong "why"?

Would like your help

And he's scary.

When I first saw Ed Marshall again, he'd seemed more pathetic than frightening, with his case of Bud, his package of fresh spinach, and the never-lasting-long-enough pain prescription. He appeared a man whose life was finished, whose existence consisted of getting through the day by whatever means possible. Seeing him near the Whitcombe house had made him seem more threatening. More devious.

Maybe I could be devious, too.

Scarier now, I wrote.

Exactly!!!!!!

You seen the news? I texted.

Yep.

Should we wait til it dies down?

Don't know. Wanna just do it.

I guess HNA won't know? I texted. I couldn't imagine her mother would approve.

HNA *would* provide better protection

Even scarier than EM

No?

We spoke late that night when I was off deadline. We would try to reach Ed Marshall by phone, and then write him a letter if he didn't respond. And I should be the one to make contact.

"Who was that?" Ray asked as he saw me getting off the call.

I tried not to look as if I'd been caught. I didn't want Ray to know what I was doing. "Just an old friend." But he was whisking past me and I wasn't sure he heard.

CHAPTER SEVENTEEN

It was officially summer. Though not yet the solstice, we'd had our last classes that day – not just for the year, but for our entire high school careers – followed by our graduation ceremony on the high school football field that evening. Now we were at the school-sponsored graduation party at the local War Memorial. My parents were allowing me to stay out all night, a recognition that soon they'd have no idea how late or early I was out or in. A rite of passage. The summer would be full of them.

The school had decorated the food tents in Newfield High School colors – there were yellow and green balloons, yellow and green cupcakes, yellow and green napkins, yellow and green cups, yellow and green slushies poured into them. "I'm surprised they didn't make the ketchup green," Luke said as he splurted some onto his hot dog. "I'm usually a mustard guy but I really don't want to add any more yellow to the decor." He pointed his hot dog to a spot behind Aggie. "Hey, Ag. Hector alert."

I looked over and saw Aggie's brother by the pretzel stand – salted green, add yellow mustard – then Ed Marshall came into view. The two of them always struck me as such as odd pair: Hector tall, muscled, as poised as a dancer as he stood on the grass – even when still he looked like an athlete; then squat Ed, shifting from one foot to the other as if he wasn't comfortable anywhere.

"Yeah," Aggie said. "He said he might come."

These reported conversations between brother and sister never failed to unsettle me. I saw little interaction between them at their house, and any conversation that did happen was laced with animosity. It was surprising that they exchanged any information at all.

"He deigned to talk to you?" I said.

Joe hid a smile.

"I don't know. I don't think I'd want to go to someone else's graduation party," Luke said.

"Hey," Jess said. "I'm here."

"Yeah, but you're our friend," Aggie said.

"And younger," Luke said. "It's cool to be at an older person's graduation party."

"Luke is the new arbiter of cool," Joe said.

"How did Ed Marshall even graduate?" I asked. We'd almost missed his name being called – the tall, skinny guy before him, who I swore I'd never seen before, not once in my four years of high school, had tossed his cap in the air against all regulations, then raised his long arms over his head and cried, "Outta here, man!" The crowd was still laughing when Ed came up next, shook the mayor's hand and slunk away.

"He has two more classes to pass," Aggie said. "This summer. But they let him take part in the ceremony."

More weird details none of us should have known.

"Risky strategy for the school, I'd say," Luke said. "Now your brother and Ed are talking to Daisy."

"Daisy Dipwit?" Aggie said.

We all looked over just as Hector and Ed left a group of friends circled around Daisy and started walking toward one of the darkened, unlit fields. Ed pulled something out of his pocket, then paused and held out an empty hand. Into it, Hector placed a lighter, and they ambled into the dark and out of sight. "Pot break," Luke said.

We were about to turn around again when a slight blonde figure rushed after them. "Hey!" Her voice was flute-like in the night. "Wait up, guys!" Daisy, dressed in a green miniskirt and yellow tank top, caught up with them and Hector put his arm around her shoulder.

"Looks like the school decorated Daisy," Luke said.

"She ever smoke pot before?" Joe asked.

"Looks like she's about to," Luke said. "Why are we here talking about people we don't even" – he stopped himself from saying *like* – "that we're not even friends with?"

"My fault," Joe said. "This is where I told my parents I'd be all night. Had to at least stop by. Beach?"

"Beach," Aggie said.

"Let's blow this clambake!" Luke said.

"So much for the arbiter of cool," I said, then felt bad when Luke's smile faltered.

We piled into Luke's car and drove the short distance to Newfield Beach, where we'd agreed to meet another group of friends. "Oh, no, what about the coyotes?" I joked as Luke turned on to the darkened beach road. On Memorial Day weekend, a group of beachgoers had seen a family of about ten coyotes at dusk, and the town had gone into a full panic about the dangers of their encroachment into our safe suburban world.

"Wouldn't that be cool?" Joe said, his voice muffled. I didn't need to turn around to know he was wrapped around Aggie, I didn't need to know if this time it was her hair or shoulder or hand that he was nuzzling, that was muting his reply. I felt sorry for Jess in the back seat with them, and also grateful for her presence, for although we were meeting another group of friends at the beach, I again felt the pressure of my friendship with Luke – the ever-present question about him, from him – which was heightened on the rare occasion it was just four of us trooping off together, instead of five.

"Jess, we're all going to come back for your graduation next year," I said.

"Is that a prophecy, Cassandra?" Aggie asked.

"Oh my god, no way," Jess said. "You guys will be well over something like high school graduation."

We parked in the lot then walked the path through a small wooded area to the beach. "Hey – a coyote!" Jess jumped before she realized Luke was joking. Joe and Aggie wandered off almost as soon as we reached the sand and the rest of us joined the circle around the bonfire, where people were already dancing. Someone had brought a portable CD player and speakers, and everyone had brought booze. I danced a little with Luke, the sand cool on my bare feet, then wandered off by myself, too. Luke started to follow. "Bathroom break," I said, and succeeded in escaping by myself to the water. I sat on the sand, close enough for the waves to hit my bare feet, and stared out into the night. Southern Connecticut was too built-up to see many stars, but I found the Big Dipper and the Little Dipper. One overeager wave caught my skirt, yet I didn't move. What was I feeling, then, at eighteen? I can no longer remember. Joe's death has settled over these memories like mist over a meadow – so if I was lonely without Aggie, or confused about Luke, or just happy to be at the beach at night with friends' voices in the background like birds at twilight, I cannot remember. I look back now and feel only dread.

The truth is, I wasn't the kind of girl who wandered mysteriously off by herself to brood, though I probably liked the idea of it. Aggie might have been impressed if she saw me; Luke would certainly be. But I didn't even think, then, let alone brood. So I stood up and returned to the party after just a few minutes, to hang out with my friends, to flirt-not-flirt with Luke, to wait for Aggie to return with Joe from her escapades, flustered and lovely. Joe's earlier curfew meant I would have time with Aggie, Joe-less, after we dropped him off, even if she talked about him all night, and I didn't care if she did, because how much longer were we going to have such nights? Maybe that was the dread I remember, simply a sense of the unforgiving relentlessness of undramatic change.

As the night went on we added wood to the fire and wine coolers to our glasses and music to the CD player – I specifically remember "Rock Lobster." Bill Henderson arrived with Sarah Dunn and a few other people I didn't know as well and I discovered I might actually like Bill. I didn't know if it was because he was drunk, or just Daisy-less, but he was funny and goofy, at one point wetting his red hair so it stuck out like Madonna's and singing "Material Girl" in a falsetto. Aggie and Joe returned from the woods. For a while I sat next to Sarah Dunn, who spoke to me in her serious way, asking me why I wanted to be a journalist, why I had chosen Northwestern, like she was a guidance counselor. "You'll be good at it," she said, then stood up as if our meeting was over, but I was pleased.

It seemed just a minute later when Aggie told me she was going with Luke to drop off Joe and Jess, before returning to the beach again. "I'll come, too!" I said, a little loudly, a little drunkenly.

Aggie smiled. "I know, you goof," she said. "That's why I came to get you."

The five of us trudged away from the party, the music and voices receding as the pine trees thickened briefly, then opened up again into the parking lot. As we headed toward Luke's car I noticed a familiar Saab, parked in a remote corner of the lot, under a canopy of low-hanging trees: Hector was here.

A door squeaked open and the interior light brought Hector, then Ed, into bright relief.

"Let's pretend we didn't just see my brother," Aggie said, and we swung farther right than needed to get to Luke's car.

Hector stood by his door as if waiting, then leaned into the back seat, and out popped Daisy Dixon – or, rather, she collapsed out, or fell out, or whatever you'd call the motions of a person almost so drunk she couldn't walk on her own. She stood for a moment next to Hector as if recovering her balance, pushing his hand away. "...fine" we heard her say, before taking a tentative step in our direction. The car doors slammed the light off and they disappeared into the darkness, except for the small orange light bobbing toward us: the nub of Ed Marshall's cigarette.

Joe had stopped without us noticing, and was now standing on his own behind us, gazing in Hector and Daisy and Ed's direction. Aggie went back and took his arm. "C'mon," she said quietly. "You'll be late." Joe didn't move.

Stones crunched under their feet like the steps of ghosts, then three figures emerged from the darkness, Daisy in the middle, her yellow tank top gleaming in the shadows, leaning on Hector, each step veering her closer to him. Or maybe she was just trying to get farther away from Ed Marshall, who looked rattier than usual, his skin mottled and sickly under the sulfurous light of the streetlamp.

Aggie pulled at Joe's arm. He ignored her.

"Hey, Daisy," he called out, his voice casual, friendly. "We've been wondering where you been."

Not true. We hadn't wondered where Daisy Dixon was; we were just glad she wasn't with Bill at the beach.

"Who's that?" she said in a playful, teasing voice. In her voice. Maybe she was playing at being drunk. And then she stumbled a little, gasped, giggled, Hector catching her, and then she was batting him away again. "Fine!" She began concentrating on the ground, taking one step at a time. "I just can't *see*."

Joe stepped toward them, dipping down to catch Daisy's attention. "Daisy. It's Joe."

She lifted her pretty chin and its dimple flashed as she smiled, an instant switch to alert. "Joe! Joe! Oh my god – how are you?"

I felt my irritation growing. Fucking Daisy's suddenly Joe's friend?

"It's graduation. Tonight! And we haven't had a dance!" Daisy ran toward him, tripping and practically falling into him. He caught her, and she wrapped her arms around him.

She was shorter than him, her head barely reaching his chest, and so thin against the soft plushness of his body.

Hector and Ed watched from the shadows. Aggie laughed.

"Oh, dear," Luke said.

"Whoa!" Joe held her waist and gently pushed her further away. "What you guys up to?" He didn't look at Hector and Ed, lingering a few feet behind, but Ed took a drag on his cigarette, then answered as an exhale.

"Just hangin' at the beach like the rest of ya," he said, smoke puffing out of his nose and mouth with each word. "Not that it's any of your business."

"Just hangin'." Daisy stuttered out an exact imitation of Ed's voice, then giggled. "Just a-hangin' at the beach."

Hector turned and raised his eyebrows at Ed – "She's got you down" – then took Daisy's hand. "C'mon. You said you wanted to see the water."

"I don't want to anymore."

"You wanted to go swimming. Remember?" His voice was gentle, persuasive, like he'd sounded those months ago as he caressed the bullets in the palm of his hand.

"That's right, we're going swimming!" She let herself be led away by Hector, Ed following. Then she stopped, shook her hand from Hector, and turned toward us. "Joe! Joe! You gotta come with us. You *have* to come with us and go swimming!"

"Gosh, Daisy." *Gosh*? Where had that come from? "Man, I'd love to but I gotta get home. You wanna ride home? Daisy? Bit cold for swimming. Isn't it?"

"I think I'm a little drunk," Daisy said to no one in particular.

"You're fine, girl," Ed said, patting her arm.

She batted him away. "Stop touching me!"

It was clear Daisy wasn't fine. Hector was the only one who looked halfway sober, and he stood in the background like a referee at a ball game, his arms crossed on his chest, impassive, not wanting to get in the way of play.

"Daisy," Joe said, "maybe—"

"Li-sten." Ed began heading toward Joe, his head lowered, his gait like an injured, hurting animal's. He paused, and it felt like he was pawing the ground with his foot though he was standing still. He spoke so low and slow we could barely hear him. "This. Girl's. Fine." Noise from the party on the beach – a screeching, a few whoops, maybe a guitar riff – filtered toward us.

"Didn't say she wasn't, Ed." But Joe wasn't backing down.

"Just fine. With us."

"Just fine. With us," Daisy mimicked, taunting, cruel.

Ed smiled, his lips widening to reveal a row of tiny, straight teeth as small as a child's yet still, somehow, threatening.

"Up to her. I guess," Joe said.

"You can bet" – Ed threw his cigarette to the ground and took a step closer— "she ain't" — as he reached into his back pocket for another — "gonna go home" — except something clicked and glinted in the night – "with—"

"Uh, Ed," Hector said.

"—with a fuckin'—"

Out of the dark like a strange, vivid bird of prey, a giant beach ball, blue and red and orange, flew over Ed's head and landed at his feet. Someone had magic-markered a green and yellow smiley face onto its gleaming surface, and it bounced in front of us, face up, face down, face up, face down, before rolling over to Joe. The smiling, awful yellow mouth stared up at him. More drunken teenagers, breakaways from the bonfire, were dancing round us like this was suddenly a party game, all boys except for Sarah Dunn, giddy from being the only girl. Someone was playing "We Are the Champions" on the kazoo. A boy stood across the circle from Joe to retrieve the beach ball. It was Bill Henderson.

Joe picked it up. "Lost something?" He tossed him the ball, then jerked his head in Daisy's direction.

Bill looked at Ed Marshall, then Hector, then his friend. "Daisy?" he said.

"Bill!" Daisy cried out and ran to him like she had run to Joe, but Bill wasn't going to push her away. "Bill, my Bill. My best-est friend!"

"Ouch," Luke said quietly.

"Bill, Bill, where've you been all night?"

"I've been looking for you. Where've you been?" He looked at Hector and Ed incredulously. "With these guys?"

Daisy began to pull his arm and walk back toward the beach. "I want to go swimming. These guys won't. Take me swimming."

The entire group started walking away from us and back toward the beach, with Daisy again at its center, Sarah Dunn, sensible Sarah, making her way next to her. Daisy's voice rose above the others. "I smoked pot!"

"I don't think we can let her go swimming," Sarah said, then Bill's voice, "How *much* pot?" and they were gone.

Hector and Ed had disappeared, too, like spectres that hadn't really existed, though the vessel that had delivered them to us, the Whitcombes' car – Aggie's car – was still parked under the trees. A silence descended around us. Into it, an owl hooted.

Luke picked up Ed's cigarette butt and tossed it into a trash can. "Our work here is done," he said.

Joe lingered a moment, looking toward the now empty path, then scanning the perimeter of the parking lot, then back again toward the beach. "A million times," we heard someone say. About what? As Joe turned toward us again, his shoulders dropped, his arms loosened, his face softened. He put his arm around Aggie's waist and smiled at Jess. "I'll tell Dad it's my fault we're late," though I didn't think that was why Jess looked relieved.

It was hot in the car, sticky with beach heat. It felt like we'd been trapped for hours in a closed, dark room, and we all cranked down the windows and let the salty, damp air from the Sound, springlike still and smelling of leaves, spray against our faces, toss our hair. "Did anyone else think that was like *West Side Story* or something?" I asked. No one answered.

The mood had been broken, and after we dropped Joe and Jess off, we asked Luke to drop us at Aggie's, too.

Aggie found some leftover pizza in the fridge at her house and warmed it up in the oven. The Whitcombes didn't own a microwave. "You want a glass of wine?" Aggie asked. I shook my head. "Me neither."

We waited quietly for the pizza to get hot enough. Finally, she sighed.

"I wish Joe could have stayed out all night."

"Strict parents," I said.

"He could've stayed at Luke's. Stayed out as long as he liked then. I mean, even your parents let you stay out all night. And now we're home already."

"Why didn't he?"

"Don't know. I guess he asked."

"Then?"

"I don't know. Seems there could've been a way around it."

"Or not." I was surprised to find myself sticking up for Joe. I thought of his measured gaze when he'd discerned the situation with Daisy, how he'd stopped without thinking. How I knew I wouldn't have stopped to help her. "That was pretty intense."

Aggie looked up as if she didn't know what I meant, then shrugged. "My brother's an asshole."

Then the timer pinged, and we took the pizza to her room to eat, avoiding the dining room even though we didn't expect her brother home for a few more hours.

CHAPTER EIGHTEEN

"Testing, testing." An airy, crackly tap-tap.

"I can hear ya, man!" a passerby shouted out, and the man at the microphone laughed, gave a thumbs up.

A protest march had been called for the first Saturday after Malik Washington had spoken publicly, and the community leaders and politicians who'd organized it were walking up and down the stage, hovering around the microphone – mostly men in ties and the occasional jacket, a few women mixed in, as well as a handful of ordinary citizens in jeans and T-shirts, with less formal positions and more street cred. Steps away from them the public was beginning to gather, holding signs – *Justice for Haley*, *Black Lives Matter*. A handful of white people were protesting – *Race Is Not a Black Problem – It's an American Problem* was a sign one held – but they were visitors, most of them, in someone else's residents' parking zone.

I often feel apart from the crowd as a journalist — that comes with the job — yet as I'd walked toward Will Haley's old neighborhood that morning, where the protest march was starting, I felt a more complicated, less comfortable separateness. I was, of course, white, and the closer I'd come, the Blacker the mix of people around me became, and the whiter I felt. I became stupidly self-conscious – of my staid navy knee-length skirt, put on to look more professional despite my casual leggings and flat, overpriced boots – as if their un-coolness made me more white. As if Black women didn't wear practical clothing. I clutched my large digital recorder close to me in a kind of defensiveness. And then worried I'd look like I thought someone would steal it. Of course, I could see white people arriving to protest, a city alderwoman I recognized preparing to speak, but I was a journalist. And outsider. Would people even want to talk to me, aside from Makayla and Stuart? Would I want to talk to me, another white journalist in the neighborhood only because yet another tragedy had happened, if I were these people? If I usually felt separate as a journalist, I also at the same time felt like a part of the solution – a vital cog in the wheels of democracy, playing my role. At the protest, I felt part of the problem. To pretend not to be seemed false.

When I first learned Ray wanted more audio with Makayla and Stuart, I asked if Jess wanted a ride to the protest, and then her news arrived: she was meeting Antonne. This momentous step forward – it was doubtful his guardians would allow him to meet more than one set of parents – had not prompted celebration in Jess as much as a deeper, quieter seriousness. "I'm going to have this child's life in my hands," she explained when I asked if she was OK. "Someone else's child, now. A *person*." She laughed. "I'm scared, is what I am." She'd decided to spend the weekend with a relative in Virginia, and had asked them to drive her around Alexandria, where Antonne was born and lived the first year of his life before ending up in foster care. I'd never thought about what a brave act adopting was; had only, before, considered the gift the parents were receiving, instead of the responsibility they were taking on.

I looked around for Makayla and Stuart, who'd used One Whitman to organize a student presence at today's protest, and spotted the students' orange sign first: *Whitman High Students Oppose Racist Society*. A very global message, in a script I recognized as Makayla's. I was delighted, suddenly, to be here with them. Proud somehow, like their youth and idealism made me younger and more idealistic. Then I saw there were dozens of students, Black and Latino and Asian and white. I knew Jess had been keeping their expectations down after the poor turnout at the high school; but now there were easily a hundred students there, some of the boys in T-shirts and jean jackets as if it were summer already. I spotted Makayla with Stuart and went up to them.

"Look at this crowd!" I said to Makayla. She looked more nervous than excited. Her smile was half-hearted, and a bead of sweat was slowly dripping down her temple. I resisted the urge to wipe it off. "Are you OK? How can you be sweating in this cold?"

"Yeah, fine. Not feeling great."

"But look at all these students!"

"They're not just from Whitman," she said. "We got the word out on social media. It went viral. They're from other schools, other towns. It's... uh... it's good. But it's because, you know... people are upset."

"You guys attracted a better crowd than the main organizers," I said. I gathered her and Stuart for a quick interview.

Moments before the speeches started, the police rolled in like a dark blue smoke. They weren't in formation but, with the guarded gaze on their faces, the sameness of their crew cuts and uniforms, the build that, whether muscled or just overweight, turned their walk into a kind of swagger and made their guns knock against their hips, they looked like an army marching into battle. About half of them Black, half of them white, they took their place one by one in front of the speakers' podium. The crowd quieted for a moment, the politicians, the protesters, the kids near the shops, looking over then away as if they hadn't looked. Their presence was frightening. I supposed it was meant to be – meant to intimidate, meant to quell even the idea of illegality. But at the same time, the tension rose, the air crackling with the sound of the mikes being tested, the bouncing of a basketball in a court I couldn't see, as the cops one by one stepped into place.

"I don't know what it means, that they think they need all this," Stuart said.

"Well, we can't be intimidated. Right?" Makayla said. "I mean, we got a right to be here."

"Feels weird," Stuart said. "I guess they wanna make sure nothing bad happens. But. I don't know."

I had a hard time concentrating. Were the cops that worried about violence? "Justice for Haley," the crowd began repeating, and I dutifully noted it down. Where was Stacy? Then I saw her closer to the podium, scribbling away, and felt relieved. I didn't want to be the only journalist here if problems arose with the crowd. As local residents began to speak, I began to pay attention. A woman described herself as "just a neighbor".

"I'm not a mother," she said. "I'm not a community leader. I'm just a person who lives and works in this neighborhood. But I am tired of hearing my friends who are mothers worrying about their sons every time they go out. I'm tired of reading about another Black man or woman shot by a police officer for no good reason. I'm tired of it, and that's why I'm here. So yes, justice for Haley. But justice for us all."

The organizer of the event took the microphone again. "Justice for Haley," he said, and the crowd repeated his cry. "Justice for all!" and they repeated that, too.

"Do you know if Miss Willis is here?" Makayla asked me.

I told her Jess wasn't, but knew I couldn't say why. "She had some sort of family commitment," I said.

They looked at each other and shook their heads.

"I think it's genuine!" I said, not wanting them to be disappointed in Jess. "She couldn't avoid it."

"Oh, we don't doubt it! We feel for her," Makayla said.

"Why?" I asked.

Stuart looked at Makayla, then shrugged. "I guess it's public knowledge. Are you like," he asked me, "from around here?"

I nodded.

"Well," Makayla said, "don't put this in your story today?"

"Of course," I said, with that quick jolt of excitement I remembered getting as a student reporter when someone was about to confide in me. Because they trusted me. And they trusted me with a good story.

"We think it's too hard for her. Her brother was killed when she was in high school."

"Her brother," I said. Joe.

"It wasn't by a cop or anything, but—"

"It seemed like it was a racist incident, too," Stuart said. "But maybe you know about this already? Didn't Miss Willis say you grew up around here?"

"Yeah," I said. "I know about it."

And then we heard a crash, a shattering of glass, shouting. Stuart and Makayla looked at each other, then began running toward the noise. "We were worried this would happen," Stuart said, to me, to Makayla, I wasn't sure. The crowd thickened in front of us, and Makayla found a bench and the three of us stood on top. The 7-Eleven window had been broken, and there were five cops hunkered on the ground amid broken glass. "There's a guy there," Stuart said. "I can see his sneakers."

A few more officers arrived and created a shield around the cluster. One of the officers nearby took out a megaphone. "It's all right," he said, the tinny sound of his voice echoing off the shop buildings. "Everything's fine." When the person rose – practically lifted to his feet by two cops – he was handcuffed, his head down, a cut on his arm probably from the glass.

"I don't think that kid was even at the protest," Stuart said as we climbed off the bench. "I'm gonna try not to get depressed by that."

"You guys aren't allowed to lose hope that quickly," I told them. They looked at me strangely. But in the midst of this darkness, Makayla and Stuart were hope. The way Joe was. The way all four of us were, when we were their age. Before Joe was shot. Before we lost our nerve.

The march continued on its haphazard way. I stuck by the students with my tape recorder on, hoping to catch ambient sound – the interviews from earlier were what I'd wanted. I could have gone home, really, but wanted to stay. I was there as a journalist, but, somehow, I felt my number would count.

A van of police officers unloaded next to us, then another. A response to the broken window, I imagined. A third unloaded ahead of us, spewing officers with shields. Riot gear. Really? The rally was remaining incredibly peaceful from where we were. The students began to notice, too. Makayla began stopping, looking at her phone, then looking around. Stuart put his arm around her, then came over to me. "Do you know if there's anything going on? I mean, this seems a bit of an overreaction?"

I was pleased that he'd asked my opinion. *They're just kids*, I reminded myself again. I was allegedly a journalist in the know. "I was just going to call the newsroom."

The home page editor didn't have any more news than we did. "The TVs are showing the arrest again and again," he said. "No surprise there. Oh yeah, wait. They're showing all these cops getting out of vans in fucking riot gear."

"Yeah. That's what we're seeing."

"No rioting, though." He chuckled. "I guess they're double-safe that way."

As we walked, it felt as if the crowd was getting thicker. "Aw, man. I'm getting hot," Makayla said.

"You OK?" Stuart asked her. "You're not dizzy, are you?"

She shook her head, but she didn't look well. She was sweating, but instead of looking hot, she looked cold. Wan.

"Why don't you have my energy bar?" he said.

She nodded but didn't eat it.

"She's a little hypoglycemic," he told me. "Makayla, you should eat it," he said. He took it from her, opened it up, and gave it back to her.

She looked at him and laughed. "Thanks, Dad," she said.

"Don't mention it," he said, but he wasn't smiling. "I don't like this," he said. "Something isn't right."

Our march had slowed to a crawl and seemed more and more crowded. Suddenly, I was jostling for room. I looked through the crowd. The cops were lined up on the side of the street like a human chain. "Oh, for god's sake," I said aloud, then looked to the other side of the street. Another wall of cops.

"Can you see ahead?" I asked Stuart.

"Well, not great. I mean, it looks like there's a lot of us now, but I thought we were spread out more before. I thought we were further to the back. Weren't we?"

I nodded. "Can you see more police officers?"

He squinted. "Well, yeah."

"Is the march still moving ahead?"

"Yeah, yeah, you're right. We're stalled."

"We're being kettled," I said. "I'm going to call the news desk."

"What's kettled?" he asked.

I rang but I couldn't get through to the newsroom. I decided to try Aggie but I couldn't get through at all.

"Is your phone working?" I asked them.

"I'm really not feeling well," Makayla said. "I need to sit down. It's too hot."

"It's gonna be hotter down there," Stuart said.

I took out a few tissues, wet them with my water. "Here. Rub this on your face." Then I gave her the water to drink. "Is there a curb she can sit on?"

"She can sit on my backpack," Stuart said. We went to the side of the crowd and set up a little seat for her with my bag and his backpack.

"My mom's gonna be worried, too," Makayla said, putting

her face in her hands, lifting her hair off her neck, then looking like she might topple over. Stuart caught her.

"Have more water," he said.

"I promised I'd text her once an hour."

"I'll try her, OK?" he said. But none of us could get a signal.

Makayla needed to get out of here. If she fainted, the crowd was so tight it would be hard to hold her up. I imagined her being jostled and tumbling over and trampled on.

"Let me see what I can do," I said. "Stay here."

I found the nearest police officer and asked for help in getting Makayla out of the crowd. Before I could finish explaining, he said, "No, ma'am."

"Why?" I asked. "She's ill."

He stared at me with blank eyes. *This is what they're trained to do*, I thought. Trained not to see people as people. Trained not to be people themselves. To be a person is to be weak. To have empathy is to be weak.

"She's a student at Walt Whitman High School," I said. "She's going to—"

"And so was the young man who crashed that store window," he said.

"Bullshit," I said, then remembered I was talking to a cop.

His level gaze did not falter. Trained not to become angry. So why didn't I feel safer? His calmness was as threatening as a curse.

"I advise you to step away from the perimeter, ma'am," he said.

"I'm sorry, officer, but this young woman is ill, and I'm a journalist covering the march."

"You can leave, ma'am, if you have your press card, but she cannot," he said.

I looked to the officers on either side of him, a white woman and a Black man. They did not gaze back at me. I thought of Robocop. Was that the goal?

My phone rang. The news desk! I spoke quickly before I lost the signal again. "OK, so they're kettling us here, kettling a peaceful crowd, I'm with students from Whitman High School, one is hypoglycemic and having, I think, a panic attack, and they're not letting her—"

I'd never been physically assaulted before. The blow came as if to my entire body, as if wind had become rock and been slammed into every part of me at once. It was night, then blinding light, then night again. I was on the ground as light snuck in between fingers. Cowered on the street, my arms over my head, don't hit me don't hit me don't hit me don't hit me again don't hit me *ma'am* don't hit me *ma'am ma'am* don't hit me *ma'am get up* don't hit me *ma'am*. I was standing and tumbling and then inside, quiet, a car, don't hit me don't hit me don't.

And I wasn't even hit. Not with a stick, not with a gun, not with a shield, not with a fist. All that had happened was I was pulled from the crowd and thrown behind the line of police officers on to the street. I landed on my rump. His shield had hit my arm. Grazed my arm. An accident, in truth. He hadn't meant to hurt me. But he hadn't exactly cared if he did hurt me. It was so violent. The bruises the next day deep black and purple and raised in anger as if in belated response. The side of my thigh killed, so maybe I had landed on that first. A hip pointer injury, a doctor said a few days later. Might hurt in the future, too, as I aged.

CHAPTER NINETEEN

I didn't know until the next day that Makayla ended up taken to the hospital by ambulance after she and Stuart found their way to a barrier and she fainted while pleading with a cop who wouldn't listen. Luckily, a nearby police captain sensed Makayla was about to faint, caught her before she fell, motioned for medics, and sent her and Stuart off in the ambulance together. Eleven people were arrested that day, most released that evening; only two were charged with "criminal mischief" – Connecticut's legal term for vandalism – neither people who had actually taken part in the march. The kettling incident, however, brought more national attention to the Haley shooting than any other story had so far. "And somehow, police say this is the protestors' fault," Ray told me on the phone when he called to tell me to take a few days off. The police decided not to charge me, but my arrest and injuries became a detail in the stories the next day, along with Makayla, whom the AP had located on social media after listening to my previous audio piece. "To my knowledge, the sentence for drug use and resisting arrest is not the death penalty," she told the reporter, in a quote picked up by a number of papers, "unless you're a Black man."

Aggie texted the next morning, asking how I was. *Black and blue*, I wrote.

I wasn't there, she texted. A few seconds later, *I'm sorry*.

What for, I wondered. For my injuries? Or not being there? The lack of clarity, today, pissed me off. She hadn't asked whether I'd reached Ed Marshall, and this angered me, too.

Jess stopped by in the afternoon, fresh from the airport, with smoothies and a muffin, a Cherry Blossoms Festival T-shirt from Washington, and news of Antonne. "He's adorable," she said after I finally convinced her I was fine. "He's just so sweet. Quiet and sweet, but not too sweet, I don't think, I mean he's not even two years old yet — kids *should* still be trouble at that age. He's definitely capable of being naughty. That's good, right? But he took my hand and led me upstairs to show me his room, his hand was so soft and small, so tiny, and I was simply – charmed. I mean, I guess he's like that with everybody, right, but the foster mother was beaming and I was beaming and Amy looked thrilled and, oh my god – I will be heartbroken if it doesn't work out. He's just… He's beautiful."

After the strain of the last twenty-four hours, how soft her story sounded, how hopeful. Tears sprang to my eyes.

"Oh, don't you cry!" Jess said, wiping delicately at her own face. "It'll be Niagara Falls here if we don't watch it. Besides, I wanted to talk to you about something. Something serious."

"You sound like a parent already," I said.

She nodded emphatically, as if not getting that I was teasing. "That's exactly right. I don't think it's an accident. That you were assaulted."

"Oh god, I wasn't assaulted, not really," I said.

"Do you want me to bring over a mirror?"

I put up my hands as in self-defense. "Hey, I know it's not my best hair day."

"I'm serious, Cassie. You've been involved in the Haley coverage. They know who you are."

"Some rank-and-file officer isn't going to—"

"I think he would. And…"

"*And?*" I asked.

"There's Joe, too."

I looked at her, incredulous. I'd learned long ago that taxis really didn't pick up Black passengers, that waiters really did sometimes ignore Black customers. That cops stopped Black men for no reason whatsoever. But this seemed far-fetched.

"You think they're going to forget about Joe?" Jess asked. "A son of one of their own went to prison."

"But they won't know my connection—"

"You know that Hector sought me out at the party the night Joe died?"

I felt tired suddenly, as if I'd suffered multiple blows to the head yesterday after all instead of simply grazing my face when I fell. "How would I know that?" I said.

"Putrid, smelling of pot, standing too close to me. Breathing beer in my face in the basement of that house party. Asking me where Joe'd gone."

"He asked me that, too."

"About Joe and Aggie?"

I nodded.

"I knew they were going to Aggie's – usual big brother thinking he's pulling something over on his little sister, how stupid did he think I was? – but I wasn't going to tell Hector where they were. And then, his lips shaping these words: 'I'm so glad they're together.' Dripping with, I don't know… he'd always been so strange with me – overly formal, politeness as a form of aggression – so when he stepped toward me I flinched. He laughed. 'Don't worry, Jess,' he said. 'I'm not attracted to Black girls.'"

I could imagine Hector saying it, could feel the bulk of him in the room.

"So I went home, flew through the night in the car with the windows wide open, *I'm so glad they're together*, Daddy coming out to use the bathroom when I got home, letting me know he'd been waiting on me, *I'm not attracted to Black girls,* and I switched on the light above the stove and made myself a drink, *I'm so glad they're together, together, together*, the words repeating and repeating, *Black girls I'm not attracted to Black girls to Black girls*. I'd never made myself a drink before, wasn't sure I was allowed to at home, but my mother used to make me a hot toddy when I wasn't well, so I boiled water for tea, added honey, poured whiskey from Daddy's bottle, and made myself a promise: I would never again put myself at the mercy of a person like Hector Whitcombe. I would be ever vigilant. I'd never let down my guard. I had this picture of myself with a border that went three hundred and sixty degrees around my body – not hard, not wired, but like a soft green hedge so that no one could ever cross that line because they wouldn't even know there was a line."

She stopped.

"And then in the darkness of that night the phone rang, and I knew Joe was dead, and all my promises had been made too late."

She clasped and unclasped her hands and straightened her shirt then stood, as if assembling herself, remembering her purpose.

"And now you've been assaulted—"

It was an accident, I thought, but I didn't say it aloud because maybe it didn't feel true.

"—and you gotta promise me. Ed Marshall's father is still on the police force, isn't he? And Hector? Really, Cassie. You need to be careful."

"I don't even know what to promise," I said.

As the Haley story receded from the news again, my bit part was once more in an un-bylined article in the *New York Times*, which in the sixth paragraph mentioned an unnamed journalist getting injured. Journalists look out for one another, or for the profession, or maybe they look out for themselves. In truth, I would have been embarrassed to get more attention than that, given I was alive and well, and with a mention, when so many people in cities across the United States had died, without mention.

And yet it was strange, too, for a personal event which nonetheless took place in public – in the public eye, involving a public body, using a questionable practice in public – to end up feeling so private, as if I'd instead broken my arm in a fall at home. It was weirdly isolating. I remember, years ago, when my mother had a cancer scare, I'd taken a walk in a popular park, and as I rounded a corner, lost in my own thoughts, a woman walking past me nodded to her friend and said, "Power walker." Her smugness was annoying, hurtful, but I didn't – couldn't – blame her for not knowing. It was a private affair. This was different. It felt somehow that people should know – that the person at Cam's Coffee shouldn't look away politely from the bruise on my cheek, or the attendant at the gas station, or at least the checkout woman at Deep's who usually said hello. They should know what had happened to me. They should then be able to voice their sympathy, shake their head at the unnecessary violence in our country. Go home and tell their spouses and friends. Be upset at the state of things. How Haley's friends and family dealt with the winnowing down of coverage, the decreasing public importance of their brother's or son's or friend's wrongful death, when as the days progressed their understanding of their loss instead expanded around them, growing larger and larger, I don't know. I have some inkling of their feelings because of Joe's death. My wonder now is not why I persisted against all evidence that summer, but how I ever stopped.

And I'm white, not Black. It doesn't happen to me again and again.

My first day back, the news desk bought a cake frosted with a picture of a kettle, and Smart Aleck handed me a travel-size toothbrush and tube of toothpaste with a ribbon wrapped around it. "For the intrepid journalist – don't leave home without it," Alex said. Squares of cake on flimsy paper plates were handed around, and we were a jolly, companionable crew. Then I was on the news desk for my shift, communicating again with everyone by email, my celebrity days over.

Ray lingered a few moments, and when everyone had left he rolled up a chair to speak to me. "So who do you think ordered that tactic on what was a relatively small and peaceful protest?" Ray asked me quietly. "You have a guess?"

"Hector Whitcombe?" I asked.

"Hector Whitcombe. Time to run a story on good ol' Hector Whitcombe."

I nodded and kept looking at the home page. A link needed updating, and I did it. I knew he was right, and yet a story on Hector now would not unearth anything new about Joe. And Jess was so close to adoption. I didn't want that event tainted by Hector.

Ray sat, waiting. "You want to write a first-person piece?"

"Fuck – no!" I said, surprised at my vehemence.

Ray looked surprised, too.

"What good is that going to do?" I asked.

"Doing good isn't actually our job," Ray said, "but why don't you fill me in on why you think it won't?"

How much I wanted to tell him: that I'd left three voicemails for Ed Marshall that had gone unanswered. That I'd seen his beat-up sky-blue pickup truck at the Windmill Diner at the edge of town one day about eleven in the morning. That I'd driven by the Windmill at that time on multiple mornings, multiple days of the week, and the truck was always there except on weekends.

That I'd been thinking, while recuperating at home, of just driving over to the Windmill by myself.

And that, if a story on Hector ran, Ed Marshall would never talk to Aggie and me.

"Do we have to run a story now?" I asked.

He laughed. "Are you fucking joking? Yes. It's running

maybe this Sunday. Maybe next. Why *don't* you want a story to run now?"

Ray would understand, if I was writing the story for the paper. He'd hold off. But I couldn't go to Ed Marshall as a journalist. He'd tell us nothing. Aggie would learn nothing. I would learn nothing. Jess, if there was anything Jess really wanted to know, would learn nothing.

"It'll distract from the Haley case," I said.

"I'm sorry."

"My second ambiguous apology of the week," I said.

"Who was the first from?"

"Aggie Whitcombe."

"For fuck's sake, Cassie. You want to *protect* these people?"

"Aggie never did anything wrong, and you know that."

I looked at Ray and saw him inspecting me – the bruise on my cheek, but me as well. Assessing me, until he met my gaze.

"Ed Marshall still lives in town, apparently," Ray said.

"Apparently, that's pretty common for people who grew up here."

"Stacy's tried calling him."

Shit. No wonder he hadn't returned my calls.

"Do you want to try?" Ray asked. "You knew him."

My chance to tell Ray.

"Maybe you already have."

"No – I really can't. I'm sorry."

"Oh, for Christ's sake, Cassie." Ray stood and walked away.

"Wait," I said, before he went too far. He turned back, impatient. "We're going to mention Joe Willis in the story?"

"Well, of course we fucking are. You know that."

"Why don't I look the story over, before it runs?" I suggested. "At least make sure we don't get something wrong." I could help, at least, in that way. And I could warn Jess, too, before it ran.

"As long as you don't tell your little friends," Ray said as if he'd been reading my thoughts.

"I certainly wouldn't tell the Whitcombes," I said.

"The Whit*combes*? Plural?" he asked. "What, you go over for family dinners now?"

I didn't know what to say. It wasn't like that. Was it?

"You sure you don't have any inside information you might share with us? Cassie? For Christ's sake."

"I honestly don't know where to send you that wouldn't be obvious. Hector's life has been straightforward since the shooting. Aggie thinks he's changed. But I think the Whitcombe family is…"

"Is what?"

"I don't know." I thought of Aggie's face that dark night outside her parents' house, that pale, wispy ghost of her old self admitting the blank of her last minutes near Joe. How eerie it was at dinner when Mr. Whitcombe reappeared, so briefly, with all his old charm. Mr. Whitcombe's mind, too, had been emptied. Of what? What if somehow Aggie was partly to blame? Would I tell Ray that?

"Cassie, they're what?"

"Fucked up, I guess."

"By the shooting?" Ray grunted. "Poor little rich folks." And walked away again.

Before getting back to work, I texted Aggie. *I think we should have a late breakfast at the Windmill*. It would be reckless to surprise Ed – he was a violent man. But a convict couldn't own a gun – right? We'd be in plain view in the diner's parking lot. I didn't know how else to get to talk to him. Ed wasn't going to tell us what really happened. But what if he mentioned something to help Aggie remember? What if he revealed one small thread of what had happened that night which we could pull and pull and pull until the entire story unravelled at our feet?

Monday??? she texted back. *School vacation next week.*

Excellent. My bruises might still be showing. That felt like protection, in some strange way.

Then she texted, *While you still black & blue?*

Scare-y!

What was *scare-y* was how often she still knew what I was thinking.

I was glad Aggie had agreed right away, because as much as I didn't think she'd tell her brother, or even her mother, I couldn't have convinced her by letting her know about the Hector story. In a way that mimicked high school, I suspected she was closer to him than I wanted to believe. Once or twice, she'd let drop a detail about his life: that he and his ex-wife decided to take separate vacations in California the same weeks so they could share custody of their twin boys; how he'd dressed up as a clown for the kids' seventh birthday party ("*Hector?*" I couldn't help exclaiming). That he spent every other Saturday night at the Whitcombes' house and insisted his mother go out with friends. What if Hector ended up finding out before we called him for comment? I didn't want to suspect my friend.

I knew, however, that I'd tell Jess. The question I was worrying about was whether to let her know we were going to talk to Ed Marshall. It was a balance of openness against the risk of reopening wounds, or maybe making never-closed wounds worse. I felt I had to tell her, but I wondered, too, if I secretly wanted her approval. Wanted her to think me good for helping Aggie, brave for confronting Ed Marshall in order to find out more about what happened to her brother.

After I knocked on her door early the next morning, her shadow passed over the peephole, then she opened the door quickly, looking alarmed.

"You OK?" she asked.

"Yes, yes."

Her shoulders relaxed, and she motioned me in. "Come in, come in, for once I'm not late. There's more coffee. Up so early!" She sounded elated, her stride bouncy, energetic. So I told her quickly, before I lost my nerve – about the paper's story on Hector, as well as our planned talk with Ed Marshall. Though I didn't tell her we were surprising him at a diner.

Jess told me she had suspected there might be a story about Hector – "He'd ordered the kettling, right?" – and that it would end up mentioning Joe, but as I told her about Ed Marshall, she paused, facing me slowly – she'd forgotten she had offered me coffee. She stood, turning an empty white mug in her hands.

"I don't know, sometimes, with Aggie," she said. "If this is about Joe. Or if this is about Aggie."

I'd wondered the same thing. But even if it was about Aggie – about Aggie feeling better – this was so intertwined with Joe the question seemed irrelevant. "Does it matter?" I asked.

She sighed. "You're putting yourself in danger," she said. "Why?"

I don't care, I thought, but I didn't want to say that to Jess.

"You need to tell someone who you're meeting, and when you're going. Promise me?"

I nodded, though I didn't know who I'd tell.

"It can't be me. I wish it could. But... I have to concentrate on Antonne. I don't even want to think about that man when I'm with Antonne."

I realized she was speaking as if her adoption was definite. "Antonne? Is there..."

"Oh, Cassie," she said. "Look at this house! It's one of the last times it'll be mine alone. Antonne is arriving in two weeks!"

"Two weeks?" I felt shocked – so quick? "Oh, that's wonderful!" I said.

She started talking about how much she had to do – the shopping for Antonne's room and Antonne's clothes that she'd put off because she was afraid of jinxing the deal, the intent-to-adopt petition she could file once he began his placement, the paperwork for her parental leave, the childproofing of cabinets, the delightfulness of every task. "Admin never felt like so much fun!" I tried not to think about the month, when

Antonne first arrived, when Jess would spend all her time alone with her child, which adoption agencies required as a way of enabling the child to form an attachment with the new parents and establish a bond like that of mother to child. I'd miss her then, but even afterward, I'd be peripheral. I was peripheral. *Don't be selfish*, I told myself.

"Listen," Jess said, "in a moment of exuberance I promised my parents I'd come to church on Easter Sunday. It'll be our last time, now, before Antonne arrives, and, well... will you join us? You're invited for dinner after, too. You don't have to—"

"No! I'd love to. That's... I can't tell you..."

Jess bounded out of her chair. "Oh my god, now I am late! Cassie," she said, giving me a quick hug, "I'm so happy!" How completely the spectre of Ed Marshall had receded into the corners of the room, had wisped right out the windows.

CHAPTER TWENTY

"Hecccc-tor!" Mrs. Whitcombe's voice reverberated from the kitchen, and she strode swiftly and smoothly into the room and stood at the foot of the stairs. "Hector Whitcombe!"

Aggie and I were playing gin rummy on the couch when Mrs. Whitcombe slid past without seeming to notice us. It was early evening, and after pizza for dinner – Aggie's father was away at a conference – we were biding our time until Joe and Jess finished work at Deep's, when we'd agreed to pick them up and go to Luke's for the night. Aggie was restless, bored, as she often was these days when Joe wasn't around. My mother's voice spoke quietly in my head– *you'll wear out your welcome, dear* – but when I'd said I might just go home, Aggie had jumped up to order pizza for dinner. This was all the reassurance I needed to stay.

I hadn't even known Hector was home, but Mrs. Whitcombe was waiting, still and straight in cropped grey pants and a long grey sheer tunic, jingling something in her right hand. Bullets. I looked at Aggie, but she was staring studiously down at her cards as if she were the one in trouble.

"Hector." Her voice was softer but somehow sterner. "I need you down here immediately."

Hector's door opening finally echoed down to us, his slow footsteps creaking on the wooden floor above us. We could sense his presence like a shadow at the top of the stairs, though we couldn't see him. "What?" he said.

"I said down here, please." Mrs. Whitcombe stood patiently, with the relaxed stance of a dancer, loose and centered. Maybe it was the grey of her outfit, but she looked older than usual, tired, the wispy brown strands of her short cut seeming not stylish but frayed, frazzled. As Hector slowly made his way down the stairs, her fist began clenching and unclenching the bullets in her right hand.

He slouched against the banister as he approached his mother, as if this weren't important enough for him to bother expending too much energy, then stopped at the third step, towering over her. She moved aside and gestured to the spot on the floor she had just vacated. He slunk down the last three steps, and though he still towered over her – he was easily two heads taller – her precise, compact energy made her seem the larger force.

She held up her hand, palm outstretched, in which sat the bullets he had showed us the week before. "What are these, please?"

"Cartridges," he said.

"Cartridges?"

Hector shifted as she stood, waiting.

"You mean bullets," she said.

"Those technically are cartridges. The bullets—"

"Bullets. Thank you. Take them, please."

Hector looked surprised – I was, too. What was she doing giving them back? He put out his hand to accept them quickly, looking at them again as if he didn't believe they were there.

"Now put them in your pocket." Again, he hesitated, glancing at her to make sure he'd understood correctly, then quickly put them in his pocket. "How did they end up there?"

"Well, you just gave them to me and I, well, I just put them in my—"

"Exactly. And so how do you suppose they ended up in the pocket of your other jeans?"

He didn't answer.

"Because I can't see how anyone else could put them there without your knowing."

She had Hector, and he knew it.

"I guess I must've put them in my pocket without realizing when Detective Marshall was showing me how to operate his gun—"

"Lessons I have expressly forbidden you from accepting."

Hector had been bragging to Aggie about his lessons from Detective Marshall, how the accuracy of his aim was improving, how, when Ed wasn't present to hear, Mr. Marshall had called him a natural. They'd had a few extra hours shooting with him recently, preparing for hunting coyotes at the beach on the night the Whitcombes were going away – a plot he hadn't revealed to any of the adults, including Detective Marshall. It was the same night Joe was spending at Aggie's, so she was weirdly in cahoots with her brother over plans while their parents were away.

Yet Hector couldn't help arguing. "I'm not in high school anymore. You can't tell me—"

"As long as you live in this house, you live within the rules of this house, even when you're outside this house. Do you understand?"

Hector said nothing, just breathed, heavily, as if he'd raced up ten times as many stairs as he'd just slumped down. He recrossed his arms and shifted his stance. It looked like if he didn't move, he'd explode with anger.

"That's ridiculous."

"We've discussed this before."

Hector shifted again, recrossing his arms twice more, quickly. The angrier Hector seemed, the silkier and smoother Mrs. Whitcombe became, as if she could physically change herself so Hector's ire would just slip around her like water. She became quieter, even smaller. Not weaker. Just more compact.

She waited for him to disagree. He did not.

"I will not have you engaging with Detective Marshall's

guns. He is a police officer. You are not. You will not engage in any manner."

"But—"

"I won't have it. And if you argue any further, I will call Detective Marshall myself and tell him the same, and I am quite sure he will respect my wishes. Do you agree?"

The last thing Hector wanted was his mother calling Detective Marshall like Hector was still twelve years old.

"Guns are not the problem."

"I am not debating gun control with you at this moment. Is it necessary for me to call Detective Marshall?"

"No."

"Good. And if this happens, or something else like it happens, again, I will call him."

This was a powerful threat, and Hector knew it. He nodded.

"And I'm going to discuss with your father whether we can trust you enough for us to go away as planned the weekend after next."

Aggie jerked up, knocking her trio of sixes into my straight. "Uh, Mom?"

"I'm busy, Aggie."

"You don't have to cancel—"

"Now." Mrs. Whitcombe stared at Hector as if Aggie and I didn't exist.

Aggie sank back into the couch, pretending to play our game of rummy, though neither of us threw a single card.

"The bullets." Mrs. Whitcombe held her hand outstretched, palm up, like a Greek statue in her pale grey attire.

"I guess I should return them to Detective Marshall," Hector said.

"No."

She remained still, her head down as if an extra in a tragedy, waiting. Finally, Hector pulled the bullets from his pocket and dropped them from his oversized paw into Mrs. Whitcombe's tiny hand, one by one into her palm, the second clinking lightly against the first as it landed. She stared at them a moment, as if trying to divine some secret from them, then clutched them in her fist again and strode silently out of the room.

"Wow," Aggie said, looking up again. "Thanks for the show."

"Fuck off," Hector said and thundered up the stairs, then paused halfway up. "Won't be nothing compared to if she finds out about your plans with your boyfriend when they're out of town." His voice was echoey from the stairwell.

"You better hope your hero Detective Marshall doesn't realize he's missing a few items." She kept her voice low, so her mother couldn't hear.

Hector leaned over to speak through the spindles. "I'm not that stupid," he said, barely audible. In one motion he disappeared again. We heard his door open and shut, and a shudder as he crashed onto his bed.

"What does that mean?" I asked.

"Fuck knows. My brother's idiocy is an unsolvable mystery."

"She should have called Ed's father anyway."

"She won't. That would embarrass Hector. God forbid. As if he's not inherently embarrassing to himself. OK. It's my turn, isn't it?" She laid down three eights.

I was jarred for a moment – what was she doing? – but Aggie always made these transitions more quickly than I did.

CHAPTER TWENTY-ONE

When Jess and I filed into a pew on Easter morning next to her mother, I almost didn't recognize her. The stiff, slight woman who embraced me briefly that morning with a cardboard hug before returning to her prayers didn't seem like the helpful, smiling, quiet person who used to try to draw us out as we sat awkwardly in her living room. Her hair was now greying and pulled into an austere bun, which suited her muted mauve blouse and brown skirt. Above her forehead, wrinkled in prayer, hovered a small lace veil from a black pillbox hat. It seemed strange to be wearing black on Easter. Was she still in mourning, after all these years, the veil a physical symbol, like Joe's still-preserved room, that she couldn't give up? Or did she possess only one hat for church? Jess, in her bright blue dress, blue hat and blue shoes, white jacket and bag – how did she find the time to always look so stunning? – seemed like a model this humble woman might look at in a magazine, not her daughter.

A man nodded to the choir to begin singing, and then I registered that he was Mr. Willis. If his wife had aged too much, Jess's father looked as if he hadn't aged a day since I'd last seen him twenty years ago at Joe's funeral. When he closed his eyes for the opening prayers, his face became smooth, still, serene; a kind of eerie blankness wiped away any expression, as if all had been forgotten except for the idea of a lord, a Jesus, a savior. As if faith required emptiness.

I'd always loved how joyful Black churches made their services. They seemed to be truly praising God, at least compared to the dour Catholic Masses I'd been brought up on, where Dave Donahue would sing dour songs in a dour voice over a dour organ, and the congregation would half-heartedly join in, except for our elementary school music teacher, who would sit in the front pew and trill the hymns in a voluminous vibrato as if on an opera stage. Here, there was clapping and gospel songs from a choir of men and women, girls and boys, all swaying to the music, the congregation clapping and singing when invited, sometimes even when not, the occasional "Amen" rising over the room like an exclamation point.

They began to read from the Scriptures, then sang, thanking God for rising from the dead on this Easter day to save us from our sins, for the sunny weather, for bringing us all to the church safely, for the dinners we'd eat with our families, for the church itself, for the children. More songs, more readings, then we held hands and prayed to the Lord for whomever they wished to name aloud – a William Jackson still in the hospital, Mrs. Jennings's children, President Obama, for Will Haley, for the protestors who'd marched against Will Haley's death the week before, and then, for the Bridgeton police chief, our leaders in Congress – House Speaker John Boehner, Paul Ryan at the end, they prayed for all the people who had fucked them over, too. The act of thankfulness felt to me like submission of a sort – to fate, to God – and I didn't understand it. Was I supposed to pray for Hector and Ed? Maybe I ought to, ought to pray they see the light of Jesus, if that light meant they would change who they were. "Thank God there's occasionally something to thank the Lord for," Jess would say after, as we drove to her parents' house. At the same time, as the singing began echoing again across the church (*He's got the wind and rain in his hands*) and a boy in the choir, about three years old, stepped from foot to foot out of time, gazing around him in wonder, I could see why Jess might want to start going to church again now that she was the mother of a Black son.

Mr. Willis's prayer came instead at lunch, at home, with his brother and sister-in-law, head bowed so that a pinky-brown bald patch I hadn't noticed before shone in the sun, the spotty shadow cast by the lacy curtains framing the window like the veil on his wife's pillbox hat. As he thanked God for many of the things we'd already thanked God for in church, his face again smoothed into a line-less blank calm. Was this what such a strong belief in God provided? "And we thank you Lord for saving our son Joe and bringing him to heaven."

"Amen," Mrs. Willis said quietly.

"And we pray too to keep safe my daughter Jess and her friend Cassandra and our soon-to-be..." And here he hesitated, and a smile rippled wrinkles outward across his cheeks, onto his forehead, clearing away the sad, clear peacefulness that had pacified his face, the wrinkles adding not pain to his features, but life. "Our soon-to-be, if God wills it"—his fingers gripping the hands of his wife and daughter harder as if he needed sustenance to bear his happiness – "the soon-to-be son of my daughter Jess, Antonne."

"Yes, Jesus." Mr. Willis's brother this time

"And also a son of this house, and help us, Lord, because we need your help, because we are not as good or as strong as you, oh Lord, please help us direct all the goodness you have endowed in us to save him. Amen."

"Amen, Daddy," Jess said, not looking up for a moment, squeezing her father's hand before letting go.

With the help of Mr. Willis's brother and sister-in-law, the day became jollier as people talked about various church members, the Mets, Antonne, Jess's job, the Will Haley protest, more church gossip. I was grateful that the story on Hector hadn't run yet, though Jess had warned her parents of it. They didn't seem to connect me to the paper, though, nor did they mention the journalist injured in the Haley protest, and I was relieved Jess didn't bring it up. Jess's uncle seemed a bigger, stronger version of her father, his laugh deep and bassy, and his wife reminded me of Jess: her skin the same warm brown, her colorful, though more conservative, dress.

We were about to finish dessert when Mrs. Willis turned to me. "Maybe, Cassie, you'd like to see Joe's room after lunch." Soft, almost pleading, with a smile that had the opposite effect of Mr. Willis's: smoothing her skin, bringing a blush to her cheeks, making her younger.

The table fell silent, and Jess's uncle and aunt exchanged a glance. While Mrs. Willis had agreed that Antonne would not sleep in Joe's old room – her grandson could have the smaller room that had been Jess's instead – Jess was still trying to convince her mother that Antonne's arrival was a chance to redecorate Joe's room for a joyous reason, not a sad one. She'd promised Jess last week to think it through.

"Momma," Jess said.

I knew I was supposed to say no, but as Jess's mother appealed to me, fondling her necklace, first the cross, then the locket that Jess had told me held a few strands of Joe's hair, I found it impossible to speak. The truth was, I wanted to see Joe's room.

"I think Cassie would find that too difficult," Jess said quietly.

Her mother sat back, looking down at the locket as if she might open it and show me the tuft of Joe's hair instead. "OK, honey." She returned her hands to her lap. "She was friends with Joe, too." As if I wasn't there.

After coffee in the front room – which I was pleased, after all these years, to accept – Jess said she was ready to go. I asked to use the bathroom and was directed upstairs, second door on the left. On the right was another door, closed. Joe's? I tried the doorknob. Unlocked. The Willis' voices murmured from below, steady, no one standing and moving toward the kitchen or the stairs. I went in.

The room was cheerful and immaculate. Light streamed in through windows. Did Mrs. Willis dust in here every day? Twice a day? The posters on the wall looked as fresh as if they had been put up yesterday: Jesse Jackson, from his campaign in '88; the movie poster for *Do the Right Thing*; Jimi Hendrix; Madonna in her black-hair guise. I laughed. I'd forgotten Joe had liked Madonna. "She's got spirit," he used to say. Madonna posed in a black sleeveless dress, a hard-looking bustier propping up her gleaming white breasts. It was amazing Mrs. Willis had let him put it up to begin with, let alone left it there. There was a cross above his bed. Over his desk was the framed National Honor Society certificate and, unframed, his acceptance letter from Penn. On the desk, more Penn paraphernalia: a Penn key ring, a Penn notebook, a Penn baseball cap. There was something classically American about a baseball cap – I imagined him trying it on, looking in the mirror, seeing how it looked forward then backward, Spike Lee style – then thinking of Bill Henderson and putting it down. Was that why I had never seen him wear it?

On the wall beside his bed hung another poster: a black-and-white photo of Joe and Aggie, goofing around. I'd never seen it. Aggie had her tongue out and a silly expression on her face, and Joe seemed to be looking at the camera and Aggie at once, laughing. They must have taken it at the mall in senior year. Aggie's skin was luminescent, her arms, her face shining and white, the brightest part of the picture. And she was so young. Joe looked the same as I remembered him, but there was no older Joe to compare him against – he was who he had been. Joe had placed the poster not above the headboard, where he wouldn't have been able to see it, but on the wall alongside his bed, where he could look at it when he woke up in the morning, went to sleep at night, when he read, when he masturbated maybe in the middle of the afternoon when he should have been studying. I was surprised Mrs. Willis had left it up – it couldn't have been the most comfortable image to look at, given how he died, yet there she was, Aggie, looming over the room.

It was only by looking carefully that one could see how much time had passed – the barely legible print on concert tickets for Public Enemy and Whitney Houston; the orange tint to some of the photographs on the bulletin board. It felt preserved – not occupied – and at the same time, the room felt in transition, as if on the cusp of being outgrown. Who was responsible for this? Ed Marshall's face floated before me, his eyes sullen, empty, the tattoo faded as if worn from being touched again and again like a talisman, and then Hector, as he was at nineteen, standing poised and still a few feet behind him. What really happened that night? I had to find out. Joe's never-lived life around me, the shut-off possibilities, was as palpable in the room as his possessions – his baseball cap, his pen – unseen but physical. Present.

I turned and Jess was leaning against the door frame, her arms loosely crossed, her gaze traveling across the room – from Spike Lee, to Madonna, to the Penn hat, to the poster of Joe and Aggie, then resting on me.

"I'm sorry," I said.

"If you wanted to see Joe's room you should have told me. My mother would have preferred to show you."

"It's OK." Mrs. Willis appeared from behind Jess and stood against the opposite side of the door frame in a kind of mirror image of her daughter. "Cassie needed private time with Joe. We all do."

How different they looked, daughter tall and straight, in her cobalt-blue dress, her mother muted in both her posture and her old-fashioned blouse and skirt, and then again, how alike. Jess had her mother's cheekbones, her wide, bony shoulders, her quietude, even if it was made of stronger, more modern, material.

"Are you going to dismantle this?" I asked Mrs. Willis.

I wished I could find a museum where we could put it all – make room for a new life here, without losing these remnants of Joe.

"No. Antonne will have Jess's room when he stays over. We'll just have to paint her walls another color besides pink, is all."

Jess would tell me on the way home that she probably always knew her mother wouldn't change her mind, that agreeing Antonne wouldn't sleep in Joe's room was always the best she could manage. But right then, her expression aloof as she reached to close Joe's door, I knew she was struggling to acquiesce, even if the only way she could acquiesce was by not struggling – a Willis trait. "I guess you better get cracking on my room," she told her mother.

CHAPTER TWENTY-TWO

"*Hector*'s going to pick us up?"

Joe's voice was loud despite the clattering of dishes and glasses on the Formica counters and tables of Friendly's. A middle-aged couple sitting two booths away looked over, though I had also noticed them glancing up at us when we came into the place – glancing up at Joe.

Aggie hadn't answered.

Was I becoming sensitized, or oversensitive?

"Aggie." Joe had leaned away from her in the booth so he could face her. He hadn't lowered his voice, and the couple looked again. "Hector?"

When Luke's parents decided they needed the car the day the five of us were going to New York City, Aggie said her father would be happy to pick us up. We'd just learned that her mother had delegated the task to Hector.

"Well, you know." She sipped her milkshake, squinting at him sideways then staring down into its pink frothiness. She was the only person I knew over five years old who still ordered strawberry. "He needs to do something useful in his life."

Aggie waited for him to look at her, then moved closer again when he didn't, even though his arm wrapped instinctively around her waist. He fiddled with his spoon, his ice cream soda long emptied. Her shake was three-quarters full. She offered him her straw. Joe waved it aside.

"Why does he have to be involved?" he asked.

"He's not *involved*."

"He's picking us up. We're going to end our great day in New York City with your brother picking us up?"

"There'll be five of us. Right? He's not just picking *us* up."

Joe moved his arm from Aggie's waist as if to take a sip from his empty glass. He rested his elbows on the table. Aggie pretended not to notice.

"It's not the best way to end the day," I ventured. I hadn't learned yet to stay out of a couple's argument. I was ignored anyway.

Joe and Aggie sat quietly, their bodies only an inch apart, but it seemed like a mile compared to their usual touchy-feely can't-keep-hands-off mode. I missed their natural, comfortable physicality. How strange it was to see them argue.

Aggie finally patted his knee. "It'll be fine."

"No. No, it won't be fine. Everything he says has a double meaning. Or maybe just one meaning. It's impossible to have a normal conversation with him. An *easy* conversation. He's always cutting."

Aggie kept quiet. Maybe, like me, she was used to affable, flexible, go-with-the-flow Joe. Not this insistent, stubborn, slightly overemotional Joe.

"Especially with me," he added quietly.

She chewed on her straw, not drinking. Aggie had the appetite of a bee. I thought of her mother's refrain: *Your brother's going through a hard time, dear*, the fury Aggie expressed when she said that, her silence now. Then Hector's voice, not deep, not loud, but jagged with derision, sarcasm. *Not everyone thinks he's the Great Black Hope.*

"His voice is full of nails," I said.

Neither Joe nor Aggie laughed.

"Aggie?" Joe said.

"I'm sorry," she said. "I can't change the fact that he's my brother. Right? We live in the same house. We eat together; we go on family vacations. He picks me up from stuff."

Joe said nothing.

"Mom threw us in the bath together when we were little. There's photos. I mean. Yuck! But." She shrugged her shoulders and went back to chewing her straw.

A strained silence. Joe was sitting completely still in his seat next to her, just his white T-shirt moving, only barely, up and down, as if wafting in a summer breeze. Then I understood this was his chest, moving with his breaths, quick and heavy with some emotion. Was it anger? I'd never seen Joe angry.

I adopted an exaggerated Valley Girl accent. "Oh my god, so, like, you stopped when you were sixteen, right?"

Aggie laughed and cupped her hand around Joe's arm, then shook his shoulder – "Hey" – and nudged his elbow with her own – "C'mon, yeah?" – gently tickling his waist, until he dropped his head and I could see he was smiling. He swung his body round in the booth to face her. Soft again, he placed his forehead on hers.

"I should make this harder, shouldn't I?"

"Pushover," she said.

"I couldn't stay mad at you for long if I tried."

"You couldn't stay mad at anybody if you tried."

His body stayed loose, but his voice tightened. "Yes, I could," he said, quiet, and Aggie didn't contest it. I was surprised. But I believed him, too.

The next day, he announced his parents would pick us up. Didn't matter what time we arrived back, he said. They'd be fine.

I overheard Aggie whispering to him in the car that night at the beach when I left Luke and Jess to retrieve a sweater from the car where Joe and Aggie had decided to stay. Just snippets of phrases as I paused, not sure whether to retreat, not wanting to retreat, hearing what I shouldn't have stayed to hear before returning to the beach empty-handed. "Listen, I love you, I'm sorry… I do not approve of his behavior, I abhor… my father… abhors it, too, I promise… just two weeks now, we're going to my bed to fuck, oh yes, to my bed to fuck, I'll lock the door, to fuck, I'll lock the door."

CHAPTER TWENTY-THREE

Whether Ed Marshall was looking straight at Aggie and me, or seeing past us as if we weren't standing by his battle-scarred sky-blue pickup truck in the Windmill Diner parking lot, was impossible to say: he didn't hesitate, didn't change his expression, just kept striding forward with that uneven walk he had, his right leg dragging slightly behind then catching up, quick, as if to make up for the lost time. He gazed up into the grey sky, maybe checking for rain, then looked up again when he was just a few feet from us, still looking skyward as he said: "I know who you are now. I ain't talking to the newspaper." And he was past us and hopping, one, two, three and into the high cab, door slamming shut, engine coughing then turning over.

Shit, we weren't going to get a chance to say anything at all.

"Ed!" I had to yell over the engine and through the car window. "I'm not here for the paper." He looked ahead and drove away.

Three mornings in a row we waited. Three mornings in a row he refused to stop.

The fourth day was Friday, and I felt desperate – the story on Hector was still on the budget for Sunday, just two days away. "I'm not here for the paper!" I yelled out again before he'd reached the gravelled surface of the parking lot.

Finally, he looked at me. "And why would I fucking believe that?" He hopped, hopped up into the truck and slammed the door with a bang. The engine sputtered on, shifted noisily, then shifted back. He rolled down his window. It was a crank, not a power window. It took some time and Aggie and I watched, mute, a little terrified.

He'd changed more than I'd understood from seeing him at a distance. He still had those long eyelashes and petite face but he was nothing like pretty. His skin looked not pale but deadened, and puffy like an alcoholic's. Which he just might be. His hair still clung to his head in tight curls, but it was dull, a blonde shade that hadn't so much darkened as dried like straw. As he turned to speak, his swastika tattoo came into view.

"You don't need to talk to me. You could still print anything you wanted in the fucking paper. I'm not stupid."

"You're right," I said. "I could. You're right. So why am I here?" He looked ahead but didn't drive off. "Aggie and I just want to hear your side. Just me and Aggie. We never heard your side. Not straight from you."

He turned toward us again and I tried not to stare at the swastika. I could tell Aggie was avoiding it, too. While the edges of tattoos tended to bleed, his was sharply defined, as if he wanted no one to mistake it for anything but a swastika. I wondered if you needed to pay extra for that effect.

"I've seen you at Deep's," he said in my direction, though his low gaze was looking past us. "You following me?"

I shook my head. "Everyone shops at Deep's."

He leaned over and threw open the passenger side door. "Get in," he said. The truck was the kind with a long single seat in the front and just a cab in the back. He motioned to both of us, swishing his arm forward as if herding cattle through a gate, though we were outside, out of reach.

"I don't want to go anywhere," Aggie said.

"I'm not gonna take you anywhere. And you're not gonna put what I say in the paper," he said.

A bargain. Or a threat. What if this was a ploy to lure us inside then drive us away? We must have watched thirty customers walk in and out of the diner that particular morning. Had any of them seen us? Would any of them have noted the old, dented pickup parked outside that could be traced to Ed Marshall? Despite Jess's advice, I hadn't told anyone what we were doing.

But we had approached him. We were luring him.

Aggie moved first, crossing in front of the truck to reach the passenger side. I followed. Aggie hopped several times to make the high step and I helped her up, then climbed in as well.

The truck inside smelled like stale smoke, and Ed lit up, but put his hand with the cigarette out the window. For our sake. I'd forgotten the small touches of thoughtfulness he sporadically made, like a good upbringing he couldn't break free of.

"OK, what do you want?" He was looking straight at us now. "You ain't here for a" – he smirked – "social call."

Aggie began talking quickly, her words rushing together so she could voice them before he threw us out of the truck. "Listen, whatever happened that night, you've served your time, right?"

"You're damned right I—"

"And that means you can't serve any more time for it, no matter what comes out now. No matter what happened. And so we're here so you can tell us your side of the story, Ed. Your side of what happened that night at my house. What you and my brother were doing there…"

As Aggie spoke, beseeching Ed, trying to convince him, turning to face him now with no fear whatsoever, with no hesitation, speaking at his level but not condescending, I began to see the old Aggie again, confident, direct, even beguiling. I kept forgetting who she'd been but here she was again, that self-assured young girl, moving through the world with ease and the sense that she would get what she wanted from it, too. How much I had missed her. How long she had been gone.

"...and how it all happened, why you had your father's gun, how it went off, because it would be so important to know what exactly..."

"You think I got nothing to lose?" He'd just then caught up to how she had started. Ed began laughing, a low, skipping chuckle that might have been infectious if it weren't coming from him. "I got plenty to lose with you girls in my truck."

"...important to know." Aggie paused. Next to me, her hand began shaking. She clenched her fist to make it stop. "What would you lose? Ed?"

He shook his head, slowly, first as if refusing to tell us anything, then as if refusing to believe himself, what he was about to do or not do, what he had or hadn't done, what he was about to say or not say. "Listen, I *would* talk to you girls, but I got nothing to say. Nothing happened," he said.

"What do you mean?" Aggie's voice was polite, aiming at respectful.

"Nothing happened."

We had been prepared for a declaration of innocence – wasn't every convict innocent? But not a denial of reality. "Joe's *dead*," Aggie said.

"Didn't happen. I don't remember it. So it didn't happen."

"Oh, c'mon, Ed," I said. "I mean, were you at the moon landing? World War II? Did those not happen?"

"Before my lifetime. That's history."

I didn't know what to say. It was like arguing with someone from the Flat Earth Society. "But I saw you that night, at the party," I said. "That night *existed*. Just because you don't remember what happened doesn't mean *nothing* happened."

But Ed was looking now just at Aggie. "I remember you that night," he said.

Aggie stiffened, her posture getting straighter. "You do?"

"In that flimsy, pretty dress. Like the inside of a shell.

Almost the color of your skin. Like you'd come out of the shower. Or out of the sun. Wearing that dress like you was almost wearing nothing at all." He reached to touch her knee and she shifted toward me. Ed smiled and returned his hand to the steering wheel.

"I wasn't wearing that dress at the house—"

"I said nothing happened at the house. I don't remember the house. I don't remember the house. Don't you know that? I don't fucking remember the fucking house 'cause as far as I'm concerned I wasn't fucking there."

What were we doing in Ed's truck? What were we doing talking to this insane, racist, violent man? Why did I think he hadn't just shot Joe? Why had I doubted that? I felt the door to locate the handle. I wanted to be ready to get out quick if we needed to, in case Ed started driving away. His fingers were playing with the keys in the ignition.

"Neither do I," Aggie said.

"Neither do you what?" he asked.

"Aggie." I murmured a warning. I didn't want her to make herself vulnerable. To tell him the truth.

"I don't remember anything about the house. Not a thing about the shooting. And nothing after."

He scoffed or grunted or something. "I guess your mother did a number on you, too."

"What?" Aggie said.

"You remember Aggie at the party?" I asked. Maybe we could lead him to talk about the house if he talked first about the party.

"I sure do." He was smiling still in Aggie's direction, a lurid, slow, sexual smile.

Aggie had gone quiet. I sculpted my hand around the door handle, trying to remember how it worked, which motion I'd have to use to release the latch. "And then what?" I asked.

He said nothing.

"And then you decided to get your father's gun to shoot coyotes at the beach?" Nothing.

"C'mon, Ed. Nothing can happen to you for this anymore. Just talk to us! We just want to know—"

"Nothing will happen to me?" He leaned over the steering wheel so he could see past Aggie, his eyes wild, his face contorted, before slamming back into his seat. The truck shook with his motion. "It's already fucking happened. All because of some fuck-ass Black ni—"

"Don't say that!"

"Some uppity Black fucking…" He stopped, as if something had calmed him. "I know you been looking at my badge."

Aggie and I glanced at each other, then back at Ed. What the hell was he talking about? Then we took in what he meant.

"You have a swastika," Aggie said. "Tattoo."

"Yeah. I fucking do. And do you know what woulda happened to me in prison if I didn't have this swastika? Every Black fucker woulda fucked me up thirty ways. Every time some Black fucker walked past me, I woulda happily had another swastika burned into me. Every time, a new swastika burned into my white skin. I'd a been happy to have my entire body covered with them. Every inch. I woulda had one on my dick. Just for fun."

Aggie was looking down at her lap, her fingers twining into themselves and untwining, then sitting, tight, still, on her lap.

"Were you really looking for coyotes?" I asked.

"We was looking for coyotes. The fuckers were contaminatin' our beaches." Ed paused. Was it really that simple? "At night. When we was trying to have fun."

Graduation night. Joe. Was he talking about Joe?

A silence filled the truck. Tears dropped onto Aggie's clutched hands but she made not a sound. Ed watched them fall. He moved slightly forward, gently, as if he might look for a tissue or even take her hand, then sat back again.

"And you went to get your father's gun," I said, "but you knew Joe was there, at the house. You and Hector. Didn't you? Know it was Joe when you shot him?"

Ed shook his head, smiling like this was some game for which he wasn't sure of the rules but was having fun figuring out. "Nope, nope, didn't happen. Nothing happened. I kept telling everybody I didn't remember shit, and somehow that was proof against me. That I couldn't shoot worth shit, and that was proof against me, too."

"But you went looking for Joe?" Aggie cried out.

"We was looking for coyotes, and we knew where to find them, too," he said. Then suddenly he was starting the truck and pushing Aggie's shoulder – "Get out. Get out. Get out of here. Get out." – and I was opening the door and he was moving the gear into drive as he kept pushing Aggie out with his elbow, then his hand – "Get out get out get out. Out. *Out!*" – and Aggie seemed immobilized so I pulled her out. She almost fell onto me, then she was leaning over by her waist as if she were going to puke, a low, keening cry emerging from her body like some ancient wound, and I hugged her as Ed screeched out of the parking lot. He took an abrupt left into traffic, forcing an SUV to brake quickly then blow its horn. By then, Ed was long gone.

I took off my jacket and put it over Aggie's shoulders. She was shivering, and I placed her in my car as if she were a blind person, holding her head so she wouldn't hit herself sitting down, tucking her purse on her lap, making sure she was in before shutting the door and running to the driver's side. Though our route would have us follow Ed's truck to the left, I turned right, not wanting to risk running into him, not that day, or any other day.

CHAPTER TWENTY-FOUR

As we drove to her place, Aggie brought her knees up to her face and continued crying. "I'm sorry," she said at one point. I reached over and patted her arm, but it was hard to concentrate on her and drive with a third distraction: Ed's words ringing in my ear. *That flimsy, pretty dress.* I stopped at a red light. Aggie the night of the party wavered before me, turning to look behind her as she walked away with Joe, a pale flowing shape in the night. The light turned green. I drove. *We was looking for coyotes.* His tone as much as his words swirling around me as I drove blindly to Aggie's place. As if coyotes was another pejorative for Black people. As I parked outside her house, I saw she had quieted and was sitting upright in her seat.

"I believe him," she said.

"Believe what?"

"That they were *looking* for Joe."

Aggie moved to open the door and I remembered the cool of the handle on my palm. My fear. "What if he was just pissing us off?" I said. "Trying to scare us?"

"Oh, he was." She laughed. "He did. But... it's strange. Isn't it? People speak the truth. As if they can't help it."

"That flimsy, pretty dress."

I'd said it aloud – I hadn't meant to – and Aggie flinched. "I should be grateful to him for that," she said.

"For what?"

"You know I hadn't remembered what I was wearing that night? I remember now. Now I remember what I was wearing on the night he says didn't happen."

The night I've never heard about, I thought.

"Come in, will you? I'm not ready to be alone yet."

I shouldn't have been surprised by Aggie's house. First of all, it was a house – not an apartment-sized condo like Jess and I had each bought, using the slim savings the two of us had each managed as single working women – and a house in Newfield, not downtrodden Bridgeton. So even though the neighborhood wasn't the toniest, I'd known the house would be expensive. Aggie's family had money. She'd probably had help on a down payment from her parents. Yet Aggie never dressed like she had money, didn't seem to care about money, and so when I stepped inside I was expecting the ramshackle, run-down quality that might resemble what she wore. Who she was.

The rooms were sumptuous. Two large, fat yellow love seats were facing the picture window in L-formation, over a white rug with a yellow and blue geometric design, which sat over wood the color of walnut. Was it walnut? The wide beams swept toward the kitchen and segued into blue and yellow and green tiles, where there was also a small opening that made the kitchen slightly but not entirely open-plan. A hallway to bedrooms (two? three? four?) went off to the left, and I followed Aggie in the opposite direction into the kitchen and discovered a wall of windows at the back, angled at the top like a greenhouse. A wooden table surrounded by six cornflower-blue upholstered chairs was decorated with cloth place settings. Another high counter divided the kitchen from the table, where more stools were awaiting. "Keep me company," she said. "Let me see what I have to eat."

It was strange, every new understanding of my place

in the world. Of Aggie's place. I didn't resent it. It came with a price I didn't want to pay. And yet I knew she didn't comprehend it. Not really. As she invited me to sit on a stool at the high counter of her kitchen, a skylight above us, beautiful implements assembled themselves around Aggie – a peacock-blue Le Creuset frying pan, a brushed stainless steel spatula, olive oil I recognized from the Italian gift shop in town where I'd bought Jess sea salt that I thought was expensive at six dollars. Cherry tomatoes on the vine from Whole Foods, two green goblets for wine, and a bottle of white from underneath the counter. A wine rack under the counter of course, but the wine was chilled: it was a wine cooler.

"Came with the house," Aggie said, watching me watch her. Out came an elegant red metal corkscrew that extracted the cork as seamlessly as I switched on a light. "I never thought I'd use it, but it's fabulous! Ridiculous, isn't it?" I realized she meant the wine cooler, not the corkscrew.

The sun broke through the clouds and a warm yellow light streamed in through the windows behind me. "Do you like butter?" I remembered Aggie asking me one day in high school, taking my face in her small hand and holding the buttercup under my chin, then telling me to do the same to her. The room turned that color yellow. I felt warm for the first time all day.

I could have become rich easily enough, if I'd wanted to, I reminded myself. Richer, at least. I didn't have to choose to work in journalism. Doing PR for a modestly capitalist company wouldn't have counted as selling my soul. Someplace like Ford. Even Microsoft these days was OK. I didn't have to work for the tobacco industry to get rich. I'd made my choices. But as beautiful Italian or Spanish or Moroccan (for all I knew) dishes glided into place laden with salad and salmon, I couldn't help but wonder: *What is it like? What is it like to take all of this for granted?*

It would be a mistake to tell her about the Hector story.

Then I saw she was crying again. I felt like an idiot. Did I really think Aggie was protected? "What is it?" I asked gently, hearing the stupidity of the question even as I voiced it. But she knew what I meant.

"That was horrible," she said.

I thought of Ed's anger at the end, the leering sexuality of his gaze on Aggie, the clear shape of the swastika; the word he'd called Joe which I didn't want to enunciate even in my head. *We knew where to find them.* "Which bit? It was all horrible."

She wiped her eyes with a bright yellow cloth napkin that matched the dishes, a detail that now, instead of prompting jealousy, made me sadder. "I just wish I could remember more." Aggie stared to her right as if searching the landscape out her window for more clues, and then I saw the photograph of Joe.

It was just a snapshot, four by six, vertical. Joe by himself, in a tarnished silver-colored thin frame that must have been its original home. Had I ever seen him by himself? The boy of many friends? He was half sitting, half leaning on a porch railing that I did not recognize as Aggie's house – a restaurant? a friend's? – in jeans and in a dark blue buttoned shirt that, in the photograph, at least, had faded over the years, yellowed near one shoulder. He was smiling straight at the camera. Straight at Aggie. So uncomplicated, Joe's gaze. His smile a ready gift. And he was so young! All my memories caught him up to our age now, somehow; I couldn't see myself or anyone else then for as young as we were, remembered us through the eyes of our younger selves who hadn't recognized ourselves as young at all. But he was staring at me where I was now, and from an earlier place and time I didn't remember. Separate. And he looked so young.

"Don't tell Jess," she said.

Joe's expression didn't change. I wished it could.

"Don't tell her what?" I thought of the comfortable luxury of Aggie's house, the conversation with Ed Marshall.

"I need to have him somewhere," Aggie said.

"The photograph?" I asked, incredulous. "Do you really think she'd mind?"

"I don't deserve him," she said.

CHAPTER TWENTY-FIVE

Again, and again, and again, I look back and picture these scenes – see the threat inside our idyll. It's their progression that I find hardest, because I can't stop it. I can only relate them. And then I see that the beach, Aggie's porch, the ice cream shop, my job at the newspaper, Aggie's room after dinner, are not idylls at all. Even if they should have been.

Hector always shows up abruptly, his voice grating even when smooth and friendly, his face hard in the soft green lushness of that summer. And now he's on the porch as Aggie and I swap cards in our lazy game of crazy eights, which I've just won. I usually won. I wasn't necessarily any better at cards. I just cared more about winning at cards.

"You're listening to soft rock again," Hector said.

"Right," Aggie said. She left the table and went back over to the swing. "Like I didn't first hear REM when you were playing them. I was in eighth grade. Nebraska."

Hector stood unreadable in his sunglasses. "I grew out of them."

"Or you decided it was cool to be stupid and like stupid music."

"Jim Morrison isn't stupid."

"No. But it's so thirty years ago."

"Twenty-one to be exact. He died the year of my birth."

"Listen, I like The Doors, I just get sick of hearing the

same five songs over and over again. And there is something stupid-*sounding* about them. Something animal in them."

"All music is like that. It shouldn't be pretentious and intellectual."

"OK, OK, but it's not like REM is John Cage. I like the intelligence behind it."

I didn't know who John Cage was.

"So why don't you like Dire Straits?" Hector asked. "They're intelligent."

"Oh, god, they're so *dire*. Aren't they? Their name is perfect. They're so boring. Give me The Doors any day."

"C'mon, Cassandra-teller-of-truths. Aren't you going to pitch in here?"

Hector's voice – even my nickname – didn't have its usual edge. He was actually including me. I felt put on the spot.

"She likes Costello," Aggie said.

"Oh, c'mon. He's so soppy."

"He's not!" I said. "If he looked like Springsteen he'd be as popular."

"No way," Hector said. "Now Bruce is it. Smart, but from the gut. Elvis is too smart for his own good."

I didn't even know Hector was aware of Elvis Costello, let alone ever owned an REM album. Who knew? I wondered what had happened between Nebraska and Newfield.

They went on but not in the antagonistic way I was used to. Their back-and-forth was comfortable, relaxed, like banter rather than warfare. Hector even looked softer today. He sat down on the steps then leaned back with a long strand of grass in his mouth – then sat up again and stretched out his legs. He kicked off his flip-flops and his bare feet looked tender some-how, vulnerable. It was like I'd forgotten Hector was human.

"It's just that REM always sound the same. Even when they switch around and have Mike Mills sing, he still sounds like Michael Stipe."

"You know," I admitted, "I always thought he was singing about his orange *bus*." They ignored me.

196

"But all bands are like that," Aggie said. "You can identify bands always, can't you? You can recognize The Doors's sound quicker than REM."

"That's distinctive, not repetitive. Listen, this song is just like 'Fall on Me'." And Hector began to sing in a high, soft voice, crooning like a modern-day Sinatra.

I was astonished he knew the words, but more astonished at his singing, at his soft, melodic voice.

"But that doesn't sound anything like 'Me in Honey'!" Aggie said. "I mean, this is much harsher, though it's sweet, too."

"They're exactly the same."

"Oh, c'mon. I can see some songs might sound similar, but that's ridiculous."

"Uh, Aggie, what did you just say? Some songs might sound similar?"

"Now, you know that's not what I meant."

"Gotcha." He did a little dance of delight, silly, light, as he sang again.

"Gosh, Hector. You should have been in a choir."

I didn't mean it as a jab but Aggie laughed, and Hector looked almost hurt.

"I'm not being sarcastic," I said.

"Yeah," Aggie said. "Next he'll take up the flute."

But the mood had changed. Hector stood up and it was like his entire body hardened as he rose, as if armor was being clamped on to his calves, thighs, arms, chest.

"So where's the Great Black Hope today?" he asked.

I might have gasped. I looked to Aggie to protest but she kept swinging in the chair, her toe just touching the floor when she needed another light push.

"Bodyguard of Bimbos. Guardian of Gals. Defender—"

"Working," she said.

"Ed'll never forgive him for fucking up his big chance with—"

"Daisy was drunk," I said.

Hector turned to me and took off his sunglasses, his clear blue eyes staring not quite at me but somewhere behind me.

"Too fucking drunk to—"

"She came with us willingly, I remember. Quite distinctly." He began crooning again, picking up the song as if it'd been playing all along in his head. His voice this time held its usual edge, a veiled threat behind those pretty words, and he closed his eyes and I could see a pulsing blue vein on one eyelid. Then he looked at me directly, his eyes blank and hard, and went inside.

The CD had finished. The street was silent, and the creaking from Aggie's swing slowed and quieted. Birdsong came through the afternoon hush and, near my head, a wasp's buzzing. I stood up to avoid it.

"If you move, it just follows you," Aggie said.

"What am I supposed to do?"

"Stay still."

I did. It flew closer to my ear – "Stay still!" Aggie hissed – and the wasp buzzed closer then flew away.

"See?" she said, and started swinging again. I sat down but couldn't get rid of the sound of the wasp in my ear.

"Does he call him that all the time?" I asked.

"What?"

Did she really not know what I was talking about? "You know," I said. I didn't want to repeat the words.

"Oh, that," she said. "He does it to piss me off. If I react he says worse things than that."

Really? Something else I hadn't known. "Like what?" I asked.

She shook her head. "What do you want to hear?" she asked, and then went inside to change the CD. I didn't answer. "Cassie?" she called from inside. "What do you feel like?"

"Whatever," I said. I didn't think she could hear me, and I didn't care. "Madonna?" I said, thinking of Joe. Joe liked Madonna and Hector certainly didn't and I almost wanted him to come down in a rage and for him and Aggie to argue about it, because Aggie had chosen the music, not me, because

198

Aggie had chosen the music to piss off her brother. Because Aggie should argue with her brother about something. But it was as if it didn't matter to her, as if she was truly capable of being unaffected by what'd just been said and she would just choose music based on her own mood, just for herself.

Then Elvis Costello came blaring out the windows – she'd chosen for me. Or maybe Hector had liked Elvis in a previous life, too.

"Want the swing?" she asked.

I shook my head. "My mom wants me home tonight." My mom would have preferred me home every night but I usually ignored her.

"Wanna call her?"

"Nah. I think I should just go."

As I walked to my car, she called out: "But the *title* is 'Orange Crush'." I didn't turn around.

In the car, The Doors came on and I switched them off. I drove in silence except for Hector's crooning in my head and Aggie's laughter, until I couldn't stand that either and I switched on the radio again and put the dial between stations so static blared in my ears and drowned out the sounds of the Whitcombe brother and sister. It sounded like the wasp. *I should tell Joe what Hector said*, I thought, and wondered about driving over to Deep's, but I stayed on course for home. I couldn't betray Aggie. I couldn't have known how insidious it all was – didn't, couldn't, know how dangerous Hector was. Right? But I did know. We all knew. Being teenagers was no excuse for not knowing. Being teenagers and closer to our instincts, our beginnings, being less civilized, less used to the fakery that adult life promulgates, and false truths, means we should have known. Means we did know. We did.

And I didn't do anything. Just went along. Thought, *I guess Aggie knows how to handle her brother.*

CHAPTER TWENTY-SIX

The story on Hector, delayed by concerns on the part of the paper's attorney, ran two Sundays later – the day Jess was flying to D.C. to pick up Antonne and bring him home to begin his placement, to begin living with her. She told me about seeing the headline in a newsstand after she'd cleared security and standing, silent, amid the flow of Sunday morning passengers click-clacking past with their wheelie bags. *Official Overseeing Haley Protest Witnessed '92 Shooting.* Should she read the story? She wondered. Should she leave it behind? People were swerving round to get by her; a woman muttered as she passed. Jess didn't notice. Why had she moved back to Bridgeton, imbued with her brother's life, yes – the high school where she now taught, the Friendly's she passed each day, even that room preserved by her mother – but also haunted by his death? She walked on. *It is his life I will honor with Antonne*, she decided, continuing to the gate, her parenting manual in her bag along with, because he was small for his age, for reasons she couldn't share with me, twelve-month-size diapers.

I hadn't told Jess what Ed had said that day at the diner – I hadn't told anyone. My nights became restless and distraught. I'd promised Ed I wasn't there as a reporter, but that wasn't the reason that I didn't tell Ray what he'd said, why I didn't add that information to our story on Hector. I didn't know how to proceed. The implication they had been looking for Joe was certainly present, but he didn't speak those words, and even if he had, Ed was about as reliable as Aggie's father. If Ed admitted it, he could say they'd gone looking for Joe to harass him, not shoot him. And none of this changed anything for Hector. I wanted more. I wanted the law on our side. I'd seen Hector at the newspaper two days before his story ran, indistinguishable in his perfectly tailored suit from the lawyer at his side, except Hector seemed more at ease, laughing as he left the executive editor's office. He was smarter now. His edges less cutting. "Hey, you have a job to do, too," I overheard him say as they left. "Like us, you also have to make sure you're doing it right." Then he turned away and surveyed the newsroom like a lion scans a landscape for prey, his golden-skinned face becoming gaunt as if he were sucking in his cheeks, before he remembered again, and smiled, saying something softly to his lawyer.

Ed's rambling, ranting words were nothing against the smooth façade of Hector. And if they had been looking for Joe that night – even if they'd gone with their guns wanting only to harass him – I wanted the law to come down on Hector as lethally as Ed and Hector had come down on Joe.

Much to Ray's disappointment, the reporters hadn't been able to unearth anything new about Hector, so the story merely outlined his links to Joe's suspicious death more than twenty years earlier —that he'd been arrested on aiding and abetting but that his charges had quickly been dropped — and his role in deciding to kettle the Haley protesters. But no laws prohibited Hector from working for the police; one employment expert pointed out that not hiring someone because of dropped criminal charges would likely be illegal. Nonetheless, I scanned the wires and channel-jumped news stations for follows by other media outlets. Jess's was the only reaction I learned of. Was Joe's life really being ignored? Again?

Several mornings I drove past the Windmill Diner. Maybe

Ed Marshall would be more forthcoming after reading in print how he couldn't be tried for the crime again – I'd made Ray put that in the article – and after seeing how lightly the article had let Hector off and lay almost all the blame at Ed's feet. But I never saw Ed's truck. Aggie revived her disappearing act, not responding to texts. Why was I surprised? It was as though the Whitcombes lived and worked within a gated community, venturing outside of that protection only when it suited them.

I wanted to crash through those gates. *You think I got nothing to lose*, Ed Marshall had said. How about me? Did I have anything to lose? Aggie had disappeared again; Jess was in her month solo with Antonne; my faith in journalism – that it could make a difference – was being shaken. Why not talk to Hector myself? But I needed facts. Something to approach him with. Weapons to use to crash those gates. I didn't have any such weapons. Some nights on my own, with what was left of a bottle of wine I'd opened by myself, Diana Krall's voice on a CD reminding me of Maria, I felt I didn't have anything at all.

Then, about two weeks later, a feature appeared in the local section on the thirtieth anniversary of a shooting range in nearby Uniontown, a favorite haunt mainly of hunters, but also a fair number of off-duty cops. Something about it sounded familiar, and the next night I woke up before dawn knowing why: Hector. It was where Hector used to go with Detective Marshall and Ed. Sure enough, I looked up the old clips and found a mention in an early story about Joe's shooting. Maybe the owner would have heard something that Ed had told his father. Or maybe he would remember Hector.

That afternoon, a text from Aggie.

Will you help me regain the lost 18 minutes?

My own impeachable gap

The timing was so eerie I didn't respond right away. She couldn't have known what I was reading, or thinking. I'd looked up the range's phone number and the procedure for booking a shooting lesson and was going to call the next day to make an appointment. Aggie couldn't have known any of this. She couldn't.

Maybe she'd come with me to the shooting range.

I remembered the dress! she texted.

'cause of Ed.

What's next?

She reminded me at that moment of Maria, how she would become absolutely, positively convinced she was about to make a breakthrough – tell her sister about us, maybe even her mother. The difference was, I still believed Aggie.

YES, I texted back.

Start tomoro? I texted again, Aggie-style, before she could respond.

Aggie liked the idea of going to the shooting range, but we couldn't get an appointment on a weekday after school for two weeks, so we spent a few days trying to jog Aggie's memory. We brought a lunch to picnic at Newfield Beach, though we'd probably never been there so early in the year, and we drove around one night trying to find the house where the party we'd all gone to the night Joe was killed had been held. I took a vacation day so I could visit her poor father again on the only afternoon her mother wasn't going to be around and Milani, his caregiver, had a nursing exam. Her father was nearly comatose the whole time, his face grey as death when Aggie tried to prop him up in his bed, hoping that might wake him. "He's gotten worse," I said.

"No, I don't know what's wrong with him," she said. "I called Mom but she said he has days like this."

"It's awful," I said.

"It happened a few weeks ago when she was away," Aggie said as her father slumped sideways on the pillows. She sighed and had me help ease him back down again. His body was so much warmer than I expected, and smelled fresh as laundry.

"My mother has her faults," she said. "But she must be doing something right. With Dad."

The first time I met Antonne wasn't the first time I'd seen him. Just a day or two after he had arrived at his new home, I spotted Jess in the parking lot around ten in the morning, carrying the little picnic basket I'd given her, and then I saw him – so little in her arms as she put down the basket and maneuvered him into the car seat. I noticed them again the next day, and I began to look for them. If her car was in its usual spot in the parking lot, I could get a glimpse of his round face, his tight brown curls, a quick smile as I heard her voice, higher than usual to make him laugh. I wondered where they went – a park? The beach? How far did they drive? *Oh, was he wearing that little yellow shirt I had bought him*, I thought one day. I resisted getting out the binoculars. I resisted timing my departure for work to meet with their arrival home, though they were almost always back before I left.

Jess sent me the occasional email – she didn't feel right talking on the phone at night as if she had a life separate from his, she'd told me – and she sounded wonderful. She even seemed calm about the ongoing disagreements with her parents over the date of Antonne's baptism. The anniversary of Joe's death was coming up, and it seemed to them natural, right, to take advantage of the coincidence – it was even on a Sunday – and baptize Antonne on that day. *Life, Momma, I keep telling them. It's about life*, she wrote, sounding calm and clear.

Every time she wrote, she sounded more serene. Even she realized how peaceful she felt – in her head, in her body. *I recognize this peacefulness from somewhere back in my childhood but I do not know when or where – it almost feels like before childhood, from some other life – and yet it is familiar in a way which made me weep when I first felt it again. Is this what my parents feel when praying, I wonder? Though there is not a higher being present for me there is a presence – my presence perhaps but within, next to, another presence and it's not Antonne, but something separate looking over us. Maybe it's the silence making room, making space around me, allowing me to expand into wholeness. Wholly. Holy.*

When I met him – actually met him – expecting a kind of monk-like serenity, Antonne was having a meltdown, screaming in the little foyer of our condo, tears, little hands balled into fists and beating on Jess's shoulder as she held him tight, bag thumping against her thigh. "Oh my god, Cassie, can you take this?" she said, pushing the bag out with her hip. I held the bag and disentangled it from her arm, another bag, Antonne's leg. He saw me and quieted, looking at me through tear-soaked eyes – he was adorable. His face was round but not plump, with a dimple peeking out of each cheek even though he still wasn't smiling. With dark brown eyes, he stared back with a quiet intensity that seemed to contemplate me, not just see me. Then he started screaming again. Jess and I looked at each other and laughed, then couldn't stop. "So much," she sputtered out, "for that quiet, well-behaved child I told you about!" I followed her down the hall with her bag and left her be. "Thank you, Aunt Cassie." And I turned, waved, Jess trying to get Antonne to do the same as he bashed his forehead into her neck.

Two nights before our visit to the shooting range, Ray asked me to stay past my shift – a Black man had been shot and killed by a cop in Ohio who'd stopped him for speeding, and Ray wanted a link on the home page before I left. "Driving while Black," I said grimly.

"Another story to tell my two sons," Ray said. He shrugged and walked away, then went home – to them, or an empty house, I wasn't sure. An hour passed before there was a decent wire story I could use, and as I waited, Antonne's sweet face as he stared at me from his mother's arms the afternoon before kept coming into my head, as if asking me something that I couldn't possibly answer. Was this ever going to stop? I wondered what Ray would say to his sons.

I was finally driving home when my cell phone rang. Aggie. It must have been nearly two a.m. She was talking almost before I'd answered.

"...this dream again, this nightmare, all the time in Paris, every night, no one to talk to, every night, Hector, Hector is standing, my mother's voice, *Ed,* every—" She broke off. The silence deepened. My phone signalled we were still connected.

"Aggie?" Was she even breathing? I turned at the next street and raced toward her house, stopping at red lights then going through them before they turned green. No one else was on the road. At her house, I rang her bell three, five times before she finally opened the door wearing blue silk pajamas the color of the midnight sky. She peered at me, one eye shut, rubbing her other eye like a cartoon of someone woken from a deep sleep. "What are you?" she said. Then, like one of her texts, "Doing here?"

"You called me," I said.

"Did I?" She was completely calm. "My phone must've."

"You spoke to me, Aggie. Don't you remember? Your dream?"

She looked at me blankly, shook her head – "I'm sorry" – opening the door wider, raising her hand to her forehead like she had a headache. "Come in? God, I have these dreams. I think it's the sleeping pills. I called you? Do you want something?"

Had she forgotten what I just said?

"I mean, like coffee? Hot chocolate." Aggie was so out of it. What if it was an overdose, even accidental? She shouldn't go back to sleep.

"Yes," I said firmly. "Thank you."

Her kitchen was no less glamorous by night. In one corner was a Japanese lantern, the shade as thin as rice paper, light bouncing around the conical shape when she switched it on, bright but soft. I sat again on the stool.

"So I called you?" she said. "I can't even remember."

"And then you stopped talking. I thought you'd... I don't know."

"Fallen asleep?"

Died. "I thought you'd overdosed or something."

"And so you came to save me." She handed me a bottle-green mug, brimming with foamy hot chocolate. "You know, you've always been the steadfast friend. The Agamemnon. Not me." I clutched the warm mug, its rounded shape soothing in my hands. "Let me be precise. Very steadfast."

Mr. Whitcombe, as he'd been, floated for a moment on the chair in front of me before wisping away again. I felt tears threatening my eyes, and took a sip of my drink.

"Let's sit in the living room," Aggie said.

We brought our mugs into the other room and I took a seat on the overstuffed love seat near the window with Aggie sitting in the corner of the couch, not quite facing me.

She looked at me, then away again. "Do I want to know what I said?" she asked.

I tried to reconstruct her words but I found they were slipping even from my grasp. "It was about the night Joe died. Hector. Your mother. Something about Ed."

"OK."

"You said you had the same nightmare all the time in Paris."

"And that's what this was?"

I nodded.

Aggie also had her hands around her mug, full – she hadn't taken a single sip. It was like she existed on water from the air. "That was a bad time."

"I thought you said it was good? To get away from your mother."

"Yes, but I began to remember things, or dream things, or something. Things were coming to the surface. Guilt. It was hard to know what to believe. My therapist said I could be filling in memory blanks with guilt, instead of with memory. Hard to talk about it in court."

"Court? You remember stuff that could have been relevant in court?"

"It's never consistent. Sometimes Ed holds the gun. Sometimes Hector holds the gun. Sometimes I do. My mother thinks I'm dreaming things because I blame Hector."

"Hector is to blame," I said. "Whatever happened."

"I need to remember all of it, Cassie. All of it. I don't know where to put these pieces, which order they go in. I have more pieces now, more than ever! And I'm sure... I'm sure Daddy can help."

She sounded like a child, but I could understand why. Mr. Whitcombe from when we were not-quite-adults came into my head: crossing his legs like a woman as he sat in the library reading a book, black-framed glasses resting on his chest; emerging from the kitchen with a bottle and five wine glasses lifted over his head because someone hadn't put out the best ones, not irritated, but excited about getting things just right; wagging his finger at us, his way of thinking, not accusing; his turning around after Aggie's mother had taken her away at Joe's funeral, coming back to hug me, cupping my chin. "Come now," he'd said. "It's no one's fault." Why hadn't he helped Aggie, then?

And then I remembered Mr. Whitcombe in his bed, his thin, diminished frame, his empty, awful gaze. "Your father can't tell you anything now."

"But you'll come?" She stared at me from the corner of the overlarge, over-cushioned couch. "You're the only one I trust."

With her legs tucked into her chest, sunk into the richness of her couch, Aggie looked as small and young as she had in high school – smaller. She was so much slighter than her personality. Or used to be.

"You know I will," I said and rose to leave, shaking my

head when she started to get up, too. I could let myself out. Maybe she'd fall asleep there.

As I reached the door, she spoke again.

"Some say every person in your dreams is you. If that's true? Then I'm always the one who kills Joe."

CHAPTER TWENTY-SEVEN

Though in high school Aggie had probably visited the city more than all of us combined on trips with her parents to museums or plays or, with her mother, shopping, Luke was our guide to New York. He took us straight to the Village and we walked around aimlessly but with loose direction from Luke that was the perfect combination of planned and plan-less – "You guys really should see about twenty certain things," he said, "but that would ruin the experience." It seemed to me we'd already gone to a dozen CD shops and, for Luke, used-record stores, by the time we stopped in what he told us was the oldest Italian cappuccino shop in the United States. "Vinyl's gonna come back," he said as we sipped the smallest and strongest coffees and nibbled on the sweetest cookies, almond I was told, that I'd ever taste, and he explained the science of sound by delineating the intricacies of how CDs and records transmitted music differently.

"You're crazy, man," Joe said. "Vinyl scratches."

I'd looked up a bookstore to visit, and Jess had searched out another, and while we didn't admit it, we were too skittish to go off and find them on our own, so we pretended to browse through CDs in yet another store until Joe took pity on us and corralled the others to come with us. We stopped at another café on the way, and Luke dared to order a glass of wine. We waited for her to card him, but when the waitress simply wrote it on her order pad, we all asked for wine. "Would you like a bottle?" she asked.

"That would be wonderful," Luke said.

It was my first time in the city without my parents – for Jess, too – and it felt exciting and frightening and very cool and very… not adult, which would of course be boring, but as if we were carving out, finally, the kind of life we wanted to lead, with the friends we had chosen. I felt happy. This was how I wanted to live. From now on. And I could. We all could.

After talking Joe and Aggie out of pizza – "We are *not* eating pizza in New York City. We live in Connecticut, for crying out loud! Peppi's is practically down the street!" – Luke took us to an Ethiopian restaurant he hadn't been to either, and we scooped up our rather liquid dinners with the spongy, slightly sour bread in our hands as if this were our usual mode of food retrieval. Dozens of napkins smeared red and orange formed an origami pyramid around our plates.

At some point, near Washington Square Park, Joe stopped us all in the middle of the sidewalk. "Wait," he said. "I just want to make this observation: Jess and I are not the only Black people on this street." We looked around at the faces of the people of the Village, haggard, a little city-worn, and of many colors. A young woman with raven-black hair and the whitest skin I'd ever seen. An Asian man in a suit. The mahogany-black angular face of a man dressed as colorfully as the waiter in our restaurant. A woman with golden brown skin, in a taupe- and cream-colored silken blouse, skirt and jacket – even her shoes looked silk. A skinny Asian girl jogging. A white woman with a yoga mat. Two Black kids about our age in jeans and T-shirts. An Indian couple, the woman with a bindi on her forehead. Who could keep track? Who would want to keep track?

"Well, it's New York," Luke said, as if he'd invented it.

We kept walking.

On the Metro-North train home, Joe and Aggie sat on the

two-seat side, and Jess, Luke and I sat across the aisle from them on the three-seat side, and when Luke's arm slipped round my shoulders, I didn't shake him off. "I'm glad Hector isn't picking us up," he whispered to me.

"Who's Hector?" I said, and Jess giggled.

IV

1992

Another Country

CHAPTER TWENTY-EIGHT

Aggie leaned out her bedroom window wearing just her bra as my mother dropped me at her house. She was smiling widely, her pale skin looking especially wan in the still bright, humid August evening which seemed to ask for the tan or a burn of a day spent outside. "It's unlocked! Just come in," she said, her arms skinny as she motioned to me then disappeared.

This was the night the Whitcombes were out of town, the night Joe and Aggie would spend together, freed not only of her parents' presence but of Hector's, too. Her brother was planning to camp overnight on the beach with Ed in hope of discovering in which part of the woods near the beach the coyotes had built their dens. "Luckily for the coyotes, Ed's now bringing a keg just for him and Hector," Aggie had told me the day before. "They'll be plastered before dark." It was strange coming into the house at that time of day without Mr. and Mrs. Whitcombe in the kitchen or dining room or library. Their home seemed empty and a little charmless. Aggie's mother kept a dustless house, and without the messiness of people inhabiting its spaces, the rooms seemed sterile indeed. I was relieved to see an espresso cup near the chair where Mr. Whitcombe usually read; not everything had been cleaned away.

It was also strange coming empty-handed – no toothbrush, no nightgown, no extra clothes to try on. I hadn't wanted to carry a bag around with me to the party, though part of me knew I was being contrary. My jean shorts and T-shirt couldn't have been plainer, and I could have left my stuff at Aggie's.

"Nothing to try on?" Aggie looked genuinely hurt when she noticed my arms were empty.

I shrugged my shoulders. "I don't know. Wasn't in the mood. Are you ready yet?" It was against our rules for Aggie to be ready yet; besides, all she'd added since beckoning to me from the window was her robe.

"Gosh, who are you, Mom? No, I'm not ready yet. What are you going to do?"

Watch you, I thought, *like I always do*. "Maybe I could try on some of your things?" Aggie's clothes always looked cool on her, awful on me, but maybe I wanted to look awful.

"Oh, great idea!" She began to rout through her closet for me, throwing this skirt, that dress, this top, another skirt, onto the bed.

I glanced around at her room: she'd actually cleaned. There were fewer dirty clothes on the papasan chair in the corner, and the makeup on the beauty stand must have been stuffed in the drawers. I sat on the bed while Aggie rummaged through her closet for something for me to wear, and I thought: *This is where she will have sex with Joe later tonight.*

Aggie had been orchestrating this night-with-Joe-while-parents-are-out-of-town for weeks. It's easy to forget now how difficult it was to gain privacy as a teenager, let alone as a teenage couple, even in 1992, even with parents as permissive as the Whitcombes. Aggie and Joe's sex life took place almost exclusively in the back seat of his car, or, as the summer warmed up, at a certain beach whose location she refused to reveal even to me. She and Joe spending the night at her house when the Whitcombes were away was something all of us had been roped into – except Jess, as Joe didn't want her lying to their parents.

"Oh, look!" Aggie said, abandoning her search through

the closet and sitting next to me on the bed, pulling down the cover to reveal midnight-blue sheets with a subtle, rich sheen. "They're silk!" she whispered, smoothing them with her hands, lingering, until pulling up the comforter again. "Her Name's Agatha thinks they're for college." Then she kept looking through her closet.

First Aggie convinced Joe to tell his parents he was staying at Luke's house, though he didn't tell Jess this. Then, when the Whitcombes threw a spanner in the works by deciding against renting a car for the weekend and taking their own, leaving Aggie and Hector with just one family vehicle between them, I was going to drive. When my parents said they needed our car that night, Aggie enlisted Luke, who was going to be driving all of us everywhere until Ed Marshall, of all people, unwittingly offered a better solution. He'd have his father's car starting at nine, so Aggie could get the Saab once Hector arrived at the party, giving Joe and Aggie their own transport. Luke was driving me home. I always suspected Joe had engineered that part.

"What about these?" Aggie said. She'd now taken out about twelve options for me and was holding them up, one by one. I shook my head without really looking at them. "Oh, there must be something!" She flittered back to the closet.

"What are you wearing?" I asked.

"Haven't I shown you?" Aggie pulled a dress off a hanger on her closet door and swooped it in front of her. It looked plain, a dull kind of beige, and I must have looked unimpressed. "I'll put it on," she said, throwing off her robe and pulling the dress over her head. She tugged the little zip behind the neck and put her arms out, gawky, goofy. "Ta-da!"

She looked gorgeous. The tannish color was complex and rich, as if purples, reds and yellows were enriching it from beneath, the material, silky as her new sheets, moving around her thin body and hugging it, too.

"Wow," I said. "How much did that cost?"

"I know!" she said. "Mom definitely wouldn't want me to

wear it to a keg party. But you! What are you going to wear? You can't wear that," she said. "You look like you're ten years old and going to the beach when it's still too cold to swim."

I should have been insulted, but it was true. I found myself cheering up and joined her at the closet. We swished past a dress that had been for a month or so one of her favorites – it was blue with a pattern of a woman's face from a famous painting by someone famous. I know now it's Picasso's *Dora*. Aggie had worn it on her first time out with Joe.

"How about this?" I didn't particularly like it, so maybe I was testing how far her generosity would extend.

"Try it on! That'll be perfect for you."

I wrinkled my nose. "I don't know."

Like a lot of Aggie's clothes, the dress looked casual but was made of a fabric that was as soft as fur against my skin as I pulled it over my head. It felt wonderful, as gentle as Aggie's fingers when she was putting on my makeup, and when I looked in the mirror I was surprised to see it suited me – the blue darkened my hair, the waist hugged my hips. Aggie was hipless.

"Oh my god!" Aggie exclaimed. "You're not allowed to take it off."

I was pleased with the result – that I looked better than Aggie in anything at all was hard for me to believe. To look good in something that belonged to her was even nicer. It felt good to be wearing her dress, to have fabric that had hugged Aggie's skin now hugging mine.

CHAPTER TWENTY-NINE

Held in the garage of another kid whose parents weren't home
– I'm not sure I even knew him – the keg party was already
spilling out from the garage to the driveway and the yard
by the time we arrived. Apparently, no one was allowed in
the house. Clusters of teenagers stood with drinks in their
hands. We found Luke talking to Sarah Dunn and formed
our own cluster. The kid who was hosting had extended the
wiring from his parents' speakers to reach outside, and Pink
Floyd was blasting – *The Dark Side of the Moon*, which was
cool among the druggie type especially. In addition to the
keg, someone had made punch with grain alcohol. From a
distant circle of kids, someone spotted us and started walking
in our direction. Bill Henderson was making his gawky way
over. Wearing long, pink shorts that made his legs seem even
skinnier, and bright white T-shirt blooming around him. he
looked like a red-headed chicken. "Bawk bawk," I said, so
we were laughing when he arrived and pulled something out
of his back pocket.

"Hey, I wanted to show you this, Joe. Really glad I saw
you." He unfolded what was in his hand: a Penn baseball cap.
"I got in last week. Off the wait list." He smiled widely and
jumped around a bit on the lawn like a grasshopper. "After all."

I spied Daisy skulking in their group, holding a beer, but
not coming over to join us.

"Hey, man!" Joe said. "You must be psyched. I guess I'll see you there."

They talked for a while about move-in day – Bill's mother had already rented a van to take them and he offered to carry some of Joe's stuff if he didn't have room. "My mother will order the deluxe-sized van. She takes moving verrrrr-y seriously. But hey, it's not like she's gonna give me a keg to take up."

"I think they'll have some there," Joe said.

"Well," Bill said, as he put on his baseball cap to leave. "See you around."

He walked away, toward Daisy, his gait awkward on the uneven lawn, like he'd already imbibed half that keg.

"I guess another underqualified Black kid decided to go to Harvard instead," Aggie said when Bill may not have been out of earshot. He didn't turn around. Daisy tapped his Penn cap when he reached her, swivelling briefly to glance at us before going back to talking.

"Luckily," Joe said, "Penn's a big school."

"Awww. You don't want to share rides back and forth on Thanksgiving?" Aggie teased. "Join the same frat?"

"Bill would join a frat, too," Joe said.

"His voice will be full of cheap beer," Luke said.

I don't remember how much I drank but I drank a lot, more than usual, because I kept seeing Aggie that evening in her underwear, staring at me approvingly in her dress. "Maybe I should let you have the bedroom," she'd said, her skin so pale against the deep blue sheets she had shown me. Then she had laughed. "Not!" I heard her laugh again as if she were near me, and in the distance I saw her with Joe in the shadows of a tree, and suddenly the idea of them going to her house afterward and to her bed with the new blue silk sheets was something I needed to drink to forget, and seeing them together here in the half-dark of the warm night, holding hands, rubbing shoulders, their bodies luminous with the promise of the night before them, underscored something maybe I hadn't quite taken in. What they were still doing at this party was beyond me – it wasn't Aggie's scene – but Joe would be waking up with her the next morning the way I usually did and maybe even having leftover pizza for breakfast and pissing Hector off by not leaving him enough and why Aggie was here now when she could have been home alone with Joe I couldn't figure out. This was more Hector's kind of party, the kid who was throwing the party knew Ed, we'd all heard – Ed had probably brought the keg – and it wasn't my scene either but somehow I eased into it that night, as hot and still as August could get, and clear, a half-moon illuminating the clouds whisking by. The trees were full and dark green, darkened further by the night, a porous umbrella through which the midnight sky peeked through as I swooshed back more punch – Why? Why was she here? Was she here for me? – as Luke put his arm around me and I didn't shrug it off immediately so Aggie would see, but where was she now? And I saw Joe's yellow shirt and the outline of her head disappear toward the cars on the street. "Luke," I asked, "can you locate another drink for me?" with a half-thought of getting rid of him and running after Aggie.

"Sure," he said, always accommodating, always willing, a nice guy, like Joe, the kind we'd always made fun of along with these parties and the kegs and drinking and being cool. The swirly feeling I was getting must have been from the punch.

"It's called *punch* for a reason," I said when Luke came back and tucked his arm around me and he handed me another glass and his warmth felt cool in the hot air empty of Aggie. "It's got punch," I said.

"Oh, dear," Luke said. "Someone's not used to drinking."

"Are you getting me drunk, Luke-y?" I asked, finding myself flirting – did alcohol do this, too? – and he leaned over precariously to kiss me, and I turned my head so he caught the edge of my ear. "Missed," I said.

"Do you want me to get you drunk?" he asked.

"Fabulously," and I turned to kiss him on the mouth.

"Wanna go somewhere else? I'll get a few more drinks."

"For the road," I said. He laughed and said he'd be right back.

"Where's sis?" Hector loomed in front of me, smelling of beer and pot and the outdoors.

"You reek," I said. "Don't run into Detective Marshall."

"Where is she?"

"With Joe. Where else?"

"I know. When? Where'd they go?"

"Why?"

"I'm supposed to watch out for her."

I sputtered. "C'mon." Would Mrs. Whitcombe really tell him to do that? "More likely she should watch out for you."

I wondered if Aggie and Joe would drive around for a while or go right to her house. With Joe's parents thinking he was staying with Luke, they had all night. They could go to an all-night diner, drop by another party. They could drive to the Sound and make love on the beach in the dark. Maybe it'd be boring for two teenagers to merely go home so they could have sex in Aggie's bed. They could drive to New York City and stay at the Plaza. Where was the Plaza anyway? They could do anything they wanted – Aggie would do anything she wanted – and I stared at Hector's ruddy face, staring at me, unblinking. He'd do what he wanted, too. It ran in the family.

"I don't need to know really. Just as well," he said, uncharacteristically amiable. "But I know you don't like him, either."

"Don't be stupid." It came out in an angry splutter, and then, because I knew it would piss him off, or maybe I just wanted them to be interrupted: "Stupid," I said, meaning him, "they're at your house. As you know. Where else would they go tonight?"

Now, when I think about it years later, his face changed when I said it – its boyishness turned hard; his pink cheeks turned a ruddy, angry red; his full-from-drink eyes sharpened like lasers. His face became in an instant the face I know now, on the news, in the paper, when I spied on him when he came into the newspaper office to try to prevent us from running our story. Because I could see his hardness that day, behind his easy smile, his affable handshake. But the way I remember his face changing in that moment twenty years ago may be just what I think I saw, my memory layered with what I now know.

Luke came back with the drinks but I wasn't interested in any more drinks. "Let's go to the beach," I said – drunk enough to suggest it, sober enough to know what I was doing as we walked giggling to his car. I wondered if Aggie and Joe would be there after all. We drove with all the windows down, my hair fluttering wildly around my face, the kind of girl I wanted to be, the kind like Aggie who did what she wanted, tumbling, laughing, out of the car with a blanket Luke had stowed in his back seat ("Always good to be prepared for the beach," he said, which made it sound almost boring, like he'd been plotting this for months). We tossed the plaid wool blanket haphazardly on the sand – Luke because he didn't want me to change my mind, me to get it over with, because I knew by agreeing to come here with Luke that I'd agreed to have sex with him, and I was drunk enough to think maybe I wanted to, or maybe didn't know what I wanted, or didn't care.

It should have been fun, and in some ways it was – being at the beach at midnight, the stars brighter over the dark water, the weak waves tumbling onto the shore. And so I didn't think too much about the male skin against my chest, his smell, the strangeness of his cock against my leg, the way it changed shape and texture and form. Instead, I thought of Aggie, and imagined what it must be like for her to have sex with Joe, with someone she loved, and so I pretended to be her as Luke, after fumbling all night and all month and all year, became as if in one moment adept – he was over me, onto me, pushing against me – *I'm Aggie*, I thought, as he entered me and I cried out and I thought of her with Joe, the shape of her lips, the

222

pretty tilt of her neck, the feel of her foot against my leg just a week or so ago on this same beach, the cool, smooth, soft plumpness of her stomach against my fingers when we were testing whether her jeans were too tight. And I knew too in that moment that I wouldn't ever sleep with another man again. I didn't consciously think it, but when I tell myself the story of my life that's when I learned one vital aspect of who I was – that's when my body knew, or learned, or felt that truth. *This isn't right, this isn't me*, ran like a dye through my body, gently, clearly, like the waves slapping onto the shore, warm, soothing, clarifying, so that as we lay on the soft blanket after it almost felt like ecstasy: with the warm air, the cool sand that I kept digging my feet into, the occasional car whooshing by sounding as natural as a leopard, or a lion, like part of the landscape.

The next morning I remember still being pissed at Aggie – not getting up to call her because I didn't want to interrupt her and Joe, because it would make me feel pathetic to hear them giggling together over the phone as they heated up pizza that I should have been sharing with her, almost calling anyway in case she invited me over to join them, but resisting – how pathetic would that be? I decided I wouldn't tell her about the night before – I'd never tell her the secret that I'd had awkward teenage sex with awkward teenage Luke Chadwick – but the real secret was I wanted to get back at her, to hurt her, or maybe I wanted to hurt myself, because I was already hurting and I didn't know it, let alone understand why.

I discovered blood on my sheets, just as my mother knocked on my bedroom door. "Cassie?" – her voice upset as if she'd already seen the blood – "Sweetheart, I need to talk to you. You need to get up, honey." How could she know? I was panicking, half-awake, and she opened the door and sat at the edge of my bed and told me about Joe, and I kept hiding the two spots of blood, still wet, with my hand, covering up the evidence, as if anything else but Joe mattered, and as she kept talking, I caressed the wetness with my fingers, pressed it into my nail as what my mother was telling me began to come clear. Joe had been shot. Joe had been shot? In Aggie's bedroom? He was *dead*?

My mother went to hug me as I covered my face with my hands. "Cassandra, you're bleeding!"

"It doesn't matter," I said. "Please don't... it doesn't, it doesn't..."

And she hugged me as I cried although even then I couldn't comprehend what this meant. Joe was *dead*? Later that day I found blood underneath my fingers and it felt like Joe's blood, and I put a Band-Aid around it so it wouldn't wash off.

I used to wonder, later, what might have happened if Ed Marshall and Hector had shown up at the beach with their gun looking for coyotes and found Luke and me instead; if Aggie and Joe had shown up, too, then Jess, until in my memory sometimes that's how the night ended, with Hector's square body, dark and ominous, swaggering into the woods behind us, Ed following with his gun, the two of them turning first their heads, then their bodies, to face all five of us, to shoot all five of us down.

CHAPTER THIRTY

Stories began emerging in the papers, including a few in the national press, attracted to the unusual elements: the suspect a cop's son, the victim a promising Black teen, the setting a wealthy suburb on the edge of a struggling Connecticut city. This was how I learned what happened: from the newspapers, as if I didn't even know Joe. This was how the story went: Ed and Hector thought they had spied coyotes at Lighthouse Beach, where they'd been planning to camp for the night, and decided to retrieve Ed's father's Remington 870 shotgun from the locked shed outside the Marshall house, also picking up his Glock 19 semi-automatic shotgun so they'd each have a weapon. They then traveled to Hector's house to pick up some insect repellent. While there, they heard a noise in Aggie's room, ran in, and Joe was shot by Ed Marshall. Those very first stories did not make clear whether Ed Marshall had raised his weapon with the intention of shooting the intruder or if it had gone off accidentally, but, by the second day, Ed Marshall was charged with involuntary manslaughter with a firearm, not homicide, and Hector with being an accessory.

Already the story wasn't quite true. They'd been planning to shoot coyotes at that beach for weeks. But – bug spray? Why did that detail make me nauseous each time, as if someone had sprayed OFF! into my open throat.

The *New York Times* wrote the sole story that hinted

at underlying racial tensions – Joe and his sister were the only Black students in the honors program; kids voluntarily segregated by race in the cafeteria; the Confederate flag was flown at keg parties thanks to the popularity of Lynyrd Skynyrd, though most students didn't think twice about it; some in the school had raised eyebrows at Joseph Willis dating his white classmate, though neither family had been opposed to it. "I'm not sure a white boy would've been assumed to be a burglar," one resident, unnamed, told the *Times*. But in general the stories were sympathetic even to Ed Marshall. It was all a horrible mistake, a sad case, an accident that new gun laws, or better race relations, wouldn't have prevented.

The calm so-called wisdom of these contextual pieces, these feature stories after the fact – how I hated them, how I still hate them. Even at the time they seemed partial, glossing over the horrific facts, failing to capture the huge, echoing, now empty space that Joe had occupied. Whenever I fully felt his death those first few days, I'd gasp for air, as if my breath had been taken, too.

I tried and tried to reach Aggie, but no one was answering the phone at the Whitcombes'. I went to the house three times, shocked to find the door locked. On the third visit I was about to turn away again when Mrs. Whitcombe opened the door, looking cool and composed if a bit haggard. "Cassie, we're a house in mourning," she said, though she was wearing a shimmering white sleeveless dress and pearls glowed around her neck as if she were playing the role of guardian angel in an elaborate play.

"I'm here to see Aggie," I said.

"She's too upset, Cassie. It's too much for her."

I couldn't believe Aggie wouldn't want to see me; I couldn't believe they weren't taking me into their home, as always, like I was one of them – that I wasn't part of whatever was going on. Because I was part of it. Wasn't I?

"I'll tell her you stopped by when she wakes."

"But it's one o'clock in the afternoon—"

And she gently closed the door.

As the days went on, I became more and more obsessed with the idea that Joe's death wasn't an accident. Why would Hector and Ed bring a gun into the house? After spending more than an hour at the beach, they suddenly needed insect repellent? Hector and Ed hated Joe, and they knew Joe would be there. What, they *accidentally* shot him? Haunting my dreams, and my waking hours, was Hector, his voice, sometimes supple and appealing, sometimes like ice. *I know you don't like him, either.* Insinuating. Why did I ever tell him where they'd gone?

My mother came with me to Joe's funeral, held a week after he died. So many people crowded into the church that we had to take a seat in the front pew of the upper level, from where I watched the wheat field of Black and white faces undulating into the pews and aisles and the sides of the church. Some arrived in a mixed group, but people largely arrived in clusters of white people or clusters of Black people. There were more Black than white. The resulting mix in the church reminded me of a topographical map, with splotches of ivory and brown instead of green and brown, some areas mottled and mixed then changing into one color or the next.

Aggie walked in just a few minutes before the service started. She was leaning on her father while giving several quick glances backward to her mother – she looked completely dependent on them, as if she'd barely be able to feed herself, let alone attend the funeral of her eighteen-year-old boyfriend on her own. She looked small and frail, though I had to remind myself that she wasn't a big person – the hugeness of Aggie's personality, her contagious energy, sometimes made one forget that. She wore a black A-line dress that I knew her mother must have picked out for her – I'd never seen anything like it on Aggie – and she looked lost in it. It was as if someone had sent an Aggie substitute to the funeral, a poor, weak double rather than Aggie herself.

The procession began to progress up the aisle, pallbearers

I didn't recognize carrying a dull iron-silver casket with gleaming black handles, the dead silver of the casket like the bullets Hector had held in his hand. Joe is *in* there, I made myself think, but that truth didn't seem possible. His father and mother followed, clutching hands, and then Jess walked behind them on her own. If Aggie looked smaller, frailer, Jess looked larger somehow – older, taller, more dignified. Her little-girl looks had disappeared. Where Aggie's gaze was hazy and inward, as if she weren't really seeing, Jess's was outward. Her expression changed when she looked up and saw me – a half-smile, or a grimace, or a sob, began to cross her face – then she just nodded. I reached out to her as she turned away, as if I could touch her. The pallbearers walked to their pews, and I saw Luke had been on the opposite side from me; he now sat among Black men of varying ages, Joe's uncles, maybe friends from church. Aggie had met a few of them a couple of weeks before.

I became determined to talk to Aggie. I spent the funeral not listening to the pastor, not listening to the remembrances that Joe's parents and Jess had written, which Joe's slightly older cousin read out, but plotting how I would get to see Aggie. I had to talk to her. My mother saw me staring in her direction and whispered to me gently. "You can't keep bothering the Whitcombes, sweetheart. Why don't you see if Aggie comes to you?"

But as the funeral ended, I looked to see which exit Aggie was using before racing off to the closest door I could get to, leaving my mother behind. I scrambled round the back of the church and spotted Aggie and her father just as they were reaching the bottom stair and stepping on to the lawn.

"Aggie!" I called out quietly when I was close enough not to make a scene, but she'd already seen me. "Aggie, I'm so sorry! I'm so sorry!"

She clutched me as if recognizing me after years and years of absence and like she'd forgotten me in between.

"It's my fault! I told Hector where you were. I thought he knew. I couldn't believe it. I'm so sorry!"

Still she hugged me tight, the two of us clinging to each other. It was so good to see her, and I began to sob like I hadn't been able to inside the church.

Her father became a gentle presence behind Aggie, his eyes soft, his hands insistent as he nudged us apart. Mrs. Whitcombe stood several feet behind, looking away. "We have to get to the cemetery, Agatha," he said.

And she was gone.

Then Mr. Whitcombe, perhaps taking pity on me, came back and hugged me just as my mother was approaching again. "It's no one's fault, Cassie," Mr. Whitcombe said. "Come now. It was a horrible accident." He looked at my mother. "Remind your daughter of that."

Was Aggie's embrace with me that day forgiveness? It felt like it then – in that moment – as we clutched at each other like infant fists around a mother's finger, blind, needy. For five minutes I felt better. And then – had she even heard me? What if she hadn't heard me? What if she heard me but it hadn't sunk in until later and now she hated me?

The next day, my mother found me crying in the backyard by the tree I used to sit under as a child to read. "Aggie's just not well, sweetheart. You can't read into it. You heard what Mr. Whitcombe said. It was an accident. No one's blaming you, of all people."

"It wasn't an accident, Mom. Hector went there on purpose."

"Cassie, don't be silly."

"I saw his face. I saw how he treated Joe. He hated him."

"Even so, Cassie. It doesn't mean he was going to kill him."

"Then why isn't Aggie calling me?" I started crying again. "I don't understand. If she doesn't think it's my fault. I don't understand."

"It's her parents, sweetheart. I don't think it's Aggie. You're her best friend."

"They liked me."

"They're scared of something."

"Of me?"

"It's not about you. They're afraid for their whole family."

Luke called a few times, and when he finally dropped by the house, Mom insisted on letting him in. We sat in the kitchen with iced tea and chocolate chip cookies Mom had made the previous day because I wasn't eating. "It's just so awful," he said. "I mean, what the fuck were they doing? Saving the world by going after a few coyotes? It's just so stupid. It makes me so angry."

I nodded my head and started crying. I found myself spilling everything out to him – Hector asking me where Joe and Aggie were, me telling Aggie at the funeral, Aggie not calling me back. "What if it's my fault?"

"Cassie, it's not your fault. I mean, we all knew where they were going, and anyone else could have guessed. It's not like they were in Timbuktu, and Hector found them in Timbuktu." He made me laugh. "I mean, it was an accident, wasn't it?"

"I don't think it was."

"Wow," Luke said. "That's, like, serious."

I told him all my suspicions and admitted that I sometimes thought about calling a reporter whom I'd gotten to know when working at the paper that summer. He told me he'd come with me if I decided to talk to her.

When he left, he gave me a hug and tried to kiss me, but I turned my head. "I'm too upset," I said, and he nodded and just hugged me lightly, as if trying not to touch me.

But he didn't come by again.

The statewide paper – the paper I work for now – raised a few of my questions, as well as several others, in a story that ran the next day. Police, sources told them, had interviewed no one except the Whitcombes, Ed Marshall, and the Willis family. An unnamed source said Ed Marshall had attended a meeting of a group linked to the right-wing Patriot movement associated with white supremacists; Hector Whitcombe, described as a former all-state football player who later dropped out of college, had been taking shooting lessons from Marshall's father. The story hinted at the need for more investigation but also quoted the Willis's family lawyer as being satisfied with Ed Marshall's arrest. "We have a confession from a cop's son," an anonymous police source said. "Why should we investigate further?"

And then nothing.

As the days went on and Aggie still didn't return my calls, I thought about calling Jess, but it took me days to find the courage after my mother suggested it. We'd never had a friendship outside of our circle of five – we'd never spent any time together on our own. And I was afraid of Jess. My parents didn't blame me, Aggie didn't seem to, Luke hadn't – what would Jess think? When I finally dialled her number, it struck me that I'd never called Jess or Joe before. Aggie was my connection with them.

The phone rang and rang, as if the entire Willis family had disappeared as well; I imagined the ring echoing through their house, through the living room with its stiff wool-covered furniture, through the kitchen with its pale pink Formica counters that had reminded me of my grandmother's house, through the upstairs bedrooms that I imagined with white cotton bedcovers and small, square decorative pillows also like my grandmother's. I let it ring for five minutes before hanging up.

It must have been the fifth time I tried that Jess finally answered, and then I didn't know what to say. Sorry? How does one say sorry? Instead I asked if she wanted to go to the movies.

"I'm not really up for that, Cassie."

I felt stupid. The movies? Of course she didn't want to go to the movies. What was I thinking?

"Or, Friendly's?" I said weakly.

Now I can put into words all the things I was too afraid then to say: *I am so sorry, I don't believe what's happened, I can't believe Joe is dead, I can't believe what I'm reading in the paper, I can't believe the story the Whitcombes are telling, I can't believe Aggie hasn't gotten in touch with me, how could Joe be dead? I don't believe I wasn't there to stop it, why wasn't I there to stop it? Why wasn't I there to stop it? Why wasn't I there to stop it?* But I could barely think these things, let alone say them. They were like dreams, hazy and frightening and buried except for those brief moments when they broke through. They were too powerful and contradictory and they hurt too much.

So we said goodbye and I hung up.

CHAPTER THIRTY-ONE

One afternoon, when I'd begged my ever-vigilant mother to let me stay home instead of going on a quick errand to the supermarket, I decided to call the reporter I'd known at the local newspaper, Alison Best. I was surprised when she answered herself – I had this idea that reporters would have secretaries – and so I told her who I was and that I'd known Joe Willis.

"Yes," she said thoughtfully. "I looked for you in the office. I wondered if you knew him."

"He was one of my best friends!" I said.

"I'll keep you in mind if we do any more stories. Now that I can contact you. We tried you a few days after he died, you know. But someone said we had the wrong number."

"If you do any more stories?" I repeated.

"It's sort of resolved now," she said. "Unless you think you have something."

After all my surety that Joe's death wasn't an accident, I hesitated. What did I really know? That Hector asked me something that he already knew when he asked me? That he'd been a jerk about Joe? I felt myself beginning to cry. "It just doesn't make sense."

Alison was quiet on the phone. "Sometimes things don't," she said.

I tried not to sniffle – I didn't want her to hear me crying.

"Listen, why don't I take you to lunch?" she said. "We can talk about journalism, and you can tell me all about your friend. And we can think about a story for the one-month anniversary. Sound good?"

We made plans to meet the next day, and I felt better, until I began thinking about someone telling her she had the wrong number. Had Mom done that? I would have wanted to talk to Alison. I knew her. I was eighteen now! It was up to me.

I tried to ask my mother about it casually, but she caught on right away, and then I had to admit I was meeting the reporter for lunch.

"No. No. Cassie, you can't do that."

"I *know* her. I used to talk to her when she walked by the Classified department."

"Cassandra, I forbid you from doing that. You need to give up on this. It's over. Nothing you do is going to..." She paused, softened her voice, touched my hand. "Sweetheart, nothing is going to bring back Joe. I'm so sorry."

I heard my mother talking to my father that night, quietly in the kitchen, when they thought I was asleep and wouldn't hear. Or, rather, I heard my father, my mother's voice too low, too reasonable, to carry.

"The case is done!" Dad said. A low rumbling from my father, then silence, which I assumed was my mother speaking, then: "The kid's confessed, for crying out loud! Why does she..."

More rumbling, more silence. I was dying to open my door to hear better, but didn't dare, in case it squeaked, so I sat on the floor by the door, one ear near the crack, blocking my other ear with my hand.

"Not a freaking journalist. You gotta be kidding."

Is that why my mother was talking to my father? So I wouldn't talk to Alison Best?

"Do you realize she could have been over there?" Dad's

voice was suddenly booming. I heard her shush him but he ignored her. "Do you realize she could have been over there when those two hoodlums showed up with a gun? Our daughter? How many nights has Cassandra been over those people's house in the last two years? She could've been there. It could have been her who was shot."

And my father banged out of the kitchen and into the living room. Sound carried too well from there, and it was where he went if he didn't want to talk something through after I'd gone to bed. I waited to hear my mother follow him, to hear the quiet opening and shutting of the door, and then, just her voice:

"You think I don't know that?" she said. "I'm grateful every day for that gift. That it wasn't our daughter."

I didn't hear anything after that, and so I gave up and went back to bed. I wondered what they were doing then. Was my mother back in the kitchen? Were they sitting on separate couches, in some kind of stalemate? Or was she on his lap? I thought about going down and joining them, saying I couldn't sleep. "It could have been our Cassandra who was shot." My parents hadn't said that to me, afraid, probably, of upsetting me further. I liked hearing them say it. It made me want to go down to them, and get a hug from them both, first from my mother, slighter, softer, reassuring, then from my dad, like the bear hugs he used to give me when I was little, squeezing me so tight I'd giggle that I couldn't breathe, thrilled that he was hugging me that tightly. Without Aggie, they were all I had, and it made me want to go back several years as if I were fourteen again, go back to before I met Aggie, and my parents were not dull and unsophisticated but just who they were. Just my mom and dad.

My father was making pancakes when I slunk down the stairs after eleven o'clock, convinced I'd been dreaming when I woke to the smell of them. Was this part of the plan they'd discussed after I'd fallen asleep? They must have come to some sort of agreement, and the agreement became apparent after the dishes were cleared away and my mother said she was going outside to do some gardening: it would be my father who would talk to me.

"So, Cassie, I want to hear it from you. Why do you think Joe's death wasn't an accident? Hasn't that been pretty solidly established?"

So I recounted my story: how Hector, with and without Ed, taunted Aggie about Joe; how they were always making comments when Joe was around; how Hector had been taking lessons on shooting from Mr. Marshall without Mrs. Whitcombe knowing; how Hector told us Ed hated Joe for protecting Daisy that night; and how Hector had asked me, again, though he already knew, where Aggie and Joe had gone. "They knew Joe was going to be there. They wouldn't have thought he was an intruder."

"But it could still be an accident, Cassie."

"They hated him. They're racists."

"That doesn't prove they killed him on purpose. Ed was drunk off his mind! He couldn't set a mousetrap let alone carry out a murder."

"Hector could."

"Why would he? Aggie's going off to college soon anyway. He has his own life to sort out. Isn't he going somewhere, too?"

"The police haven't asked any of us anything about the party. None of us. And they're lying about that night. They'd been planning to shoot coyotes at the beach for weeks."

He sighed, and scratched the back of his head, staring into space as if that helped him think. "Listen, I know you're desperate to make sure you are heard, but I won't allow you to talk to a journalist."

"You don't trust her."

"No."

"But I want to be a journalist."

He smiled, suddenly affectionate. "You always have been a

curious little girl. Quiet, but watchful. You probably heard half of my conversation with your mother last night. Hmmmm?"

I tried not to look guilty, then decided to admit it. "Yeah."

"I figured as much. Listen – I think it's important to talk to someone about your concerns. But a journalist isn't going to know the law. Especially a journalist at 'Southern Connecticut's Largest Afternoon Daily'. All they're going to know is a good story."

"But they could bring attention to it."

"And what if it is nothing? What if your ideas about what might have happened –"

"They're not just ideas."

"…if the *information* you want to share about Hector and Ed and whatever they were doing that night holds absolutely no weight whatsoever from the point of view of the law? None whatsoever. Maybe the police already know everything you want to tell them and have decided it doesn't make a difference to their case. Have you thought of that?"

I shook my head. "I don't trust them."

"And a bad story, instead of shedding light on the situation, instead of helping the Willises, hurts the Willises. Hurts Aggie and Jess. They're going through a lot already."

I was silent, overwhelmed by his logic.

"And hurts you. You're my concern."

"The police haven't even interviewed me."

"Why should they, sweetheart? You weren't at the house."

"I was at the party."

"How many kids were at that party? Fifty? A hundred?"

"I'm Aggie's best friend!" I said, and almost started to cry.

"Don't get upset. It's not all bad news! Now listen – what if I make an appointment for us to go talk to the prosecutor?"

"Will you?"

"I would send you by yourself, but I think they're more likely to listen to you if it's clear I'm supporting you by being there. I won't say anything. And it's not because I don't think you can handle it on your own."

I nodded. "OK."

"And I want you to know that I agree with you."

I heard a silence, as the clip-clip of my mother's garden shears, which had been sounding quietly through our screen windows, paused. "You do?"

"I'm not saying I think your conclusions are right. But I believe you have information that should be shared. That they should have asked you about."

I nodded again. I felt a weight lifted off me and, in its place, a little hope.

"And then," my father said, "will you come with me to a Mets game?"

"What, you're bribing me now?"

He laughed, looking pleased. "I'm bribing myself. I mean, you haven't left me much choice, Maiden of the Stubborn Heart. Have you? And here all this time I didn't think you were like me. I thought you were all your mother. Well. The things we parents learn."

My father was able to make an appointment, and we met with the prosecutor for forty-five minutes. At the end, he shook my hand and thanked us for the information, and we never heard from him again.

My mother began organizing my life for college – taking me shopping, getting a suggested reading list from the journalism department. Suddenly, I was leaving in two weeks. My mother kept a close eye on me, and she changed the subject when I brought up Aggie, until I didn't bring her up anymore. While I don't believe my mother would have precipitated my division from Aggie, I do think she was relieved I was out of the clutches of the Whitcombes.

She found the address of my roommate so I could write to her, but I didn't want to, then the roommate sent me a postcard and my mother insisted I write back. "I'll have to tell her about Joe," I said. The thought of putting into words, trying to explain it to a complete stranger, seemed impossible. I could write and write and write and I still wouldn't be able to capture the enormity of what had happened.

"Tell her about it in person," my mother said. "It's too difficult to write in a letter. But if you don't write at all, she'll think you don't like her already, Cassie." And so I wrote, not mentioning Aggie or Joe or anything but what my major was and when was she arriving and did she know what classes she was taking.

I thought it would feel horrible to leave it all out. Not to mention my best friend. Or Joe. But then, how light I felt for a moment as the letter floated away, another, different Cassandra with it. A Cassandra not obligated to tell everything all the time. A Cassandra who didn't just blurt out the truth.

It would be possible to just walk away.

And I did, pretty much.

On the day before I left for college, I told my mother I was going to buy that electric kettle I'd not let her purchase for my room – "Great!" she said, pleased I was taking the initiative – and drove to Aggie's house one last time. There was a For Sale sign out front. I was shocked. I left the car and ran to the door, knocking frantically. No answer. I walked around the porch and saw that the curtain to the library wasn't fully closed. Inside, the room was empty, and immaculately clean: the walnut bookshelves shone with new wax; the walls gleamed with fresh ivory paint – it must have taken many layers to cover the dark red walls that I had loved – and the oak floor looked lighter and brighter. They were gone. The Whitcombes were completely gone.

I tried, that first semester, to find Aggie at Smith. I rang the college a dozen times before a clerk recognized my voice and told me against the rules that Aggie had never shown up.

I tried all five of the other universities she'd applied to – she'd been accepted at every one – to no avail. I even tried Penn, though I knew it would be impossible to get into Penn after the fact, but the Whitcombes could do anything they put their minds to. No one knew anything about her. I followed the coverage of Ed Marshall's brief trial, then guilty plea. While Hector's name often came up, there was no mention of Aggie. In time, I stopped looking.

V

2014

The Same Country

CHAPTER THIRTY-TWO

When Aggie called the morning after her strange phone call and my late-night visit to her house, I was the one in a half-dream state – something about Maria, whispering to me, but I couldn't hear her, not in the dream and not now, and I hadn't dreamt of her in so long I didn't want to let her go. It took a few minutes for me to wake up. "Aggie," I finally said. "Can you start over?"

She'd received a call from her mother first thing, saying an emergency had come up for her father's caregiver Milani and could Aggie possibly call in sick to come over to watch her father while Mrs. Whitcombe went to a luncheon. "I'm leaving now, so my mother has time to get dressed, which means I can skip giving Dad his medication this morning without my mother knowing – I swear it makes him more befuddled, not less. She's not home until four or so. Can you come to my parents' house at eleven thirty?"

I didn't answer. As if still in my dream, I felt something instinctual that I couldn't name. Fear, maybe. Dread.

She took my silence for agreement. "Park around the corner – not on Dover Street, she'll drive that way, try Park – then wait in your car and I'll let you know when she's actually left. I know it's a long shot, I'd rather have a whole weekend with him, but this is good. My father's best around this time of day. He doesn't take the drug that I think makes him sleepiest until after lunch. Cassie?"

I agreed to be there as soon as I could. But I didn't want to go. I didn't want to be in her mother's house, I didn't want to see Mr. Whitcombe again, I didn't want to help Aggie with her hair-brained scheme. I felt all of me resisting the idea, the kind of resistance that Maria would have told me to listen to. I went into the kitchen instead of showering and sat in the sun at the small round table where I liked to sit in the mornings and drink coffee and wondered if I could call Aggie back and cancel. Not turn up at all. *Don't go,* Maria whispered.

Outside, a whistle, like a teenager trying to get someone's attention. I looked out blankly and Jess stood holding Antonne on her hip, looking up at me, waving wildly at me, then taking Antonne's hand and waving it, more gently, for him. I swear he looked bigger than he had the week before, the purple T-shirt she'd bought when I was with her no longer hanging off his shoulders. The doctors had said he might grow quickly after a few weeks of good rest and good diet, as the foster home he'd been in had taken good care of him, too. Time for a growth spurt, they'd said. I opened the window and leaned out. "Where you two going?"

"The beach!" Jess called out. "Come with us next week."

Jess's month alone with Antonne was coming to an end already. Already? And I'd been invited to spend time with them.

"Love to," I yelled down, then gave a thumbs up, too. Jess placed Antonne smoothly into his car seat and then beeped merrily as she drove off. *Even if it's just the beach with Jess and Antonne*, I thought, *the future awaits*. Then I began getting ready to head off to Aggie's.

Mr. Whitcombe was out of bed this time when I arrived, sitting in the chair where Milani had been sentried on my first visit, staring with the same blank stare out the window. He seemed no better than before, but the room at least was fresh. Aggie had opened the windows wide and a slightly salty breeze was blowing in from the Sound. It was one of those New England days that was hot in the sun but cool in the shade – another familiar feel to the weather. Three seasons had passed since I'd moved back to Bridgeton. A fourth was now beginning. Their variations were mine again. And now here I was, back at the Whitcombes'.

Her father had not looked at me when I walked in – "You remember Cassie, Dad?" Aggie had said again, again without him responding. He kept grasping at a blanket on his lap as if to pull it closer, until he pushed it off by accident. Aggie retrieved it from his feet almost as it fell and folded it to place on his bed. "The way my mom cocoons him in here, no wonder he's half-asleep the whole day," Aggie said quietly.

"He does look cold," I said. Mr. Whitcombe turned his head in my direction, then back toward the window, clutching at his elbows, then reaching for the now absent blanket. "Mr. Whitcombe, do you feel chilly?" I asked loudly. He didn't respond.

"You think?" Aggie's brow wrinkled, and she went into the hallway. I stood at the threshold as she opened a closet door to reveal shelves and shelves of blankets. "Of course, he never *moves,*" she said, still speaking quietly even though Mr. Whitcombe wouldn't be able to hear her now. She pulled one out and headed back to me. "I know he can't exercise, but shouldn't he be doing something? I was reading the other day that nutritional supplements might help his energy. Mom's not into the exercise idea, but how could she say no to nutritional supplements? She's going to talk to his doctor next week. One of his doctors. I think he has about ten." She re-entered the room. "Dad? Dad?" She unfolded the blanket and tucked it around his waist, stood before him, then squatted so she could hug him.

"Aggie," he said, and she beamed.

"Yes, it's Aggie!" She gave him another hug, then began rearranging the room, pulled another chair over for me, so there were three of us around a small table. She leaned over to fuss with the blanket again, her father not seeming to notice.

"Do you think we're being unrealistic, about today?" she asked me. "Selfish, really. Dad, let's just have a nice lunch today, me, you and Cassie. What do you think?"

I shouldn't have felt relieved, after all these years of wondering what had happened. But I was. Perhaps this was enough now. Helping Jess with Antonne. Staying on the Haley story. Today, taking care of Aggie's father. "That's probably better," I said.

So we spent the day with Mr. Whitcombe. The sun strengthened as the morning went on, warming the room, both the temperature – Aggie's father began to look less pale, less shrivelled – and the colors. It was a beautiful space after all, put together with love. Maybe Mr. Whitcombe wasn't well enough to sit in his chair very often, but it was both soft and firm, positioned at the window so that he could look, when he looked, past the red and black roofs of neighborhood houses, picturesque in themselves, to a sliver of the Sound, blue and sparkling in the distance. The small iron table with a mosaic-tiled surface, the two chairs Aggie and I occupied, low and armless, draped with linen so elegant it could have come from one of Mrs. Whitcombe's dresses, made it feel like the outdoor café of a fancy hotel. But of course. The room had been set up this way on purpose, as if Mr. Whitcombe would be receiving guests daily. He'd barely been out of bed, according to Aggie, let alone had any company. It was hard to believe Mrs. Whitcombe had indulged in that little fantasy, and I felt myself soften toward her. She'd always been a doting wife. How much she must miss him.

Aggie and I took turns going downstairs to bring up drinks and snacks. Aggie had bought empanadas from the Bridgeton shop the day before, and I enjoyed heating them up in the Whitcombe kitchen. As always, the Whitcombes owned the best of everything, and I rummaged through their cabinets for the most beautiful objects: terracotta and blue plates for the empanadas, thick glasses with blue rims from Mexico for an organic mint lemonade I found in their fridge, and delicate forks with blue flowered ceramic handles that I was delighted to remember from high school.

"Where did you find *these*?" Aggie asked in amazement as she handed one to her father.

"Don't you usually feed him?" I asked quietly.

"Mom and Milani do right away," she said. "Dad, I give you a chance, at least, don't I?"

Her father was holding the fork in his hand, turning it round in his fingers as if deciding whether he would use it. "Mallorca, 1965," he said, then handed the fork back to her.

"Mallorca!" she said, looking at me excitedly then back to him. "But I thought you and Mom went to Madrid for your honeymoon."

Mr. Whitcombe was now holding up his plate, and we waited for a place and date on that. Then he pulled his hands away and the plate dropped to the floor, cracking into two clean pieces. The empanada rolled toward Aggie. Mr. Whitcombe didn't seem to notice any of it.

"Shit," she said, picking up the pieces, dusting off the empanada and putting it on her own plate. "I forgot Mom has him use plastic up here."

"Is it valuable?"

"Got me." She spied on a side table a plastic plate in a muted '50s blue – even plastic was vintage here. Aggie put her own empanada on his plate then tore off a piece and held it near her father's mouth, but he turned his face away. She tried again, and this time he accepted the food. "Empanadas, Dad," she said. "From Julia's Jamaican Bakery. Remember?"

He nodded, but it was hard to know what he was agreeing to.

She fed him several bites before he started turning his head again. She offered him a drink of lemonade, then sat back in her chair. Her own food remained untouched. "Do you remember?" Aggie said again. Then I saw she was looking at me. "Do you remember the first time I talked to Joe? I mean, *really* talked to Joe?"

I didn't. "I always thought it happened so quickly."

"It was quick! Oh my god, it was quick, once I'd really talked to him. But don't you remember that? We'd run into him and Luke at the McDonald's – we hated the scene at Mickey Dee's but we both wanted a chocolate sundae – and Luke came over because of you, and I ended up talking to Joe."

The feel of the blacktop, dark and dirty, when we'd park our car at McDonald's at night, the awkwardness of passing kids we knew but didn't particularly like sitting on the hoods of their cars drinking, the neon brightness once inside, the orange chairs attached to the floor and wood-veneer plastic tables, the smell of French fries – all of that came back to me like a hazy almost-memory. But I could not remember this particular night. I couldn't remember any particular night at McDonald's.

"It's like I can live in that exact moment," Aggie said, "not the words we were speaking, not what he was wearing, nothing specific, no details, but the moment, the split-second moment, we hit it off. Like two metals rubbing together. I don't think we touched but I felt I was bouncing off of him, he was bouncing off of me, something forming between us, new – it is chemistry. Isn't it? That spark between two people."

Aggie looked over to her father. He was staring at her, but I couldn't tell if he was actually taking her in, if he was in this world or in some other world. He looked cold again.

"Poor Daddy," she said. She patted his knee and tucked his blanket more firmly around his waist. "This never was going to work. Was it?"

She sat back again, her hands clasped in her lap, hunched slightly, knees together, feet splayed out. It was one of those poses that would look awkward on anyone else but that made Aggie appear awkwardly graceful, like a young girl with too-long limbs in ballet class. Beautiful because of her awkwardness. Could I still love Aggie after all these years? Her dark hair wisping thinly around her pale, angular, now lightly lined, older face. Oblivious to me. She was innocent, somehow, even now. Maybe that's what was so appealing about Aggie – her energy, her spirit, was like a child's. She never held back. Not with Joe. Not with me. She was full on.

Her father spoke quietly but firmly. "Please turn out the light. Diana."

Aggie stood to gather the plates. "It's daytime, Dad." She stepped toward him, leaning on one arm, and put her face close to his. "Don't you know even that, Daddy?" She straightened again and sighed, then put the plates back down on the table and stood at the window, looking out. The light was already turning toward the darker yellow of late afternoon. Another day passing.

"What happened that night?" I asked. "The night Joe died." *The night Joe was killed,* Jess correcting me in my ear.

She didn't move, but I could see her stiffen, her breath pause.

"I never saw you after that," I said. "Except at the funeral. We never talked about it." I thought about what happened to me that night, at the beach with Luke. I'd not told anyone, not even Maria. But what happened to me didn't really matter anymore. This did. "Aggie?"

She began talking, slowly at first, telling me again she couldn't remember it all, making me ask questions before she began to talk more freely, telling me everything she could remember about her last night with Joe.

CHAPTER THIRTY-THREE

They were shy when they first reached her room, where he'd never been, not really, only briefly on one visit when she'd pulled him in on his way back from using the bathroom, pulled him in to kiss him hard but quick, before her parents would wonder where they'd disappeared to, waiting for them downstairs with wine glasses in their hands. No, he'd never really been in her room and they'd felt shy at first, Joe wandering around, touching the antique dressing table, the ivory hairbrush, the blue silk sheets she revealed to him, how he liked touching the objects she touched every day, he said, ordinary objects. She sat on the cool sheets and watched him graze his fingers over the wood and ivory mantel clock, touch the tassel of her lamp, open the closet door and flick through the hanging clothes, pulling out a purple skirt – "I've never seen you in this" – moving on. What was he waiting for? "Oh, for Christ's sake," she said and ran and jumped and wrapped herself around his torso, falling, up again, him turning toward her, lifting her up as she wrapped her legs around his waist, carrying her to the bed, "What the fuck," he whispered and she could feel him hard against her, "was I... waiting...", the rest of the words lost and they were wild, and hungry, and free, finally nobody else was around, nobody, and she couldn't possibly say how much she wanted him, and it felt like hours of that, nights upon nights, just the two of them, intertwined, alone, no world outside theirs. As if their world could last forever. Not just for two hours and four minutes, which she later would calculate that time had measured. As the first call to 911 was made at 12:58. According to the police log.

Aggie stopped then. As she looked out the window I felt as if I was in her old room, too, with its blue walls and blue rug and its view of the city, not the Sound. I glanced at Mr. Whitcombe. His eyes were closed. He was asleep.

"Keep going," I said.

"Why?" She turned to face me.

I didn't answer. I didn't know the answer. But it was getting late, and her mother would be returning soon, and then this long-lost closeness I felt with Aggie and even, today, with her father, would disappear.

"I thought you wanted to remember," I said.

She nodded, chastened, and slowly she closed her fingers around the edge of her chair as if for courage to go on. "I had to go to the bathroom. I wanted Joe to come with me. I didn't want to leave him for a second. But he said he wanted to stay in my room, liked the idea of staying there, and I liked that idea, too, and I thought about him being in my room as I went to the bathroom, took my time, daydreaming on the toilet about him waiting for me in my bedroom, pretending for a moment that he wasn't there, that it was my imagination, then reminding myself he was there, waiting for me, thinking about me, too, longing for me to return. And then…" She paused, half-turned toward me, brought her hands to her face. "And…" Her voice broke before she went on. "Joe waiting for me in my bed and finally I couldn't bear waiting any longer and I heard this big boom – like a car had exploded outside it sounded so loud to me – I swung open the bathroom door and it was like I was blinded, it was bright for some reason, then dark again, like I was momentarily blinded, and I went running toward my room and there are all these people in my room – where did they come from? – my parents, Hector, Ed Marshall of all people, what were they doing here? And Hector is looking at his hand like it's a foreign object. 'Where's Joe? Where's Joe?' and Dad is trying to hold me back, to cover my eyes, 'Don't look,' he says, and I don't know what I'm not supposed to look at, I just want to find Joe. And I swear I remember Hector. Hector was… Hector…"

Mr. Whitcombe spoke, his eyes still shut. "Hector was holding the… Hector. And it was Hector holding the…" He was silent and for a moment I thought he'd forgotten he was speaking. "And we walked in and it was Hector holding the…"

Aggie turned to me, pleading. She couldn't provide the word for him. Couldn't give him the word he needed. So I did.

"The gun, Mr. Whitcombe?"

"Yes!" Mr. Whitcombe opened his eyes wide and his gaze was sharp, his eyes blue again, steely blue. "Thank you, Cassandra. I walked into the room with your mother and it was Hector holding the gun, on his knees like he'd fallen and it was Hector holding the gun, Hector…"

"Mr. Whitcombe, *you* saw Hector?"

"Yes, holding the gun and he was on his knees with—"

"Edmond –" Mrs. Whitcombe's voice filled the room – "Edmond shouldn't have shot Joe." Her words sounded as clear and precise as they had in my dreams weeks before, so like they sounded on those hazy nights that I thought I had imagined her voice until Aggie and her father turned slowly toward the door and I saw she had appeared as silently as an apparition, this ghost from our past. But she was solid, in her cream-colored silky soft suit. Corporeal.

"Edmond should never have shot Joe," she said. "It was really wrong of him, wasn't it?"

Mr. Whitcombe continued, his eyes open now and gazing at his wife, pleading with his wife. "And we walked in and it was Hector…"

"Yes!" Aggie said. "I remember now! Hector was holding something I couldn't tell what it was—"

"…holding the gun. It was Hector holding the gun. Holding the gun." Now that he'd found the word, Mr. Whitcombe couldn't let it go. "We came in the room and Hector was holding the gun, the gun, holding the gun when we walked in the room, and then Diana said, 'Hector, put the gun down.'"

Mr. Whitcombe had known all this time? Mrs. Whitcombe? All the Whitcombes had known?

"Hector looking at his hand like it was a foreign object instead of his hand—" Aggie said.

"Edmond shouldn't have shot Joe," Mrs. Whitcombe said. "But he did. If you girls think you heard something different today, you're wrong."

Aggie was covering her eyes with her hands, then holding them to her forehead, as if her mother's mere presence could muddle her memories again. "A gun?" Aggie said. "You saw Hector holding a gun when you walked in? You saw *Hector*?"

"Your father is confused. He's wrong. It was all a long time ago."

"And you've been covering up for him for twenty years?"

Mr. Whitcombe was beginning to struggle in his chair, moving as if to get up but unable to. "Hector was holding the gun, the gun, the—"

I went to him and gripped his hands, hard as I could. "Stop it. Stop it." I wanted to shake him until he shut up.

Aggie raised her chin high, put her hand to her hips, and turned fully toward her mother – her old stance, the old Aggie, back. "What about Jess? Or Joe's parents, or… or *me*? Did you think about helping me? Why did Ed Marshall ever—"

Mr. Whitcombe kept going. "Hector was holding the—"

"I don't see how you can believe your father, Agatha. He'll say anything you suggest to him. No one else will believe him either. Oh, except for our Cassandra." She smiled coldly in my direction.

"I was there, Mom. Don't you remember? I was there, too. I saw Hector holding the gun."

"Not when…" She stopped.

"Not when what?"

"We were there before you, dear. We saw Edmond put down the gun."

"I saw Hector..."

"You can't change your story after two decades."

"...I saw Hector holding the gun, I've been dreaming for years about that night. And in my dream when I walk in Hector is holding out his hand, staring at his hand, and then I see he's holding a gun. It's all weird and in slow motion, always, everyone misshapen, first elongated, then wide, and so I've thought all these years – you told me, you let me think all these years – that I was dreaming, that I'd given the gun to Hector in my dreams because I blamed him for Joe's death. That therapist you found me – was she part of it, too?"

"Edmond shouldn't have shot poor Joe."

"And..." Aggie looked at me – no, not at me, at her father, but maybe not seeing anything. "Dad knew? Dad?"

Mr. Whitcombe was babbling to himself, a strange expression on his face, excited, smiling, yet fearful, too. I tried to extract my hands from his but now he gripped me, wouldn't let me go.

"Edmond confessed."

"But then he said he couldn't remember."

"We weren't there, Agatha, when Joe was shot. None of us were. And there's no way my Hector would do that – shoot another person, a friend of the family, like that."

"Like what?"

She hesitated. "Even by accident."

"Don't you understand, Mom? This dream I've had for years? I remember it so clearly now. I rush into my room and you're there? And Dad? And Hector, looking at his hand like it's a foreign object, 'Where's Joe? Where's Joe?' Dad trying to hold me back, covering my eyes, 'Don't look,' and I don't know what I'm not supposed to look at I just want to find Joe, and then I look down and I see him on the floor, what is he doing there? His head propped up by the leg of my bed, on some dark blanket I didn't know I owned, dark and spreading like molten coffee, I try to get to him but Dad's stronger than I've ever known him to be, he holds me back, Joe's not answering or looking at me and 'Is he bleeding?' and Dad's around me and it's dark and raucous in my head, it must have been silent in the room but it's raucous, I can barely hear, the room like a hurricane, and I hear you, Mom, so clear and precise, 'Put the gun down, Hector,' and there's a gun, a *gun*? 'Now, Ed, please put on the safety,' and then I hear this other voice in the room as Ed Marshall dips down to the floor, the voice high and keening, speaking in fragments of syllables, 'J—', 'J—', 'Wh—', over and over, until the half-syllables turned into screeching, unintelligible sound, and at some point I think it must be my voice because my throat stopped hurting when the noise stopped, as Dad holds me back from running at Joe, running at Hector, what had he fucking done, I'm fighting Dad, hitting his thighs and arms and face, but at the same time his hold is soothing, too, soothing to me, because he's there, protecting me, when I don't understand what's going on, I'd have bruises the next day but part of me is glad he's protecting me from all the horrible things in the room, and then you again, Mom, I don't know what you mean, 'You've shot Joe, Edmond,' you keep saying it again and again, looking at Hector and nodding your head, 'Edmond, you shouldn't have shot Joe', 'I didn't... I didn't...', 'I know you didn't mean to, Edmond', 'I didn't mean to, I didn't...', Ed still gibbering on and on when the cops finally arrive and white coats fill the room and the world blinks, blanks, and Joe, Joe just, where is Joe? I didn't understand, I didn't, I didn't..."

Aggie was crying so hard she was making no noise. Speaking no more words. We didn't need any more words. Not even Mr. Whitcombe could be helped by any more words now.

It was he who broke the silence of Aggie's sobbing, as if he hadn't heard her words or her silence.

"Because the light was on, and it was awful!" He spoke in a sudden, loud, terrified roar. "Diana, turn out the, the... it's too horrible to look, please Diana, turn out the… turn out… turn out the…"

"Gun?" Mrs. Whitcombe said. "Turn out the gun, dear?"

"…the… the… please turn… please turn out the…"

"The light's off, dear. It's just not dark yet."

"The light's off. Thank you. I'll sleep now."

And then he was asleep, his face instantly peaceful, his hands still in mine. I unwrapped his grip and placed his hands on his lap. Mrs. Whitcombe gazed at him from her distance, then brought another blanket over and tucked it around him. "It's freezing in this room," she said. She quietly shut the windows. "You have no idea how to take care of people, Agatha. Do you?" she said, and left.

CHAPTER THIRTY-FOUR

A full year has now passed since I returned to Bridgeton, and I am still lost in the tumult of those first hours and days and weeks after learning what happened the night Joe was killed. The confusion rises again like a mist over water – it's so hard to know what I'm seeing. Though I know what's underneath, I can't make it out. But then the mist dissipates into the air and it all becomes as clear as the brightest winter's day – what the Whitcombes did.

I try to feel sympathy for Aggie, try to understand how strategically her mother manipulated her only daughter in order to save her only son, or her family, or herself. Isolating Aggie almost as much as she isolated the dangerously garrulous Mr. Whitcombe in those final years. Feeding her drugs in the months after the shooting that eased her anxiety by taking away, or keeping under wraps, her memory. Finding therapists who believed Mrs. Whitcombe first, before Aggie. Keeping people like me away from her.

Sometimes I can think of Aggie as I used to, because if she was only half herself when I met her again that evening in the produce aisle of the supermarket, if she had been only half herself ever since Joe died, Aggie was galvanized that day in her father's room, freed as if from a small, tight prison. Before, as each number of the combination lock that kept her enclosed was revealed, each click had made her shrink back – until the final number released the door and Aggie burst out. While I was still reeling, she went into motion.

"I need to tell Hector first," Aggie said as we raced out of the house to my car. Her mother had blocked hers in.

"Tell Hector what?" I said, still not sure what the hell had just happened.

"Give him one last chance."

"Don't you understand?" I said. The truth was coming to me in pieces, blinding me before letting me see another part of it. "Your father knew all along. Your *father*. Knew that Hector shot Joe." Jess came to mind, not the Jess I knew now, but the younger one, her face rounder and sweeter. How trusting she had looked when Joe was around. "And now that he has dementia, *now*, when he has no idea what he's saying or doing – *now*?"

"And then I'll go to the prosecutors."

How kindly her father acted toward me at the funeral, his words caring, wise. His affectionate touch on my arm. *It was a horrible accident.* As much for my mother's benefit as mine. Enlisting her cooperation. *Remind your daughter of that.*

"When all the time he knew," I said. "Your father! Your whole family knew. You…"

I stopped. Aggie stood before me, her pale skin gleaming in the warm light of the afternoon sun.

"…knew," she finished for me. She grasped my hands, squeezed them tight, shook them in excitement. She was almost smiling. "That's what I remembered. All this time! It's always been what I remembered. Everyone convinced me I was imagining it. But I wasn't."

"You knew," I said.

"I thought I was conjuring it out of thin air. Out of guilt. I mean… Joe. Joe should be walking this planet. And he's not. But I know now, I really know."

"I knew," I said.

An hour later, after phoning work to warn them I'd be late and going home to take a hot shower, I was sitting in Ray's office. "Jesus Christ," he said when I was finished. "We'll put the whole

Haley team on this." I could see he was planning a strategy already, figuring out which reporters to assign to which sections of the story. "Let's run it Sunday. And you confirm everything?"

I did not hesitate this time. I'd been at the Whitcombes' not as a reporter, but as a friend. Now, I was a witness. "Yes."

"And you'll write your own piece?"

Ray's face remained calm, patient. Unlike most journalists, he never let his curiosity show, and he was never in a hurry. The long game, indeed. He'd always known what my answer would be. I just had to get there.

"How many inches are you going to give me?" I asked.

He smiled. "How long is a piece of string?"

At home, at midnight, I almost missed the note slipped under my door from Jess. *Aggie stopped by. I'll be awake.* I knocked softly in case she'd fallen asleep but she answered immediately, wearing an overlarge blue terry-cloth robe that seemed too warm for the heat that had moved in that afternoon, the air now sticky and humid. "Let's sit outside," she said, leading us on to her balcony. And we sat, not saying anything for a while, listening to the sound of crickets, the hum every few minutes of a passing car, and, occasionally, a staticky peep from the baby monitor as Antonne gurgled in his sleep. It might have been the only peaceful hour I experienced for months, those minutes with Jess when we didn't try to sort it out, didn't try to understand, didn't ponder why. Just let what we'd learned sink in.

"She told me she loved Joe," Jess finally said. "Truly loved him. Still did. She didn't want me to ever think it was… light… for her. Some fad."

"Does that matter?"

"I don't know. Not to me. At least. But." Jess shrugged. "It's like she's proud of it."

An animal howled in the distance, a cat maybe. Maybe it was an owl.

"She said she'd never be with anyone else." Jess wrapped the robe more closely around herself. "I told her, 'Don't be stupid. Joe's dead.'"

After Aggie went to the police, and the stories were published, more pieces fell into place. Some made it into the paper; some didn't. Mr. Whitcombe had been over-medicated for five years; for fifteen months after the shooting, Aggie had been put on a dosage of lorazepam that was two times higher than the largest recommended dosage; the Whitcombes had been paying Ed Marshall's rent and health insurance premiums since he had been released from prison. "We'll be suing the Whitcombe family for a lot more than that," Detective Marshall was quoted as saying, though he refused to say whether their financial help was offered before the trial or if it had been a factor in Ed changing his plea to guilty.

The Willis family always refused to comment.

We'll never know if Hector shot Joe on purpose. There is simply no evidence that he did or didn't. No clues to nudge the story one way or the other. The fact that he lied for more than twenty years, let his once-friend go to prison in his stead, tells us nothing about whether Joe's death was an accident, or a murder. That information simply reveals that Hector was capable of murder. Was ruthless enough. Violent enough. But there was a reason for Hector and Mrs. Whitcombe – and, I force myself to add, Mr. Whitcombe – to send Ed to prison: it meant Hector didn't go. But to what end would Hector have hunted Joe down and shot him? Yet I have come to believe that hate needs no reason, no purpose. It just exists. So how much I want to know the full truth about Joe's death varies from day to day. Some days, anger will enter my body like a force I can barely contain; other times, the idea that we'll never know passes through me like I'm not even there.

I passed my bookshelves the other day, and Mr. Whitcombe's poetry collection caught my attention. I left it there. Now it was a reminder of what I didn't want to be. How I didn't want to live.

On the evening Aggie visited him, Hector employed every tactic possible to convince his sister not to reveal what she had discovered. First, he stonewalled. "It's just not true, Aggie. I'm sorry, I know it's still hard to accept what a stupid accident Joe's death was, I'm sorry I went over to Ed's to get that gun, I should have known Ed couldn't be trusted... if you think this doesn't haunt me still, it does, but Dad's just not right."

"But I remember now," she said. "I remember. It's not just Dad."

And then he tried logic. "You don't remember, Aggie. But, hey, let's say you're right, let's say this version is right." Then he pointed out the problems: their father's testimony would be useless, Mom's would outweigh it, no one would trust Aggie's sudden, emotional, guilt-driven revelation of what she now remembered after all these years.

She refused to budge.

Then manipulation: "Think how much it will upset Dad and Mom, you think she hasn't paid for this already? And for what? Nothing will change. Nothing you will say will make a difference, Aggie," he repeated again and again. "The Willises won't be better off. They'll be worse off. It won't matter. Not anymore. There's not gonna be any justice. Nothing you say will matter. The cops won't listen to you. They're my friends."

Then, he used threats. That had always been his strongest suit.

"You think this will be good for Joe's family? This will tear them apart. Why his parents didn't know where he was that night. They'll tear Jess up at the trial. Look at every single aspect of her work at the high school, her past. Her adoption."

Her adoption? How did Hector know about Jess's adoption?

Aggie told me that was when she hesitated. She knew her case was weak, her testimony questionable. She didn't know if Hector shot Joe. She knew only he was holding the gun. And her mother would deny even that. All this trauma – for what? To put at risk Jess's ability to adopt a child? Was she going to hurt the Willises again?

Hector sensed her weakness.

"And her son. His name's Antonne, right? I think a few of the cops in D.C. are familiar with his father. And his birth mother? Another disaster. Believe me, you and Jess don't want to know what I already know about Antonne's birth parents. And everyone else will know, too. I'll make sure of it."

The threat to Jess was his mistake. Aggie recovered herself again.

"What – now you're telling me you've used your position in the police to dig up confidential information to threaten Jessica Willis, whose brother you're pretending you didn't fucking shoot? Don't you dare," she said. "Don't you dare try to drag Jess's son into this, or Jess. Don't you dare try to fight me on this, and don't you dare drag Jess and her son into this, or that will backfire big time on you. I'm going ahead with this no matter what you say, no matter what the outcome, no matter what. Got it?"

Hector resigned the next day, but it didn't stop Aggie from going to the police with her story.

At times I envision her then as Agamemnon in the midst of the final battle in the Trojan War – her sword striking precisely at all targets – as Agamemnon the righteous warrior, serious, steady, strong. She is kingly as she stands, firm, unswayed by Hector's arguments and manipulations. She knows she is correct.

And then she's Aggie just as she was the first day I met her – her tangled, limp hair, that funny way she stood with one knee crossed over the other, both feet angled and bent outward so the soles of her shoes looked out at the world on either side of her, her arms crossed, hands clasped backward, everything askew, including her head, tilted sceptically at her brother. "Yeah, right," she says in her squeaky teenage voice. "You're gonna tell me about justice?"

But it all comes too late. Joe long dead.

Maybe I'll be able to forgive Aggie when I can forgive myself.

And then, Maria called.

"*Mi querida.*" Her voice, soft, low, a harmony of notes, like the strumming of a guitar. "*Lo siento.*"

She'd seen my story, was stunned, she said, by my story. "Stunned," she repeated. "How cruel. So cruel people are."

I let her words resound in my head; I didn't want to speak and silence their echo.

"Are you OK?" she asked.

Listening to Maria was so much like a caress and I drank it in. I hadn't realized how thirsty I was for her softness.

"Thank you." I allowed myself her name. "Maria."

"I want you to know," and her voice changed timbre, quickened into nervousness, and I braced myself for another empty promise, another hollow vow, "I wasn't going to tell you now but—"

"Please don't," I said.

"Not today, but I've told my family. My parents. My sisters. My sisters knew." She laughed, quietly, ruefully, I could imagine her shaking her head, her black curls falling across her face. "I was so stupid. So foolish. So much I've hurt you – so long. I've left it to so late. But *mi querida*." She paused, slowed down. "You are welcome here. You always were."

I do not know what I will do. How much harm love can take before it sneaks away, no one noticing it's gone. But I'll forgive Maria. I know that.

CHAPTER THIRTY-FIVE

As I took a seat at Antonne's baptism, upstairs at the church Jess and Joe had grown up attending, leaving the main floor for family and church members, I realized I was sitting in the same section my mother and I had squeezed into at Joe's funeral. Jess had worried about having the service so close to the anniversary of Joe's death, in the same church, and now here I was sitting in this same seat. But I didn't move, although Jess's aunt waved and motioned me downstairs. I wanted to stay in the seat I'd taken all those years ago. Maybe I could see what I couldn't see then. Change something, though I knew that was impossible.

I looked for Jess and Antonne and found them in the front pew with her parents. Mr. Willis hadn't performed any sacraments – not Communion, not a baptism – since Joe had died, but today, he was wearing a flowing black robe and white collar, with a baby-blue liturgical stole with a lavender cross stitched on each side – he'd decided to perform Antonne's baptism. In a moment, he would join the pastor as he walked to the altar; until then, Mr. Willis was squatting in front of Antonne, then standing and leaning over, talking to him, coaxing him into a low five. Jess, too, looked exuberant, in a royal-blue dress that I remembered from another time I'd seen her. Jess's mother still wore her black half-veil, but her dress was a silken ivory color, the same color as the little suit she had sewn for Antonne to wear. "Like a wedding, she'd told me," Jess said after. "I'm not sure that wasn't a dig."

The present was asserting itself here, in this church. Maybe this was the best start for Antonne, for Jess.

It was the only christening I'd ever been to with a sermon, and I didn't know if every AME Zion baptism had a sermon, or if this one did because of Joe. The pastor was the same man I'd heard at Easter, the same man, I'd learned since from Jess, who had officiated at Joe's funeral, though I hadn't recognized him then. In the series of compromises between Jess and her mother over the baptism, having Pastor Evans lead the service was a concession Jess said she didn't mind making.

"It's not an easy thing to raise a Black boy into a man in this world we live in today," Pastor Evans said.

"Amen."

"Yes sir."

"Ain't that the truth."

"Let alone as a single Black mother. Even with all the advantages that Jessica has given herself – with her education, her esteemed position in our school system, her closeness to her family, her involvement with this church – it's not easy. And Jessica, and her parents, of all the people in this congregation today, may know best of all how difficult it can be, as she herself lost her own dear brother Joe when he was just eighteen, about to go off to college at the University of Pennsylvania, when he was shot by a couple of young white men who claimed they were going to go shoot themselves some coyotes…"

"God have mercy."

"The Lord forgive them."

"…and shot this promising young Black man, one of the nicest young men I had ever met, shot him instead. And then he lay in this very same church, and we mourned him then, and we mourn him now."

"Amen."

"Amen," I said, mostly to myself. I had done a lot of

mourning in those weeks, and to mourn Joe, and only Joe, seemed to me something to "Amen". The sadness we all felt now, the anger, the suspicion, hadn't been present for us when Joe was alive. He'd been such an easy person. I looked for Antonne again, in the pew next to Jess. He was turning his head away, shy, then staring back across the church, and I spotted a woman in a huge pink hat playing peekaboo with him. *Ease*, I thought. I wished Antonne an ease with this world despite all its flaws.

"So Jessica knows from her own personal hard experience that she can protect and guide and teach and love and still the world can beat you down. The world can even kill you. But that's also why all of us are here – to pray for Jess and her new son and to help her raise this beautiful baby boy, Antonne Joseph Willis, to pray to Jesus to help her too and also today… every day… to celebrate… to celebrate!"

"Amen."

"Hallelujah!"

"…our Lord and this new life, because with new life can come a new and better world, for Black babies and white babies both, a new and better world in which all of us can thrive in the name of our Jesus, Amen."

May the Lord make it true, I might have said if I believed in a lord and had been raised in a church where the congregation spoke out of turn. But instead I sang along with the hymn and tried to control my tears and then felt very white and uptight for not just crying out – why not? – but then I'd feel self-conscious about that, so I discreetly wiped a few tears away and didn't dare look around until my emotions were in check. And then Jess led Antonne up to the altar, holding his hand as he looked up at her in wonder, then at her father, his grandfather; then Jess picked him up and held the back of his head as she leaned him toward the baptismal font, and Mr. Willis sprinkled water on his forehead and prayed and made the sign of the cross in the air and Antonne began to cry and Jess, her father, others in the church, including me, heartless adults that we were, began to laugh. For the first time in months, I felt joy.

We didn't know then that, the next day, officer Sean McCarthy wouldn't be indicted in the shooting of Will Haley, that the state's attorney would decide that the officer had acted reasonably in self-defense given the history of Haley's previous arrest. As we watched Jess bend her child's head toward her father, the drops of water he sprinkled catching the sun and falling, glistening, onto Antonne's skin, we didn't know quite so explicitly that the world we were welcoming Antonne into was no more just than it had been some twenty years before when Joe was still alive. Maybe it was worse.

All of that we found out the next day. Ray phoned me at home to let me know the state's attorney was making its announcement that afternoon – "I don't want you in early," he said, "just letting you know it'll be a long few days" – and so like a regular citizen I watched the news on TV, cried out when I heard there'd be no indictment, turned the TV off because I couldn't bear to watch their idiotic, simplistic coverage – "So, Jonathan," one white announcer asked another white announcer, "what do you think this will mean for the African American community?" – turned it on again when I heard sirens rushing past on Newfield Avenue, checked to see if Jess's car was in the parking lot – it wasn't, I hoped she was at the beach again, I hoped she didn't know yet, time enough for her to find out – thought about calling Aggie, didn't, then went into work early. Nothing we had done had made any difference, so maybe it was habit, or illusion, but it was still the place I went in hope that I might contribute something.

It's only in my memory that the baptism in the church is interspliced with scenes from the next day's protests: that the sirens blaring past the windows of my condo as police sped to contain a riot that didn't happen instead caused people in the church to turn their heads inquiringly toward the tall stained-glass windows; that the hymns at the church turned into the off-key "Amazing Grace" that was sung outside the police station; that the pastor's words that day became mixed in with what Ray told us at work, "The story will be over now," warning us, "if there's anything you ever wanted to get into the paper about this shooting, now's the time to do it. And do the best fucking job you can."

Not that there was much to write. A couple of news stories the first few days, a feature on the Haley family, a feature on Makayla and Stuart, with Makayla sounding calmer, more worldly, than I felt ("This is how it is, we just keep fighting"), and a round-up/analysis on Sunday. Finished. I didn't want smashing windows, fires in trash cans, young men jumping on the roofs of cars until they caved in, and, then again, I did. I had to fight to quell my anger. What else would make this world take notice? Hours would pass when I could not think of a single answer to that question.

It is only in my memory that these two images also converge, and become the only answer that brings with it any hope at all: Jess, in tears, sobbing over little Antonne's crib – "Why can't it be better for him? I want it to be better for him!" – her body hardening again as tears shake her, and then Jess holding Antonne in her arms at the church, softly lowering his head to the baptismal font, because Jess's body had become hard like muscle is hard, like earth is hard – you could hit it, you could bend it, but it would not break – Jess would not break – and then Antonne cries and Jess laughs and lifts him back into her arms in the church, at home, and her strength shines through it all.

ACKNOWLEDGMENTS

If no man, woman, or person is an island, perhaps as writers we are archipelagos? So let me name just a few of the other non-islands around me who have offered their insights, shared their friendship, and given their support during the writing of this novel.

I will start by thanking the students, teachers and principal at Woodrow Wilson High School, now Jackson-Reed High School, in Washington D.C., who opened their classrooms and minds to me in the early days of researching *The Same Country*. Principal Kimberly Martin and teachers Spencer Nissly and Jennifer McLaughlin were particularly helpful. Amilcar James and James Sarokin, then Wilson students, founded a group called "Common Ground" which served as the basis for the fictional "One Whitman." Amilcar and James are inspirations for not only this novel but for life, too.

Jewel Adams is another teacher who allowed me to watch her work in Baltimore and shared her ideas, impressing me with her quiet intelligence and dedication.

Margot Livesey first taught me how to write a novel – her voice was in my head for this one, too, her own work a model of precision, her professional advice and comradeship a model of how to be in the world.

Thanks, too, to Judy Heneghan, Janet Passehl, Amy Wack, Kevin Brennan and Holly Johnson, dear friends and trusted readers, whose clarity of mind I am lucky to have shining on my writing and life.

I am also forever grateful to Holly and Pat Merloe for the seemingly ever-available writing space in the top floor of their house – a sunlit refuge in my beloved D.C.

My novel writing group (both the writing and the group are novel) deserves their own mention: thank you Katherine Stansfield, David Towsey and Katie Munnik for your willingness to share thoughts and pizza; and to Donna Hemans and Kate North for essential reads at key moments.

Jonathan and Fiona Edwards, too, read early drafts then re-drafts – and their friendship goes well beyond these pages.

Kalisha Buckhanon became a colleague as well as a reader when she shared her responses and insights on *The Same Country* – twice! I'm also grateful to Gene Seymour for answering the call from our distant Connecticut past to provide his ideas and support.

The eagle-eyed Mary Ellen Huesken provided an early copy edit; and little nuggets of research can be credited to Ken Dixon and Colleen Murphy.

At the University of Southampton, I am grateful for the research leave which enabled early writing and research, and particularly thankful to have Rebecca Smith, Philip Hoare and now Toby Litt as colleagues and friends.

The Virginia Center for the Creative Arts has provided me with many weeks of uninterrupted time to work on this book, and friendships that have lasted well beyond those weeks. My writing life has depended on it.

The constancy of my agent Jennifer Lyons in New York, her assistant Mikaela Bender, and my agent Anna Carmichael in London has exceeded any expectation – I cannot thank you enough. How lucky I am that they found my editor at Legend Press, Cari Rosen. Unusually for me, I've not disagreed with a single suggestion from Cari – thank you for choosing my novel, and for giving it your thoughtful and intelligent attention. Everyone at Legend, especially Lucy Chamberlain and Olivia Le Maistre, have shown a dedication to my book that reflects their dedication to the world of books which they help create – all of us can be grateful for that.

I feel lucky to have a family – Karen, Eileen, Paul, Kevin, their beautiful spouses and families, and of course my "Ace" Dad – who backs me through this crazy writing thing I do, not raising skeptical eyebrows but cheering me on as if it's a sports game.

Lastly, though not one bit leastly, I will forever be grateful to Paul Edwards, whose unbending standards for his own art (and sometimes mine) has been a constant inspiration, and whose love keeps me afloat. You will be rewarded in the usual manner.